The Mountain Between Us

Marian Snowe

Other Books by Marian Snowe

Heart of Glass
Hereafter
Rescue Me
Love Birds

About the Author

My name is Marian Snowe, and I write stories about true love between women. I'm lucky enough to have found my soulmate, a beautiful and dauntless woman – and our love has inspired me to share the stories I've written about the adventures that two ladies can have falling in love. I'm entranced with the natural world, from mockingbirds to yarrow blossoms to cirrocumulus clouds, and it weaves itself into my writing as my wife and I explore it together. I hope you'll get as much happiness out of reading my stories as I do writing them! Visit me online at MarianSnowe.Wordpress.com or stop by my Facebook page, under Marian Snowe!

Learn more about Rose and Star Press, publishers of lesbian romance and fiction of distinction, at
http:///www.LesbianRomance.org

ISBN: 1539182479
ISBN-13: 978-1539182474

The
Mountain
Between Us

DEDICATION

For my parents, who've believed in me since before I could hold a pencil. It's because of you that I know how great it feels to climb a mountain.

And for Ruby, who loves the smell of a campfire.

Chapter One

"Today is the first day of the rest of my life!"

Tess Monroe was so certain of this announcement that she didn't even bother to knock wood as she stood on her front steps in the suburbs of Concord, New Hampshire. True, if she had attempted to rap her knuckles on the wooden railing, it might have fallen over; the house she rented was small and old but mostly solid, and entirely livable. "Full of character," Tess called it. You just had to make sure to keep your balance on the stairs, that's all.

Her hands firmly gripping the straps of her backpack and a determined smile on her face, Tess was ready to confront anything. It was a bright, beautiful morning in late October and a dry breeze rustled the dazzling red and orange leaves of the maple trees by the sidewalk. Blue sky, cool air, warm sun—it was the perfect day to climb a mountain.

Tess's backpack was stuffed with everything she could imagine she'd need for the hike: an extra sweatshirt and a fleece-lined windbreaker, snacks, water bottle, flashlight (not that she'd need it), and a mini first aid kit. Tess also had a small suitcase already stationed at the curb, containing essentials like her cell phone charger and toiletries, but mostly filled with all the yoga clothes she owned. The hike was only the beginning of this week of relaxation and rejuvenation. At the end of the trail, in a valley high in the White Mountains, was the Rising Star Yoga Resort. Tess felt like she should be on an episode of *Lifestyles of the Rich and Famous* just thinking about it. Then she grimaced and wondered, firstly, what ever happened to that show, and secondly, whether remembering it at all meant that she was old. Now it had probably been replaced with *Keeping Up with the Kardashians* or some *Real Housewives* show.

She hopped down onto the sidewalk, calling goodbye to her house rabbit, Sappho, through the partially open window. Any minute now, Tess's brother and sister-in-law would be by to pick her up and drive her to the trailhead where her hike would begin.

The house's white siding was nearly gray with age and weather, and the oil tank in her sliver of a yard looked like it had been installed sometime during the Kennedy presidency, but Tess ignored all that. Instead, she hung over the peeling picket fence and gazed with pride into her tiny garden.

There were only about nine square feet available for gardening, but Tess had made the most of them. This time of year, the plants were starting to die down for the winter, but in the spring and summer it had been a sight to behold. Half the garden she'd dedicated to flowers, from foxgloves to Solomon's seal to waxy sedum. The other half was an herb garden with oregano, basil, and chamomile competing for space. It was one of the biggest sources of pride in Tess's life.

Maybe the only thing.

But that was all about to change. Three days ago, Tess had cleaned out her desk at the technology company where she provided sales support. Ten years' worth of empty file folders, packets of pretzels far past their sell-by date, and cheap corporate trinkets like stress balls and paperclip magnets went into the trash. She had two weeks off before her new job started, and she was going to make the most of them.

This trip was going to be a fresh start. Tess hadn't been doing yoga for long, but she always marveled at how much better she felt after a class. A whole week of it would surely make her feel like Wonder Woman and would set the stage for her new life.

A cheery car horn beeped at the end of the street, and Tess leaned away from the fence to peer down the road. Right on time, Anthony's maroon minivan pulled around the corner and slowed to a stop in front of her house. Tess's sister-in-law, Jill, was driving. Anthony got out and opened up the sliding side passenger door for Tess.

"Hey, shortcake! Think you've got everything you need?"

"Shortcake?" Tess stuck her tongue out at him as she slung her tall hiker's backpack into the next seat over and jumped up into the van. Her brother hoisted her suitcase in after her. "Whatever, butthead. You're no basketball player yourself."

Anthony slid the door shut for her and returned to the front seat. "You're just sensitive because there are ducks taller than you."

"Ugh, why did I ask you for a ride?" Tess buckled her seatbelt and leaned back against the headrest, feigning disgust. She *was* short, and she'd be the first to admit it. But the duck comment was just insulting—no offense to ducks.

"Because it's all thanks to me you're going to this fancy-pants resort anyway," Anthony replied loftily.

"It's all thanks to your wife, you mean."

Jill chuckled as she headed the van out of the neighborhood and toward Interstate 93. "Honestly, Tess, I couldn't have used that ticket. We've got Emma and Beth's birthday party tomorrow and I'm too hyperactive for yoga, anyway." Emma and Beth were Tess's twin nieces, and their traditional joint birthday party was always a huge affair. When Jill won a week at the Rising Star Yoga Resort in a raffle at work, she and Anthony gave it to Tess as her "congratulations, you quit your job" present. There was no way Tess would have been able to afford such an expense otherwise, no matter how much she needed a vacation.

"Have I mentioned that I'm humbled by your wife's generosity?" Tess asked Anthony. "And her beauty. You should take her out to dinner more often." Jill held her hand up toward the backseat and Tess gave her a high-five. Anthony groaned.

"I hate it when you two are together."

"Oh, yeah?" Jill shot Tess a grin and turned to her husband. "Maybe I should've married Tess instead, then."

Tess cracked up laughing, but Anthony just rolled his eyes. "Not even you can meet standards that high," he said pointedly.

"You leave my standards out of this." Tess poked him in the back of the neck through the gap between his seat and headrest. He swatted her hand.

"So, what's your schedule? Lots of bending yourself into a pretzel and becoming one with the universe?"

"I think it'll be a couple more years before they let me in on that technique." Tess pulled a printed sheet from the front pocket of her backpack; there would be no cell reception at the resort, so she'd planned ahead and printed everything she needed. "Well, it'll take all of today to hike up. If we leave at nine a.m. as planned, we should get there around five o'clock tonight."

"They don't expect everybody to hike up to that resort, do they?" Jill asked. "They'd never get any business."

"Nah, there's a road that goes up to it too." Tess flipped through her printed pages to find a map of the resort area. "It's just on the other side of the mountain from the hiking trail. That's how they're taking our luggage up. Once we get up there, we've got a schedule of classes we can take and plenty of free time in between for pampering ourselves at the spa. I hear they've even got a Michelin one-star rated chef to prepare our meals."

"Wow, swanky," Anthony said. "Careful you don't get too used to that kind of life."

Tess laughed mirthlessly. "Oh, don't you worry. I'm kind of surprised they're even letting a plebe like me in the door."

She and her brother had grown up in an old duplex in a tightly-packed, rundown housing development. Their parents both worked two jobs and still made just enough money to keep food on the table. The family never went hungry, and Tess was grateful for that now, but as a child, she and Anthony spent a lot of time gazing enviously at their schoolmates' designer clothes and the cars they were given upon turning sixteen. Going on vacation to a resort like this wasn't even in Tess's worldview as a child—and it only was now because of Jill's good luck and generosity.

Soon enough the White Mountain range came into view with its patchwork of green, orange, and yellow trees laying over it like a blanket. Foliage season was in full swing, even approaching its end, and cars streamed toward the mountains like they always did on days with weather as fine as this. Tess watched out the window as the land rose in higher and higher rounded peaks and the road wound snakelike between them.

They'd left the highway behind some time ago when Jill spotted a sign on the right side of the road, proclaiming the open area behind it to be the Rising Star Resort Trailhead. Across the street was a state-run ranger station and other trails leading into the national parkland. Jill pulled off the road into the dirt parking lot.

"Wow," Tess said, glancing back at the sign and then taking in the handful of other hikers standing beside their cars and readying their gear. "They have their own trailhead. They must own all the land around the trail."

"Like I said: swanky." Anthony hopped out of the van and opened the sliding door for Tess before she could get it herself. "We're picking you up back here in a week, right?"

"Right." Tess climbed down with a smile and pulled her backpack out after her and suitcase. Anthony gave her a light slap on the shoulder.

"Don't fall off any cliffs. Don't get eaten by a bear."

Tess elbowed him good-naturedly. "Any other words of wisdom?"

"Hmm..." Anthony put his fist to his chin, affecting a thoughtful expression. "If there were ever a good time to drop those ridiculously high standards of yours and enjoy a nice hook-up, this would be it. I hear yoga people are very flexible."

"Oh, for God's sake!" Tess swung her backpack on, purposefully smacking Anthony with it, and headed toward the crowd. "Jill, take him home. See you later! Tell Emma and Beth happy birthday for me!" She waved as the van took off and then sped up when she neared the other hikers. Tess loved meeting new people—she was inherently cheerful and good at small talk, and this had helped her in her sales job at her old company. Unfortunately, she soon discovered she wasn't pushy enough to be really good at selling things.

Tess's brown eyes flicked between the faces of the assembled hikers. There was a group of younger women who all had essentially the same hairstyle and clothes; some college kids who looked like they were ready to climb Mount Everest with the amount of gear they had; and a middle-aged woman and man (the man looked less than pleased to be there). Oh, and over there was—

"Hey, Emily!" Tess dashed toward the couple standing on the other side of the lot by their car, stuffing last-minute supplies into their backpacks. Emily was part of Tess's circle of friends from college who still hung out together (one of the only straight ones, actually). It wasn't at all surprising to see Emily here, actually—she loved yoga and was a fervent athlete who frequently competed in marathons and mountain biking races. She was wearing a bright turquoise bandana over her choppy red hair and cargo pants, looking perfectly suited to the hike.

Emily looked up when she heard Tess's voice and laughed in surprise. Her boyfriend, Stefan, locked up the car while Emily came to meet Tess.

"I had no idea you'd be coming to this!" Emily said.

"Honestly, I didn't know either until a couple of days ago. My sister-in-law won a ticket for this getaway at her job, but she couldn't go, so she gave it to me." Tess searched in her pocket for a hair tie and gathered her fluffy, shoulder-length blonde hair back into a ponytail. It was already windier here than it had been at home, even though they were still at the bottom of the mountain. Stefan joined them and together they all walked back to where the group was gathered. A van sat nearby with a collection of suitcases, and Tess added hers to the pile.

"They let you take a whole week off, huh?" Emily asked Tess with lopsided smile. She knew—all of Tess's friends knew—how much she'd disliked her old job, especially its inflexibility. A triumphant smile broke out on Tess's face. She drew herself up and planted her fists on her hips.

"They didn't have to! Friday was my last day."

Emily's eyes went wide and she gave a little hop of excitement. "You're kidding! You quit? About time!"

"You're telling me," Tess agreed. "In two weeks, I'll be a full-time teacher at Sunflower Preschool."

"Oh, how perfect!" Emily clapped her hands in front of her mouth. "That's just what you wanted, right?"

"Yeah," Tess replied, pride warming her voice. "I was originally looking for position where I'd get to teach kids who were a little older, since I really want to nurture a love of math in girls especially. Preschool math is pretty much limited to counting, but it's a hundred times better than what I was doing before." Stefan, walking beside them, quirked an eyebrow.

"But doesn't being a preschool teacher pay a

18

ton less than your previous job?"

Tess shrugged uncomfortably. It had been a big decision, one that she spent many sleepless nights debating, and thinking about how tight money was going to be still made her feel a little queasy. But that was a question she was going to have to get used to answering with a career change like this.

"It does, but I was going nowhere back there. At least now I'll have a chance to do work I'm proud of."

"Besides," Emily said, veering toward Tess to bump her with her shoulder. "You have to follow your dreams."

"I'm lucky. An opportunity came up and I had the means to take it." Tess smiled weakly. Sure, she was deliriously happy to be teaching at the preschool. But starting her career all over in her mid-thirties? So much she'd planned in college just hadn't happened. All those big dreams had fizzled out like a dud firecracker. Tess couldn't help but wonder whether the opportunity for really following her dreams had passed.

The other hikers had been chatting amongst themselves, but now they fell quiet when a slim young man waved his arms in the air for attention. He had a short brown beard and his hair in a bun, and he wore a burgundy zip-up sweatshirt with a light scarf and skinny jeans.

"Hey, guys! Guys?" He waited until everyone's eyes were on him. "I'm Paul and I'll be your guide up to the resort today. We're just waiting to hear back about some weather reports that say we might get a bit of rain. It's up in the air as to whether the storm will come our way or head off in another direction, so we're going to delay the hike start time until ten o'clock, okay?"

Tess took a look at her phone's clock. It was almost nine now, the time they had planned to leave.

"You can hang out here, or there are a couple of short walking trails around," Paul continued. "Just be back by quarter of ten. If the storm comes this way, we can caravan up to the lodge on the service road on the backside of the mountain."

Tess glanced over at Emily. "I can get a ride up with you guys if we do that, right?" Emily nodded. "I'm glad you happened to come here this week too," Tess added. "Otherwise I might've had to walk up that road!"

"It's our one-year anniversary," Stefan said, taking Emily's hand. She smiled up at him and cuddled into his side.

"Oh!" Tess glanced between the two of them, a blush creeping up her neck. Crap. Was this supposed to be a romantic weekend for them, then? "Congratulations, you guys. That's awesome." Emily gave her boyfriend a peck and Tess felt her stomach sink. The last thing they needed was a third wheel. "Um... Are you going to hang out here until ten?"

"Yeah, I was thinking we would," Stefan replied. Tess glanced around the parking lot and noticed a little wooden sign that probably indicated one of the walking trails the guide had mentioned.

"Okay, I'm just going to take a little walk, then. I'll be back soon. Can you watch my stuff?" Tess took off her backpack and set it down next to where Emily and Stefan had piled theirs, and then she headed toward the sign. So much for getting to hang out with Emily for the week... Tess wanted to give them space, but she couldn't quash the disappointed feeling she suddenly had. Meeting new people was a fun prospect, but it looked to her like everybody else in the hiking group was either with a bunch of their friends or with their partner. Other than the guide, of course. If Tess couldn't break into any of the groups, she'd end up like that kid who had to eat lunch with the teacher because nobody else would sit with her.

The path into the woods looked enticing enough, though. It had been ages since Tess had spent more than a few weekends a year out hiking, and she hoped she was up for the task today. The website said that the trail up to the lodge was a fairly easy one, at least, and she could get a little warm-up here. The sign called this path "Whitethorn Loop" and it was only three-quarters of a mile long, so it definitely wouldn't take her a whole hour.

Tess deeply inhaled the autumn scent of crisp wind and drying grasses and stepped onto the tree-shaded trail.

$\mathscr{D}$

There was a good reason so many leaf-peepers flocked to these mountains every fall. Everywhere Tess looked was a kaleidoscope of colors—red, orange, yellow, and tan joined the deep green of conifers to make the forest around her look like a stained-glass window. She could feel the calm and stillness seeping into her bones already. Even though they'd only driven an hour or two to get here, this felt worlds away from the rush of traffic and the clamor of telephones. This would be the perfect vacation—she'd make sure of it.

It felt so good to just enjoy the quiet of the forest that Tess walked slower than she normally would have, meandering aimlessly while she watched the leaves rustle overhead and squirrels scoot around on either side of the path. When she came to a big bend that curved around back the way she came, Tess could see gold filtering through the tree-trunks some distance away.

She stopped, peering in that direction. There were maybe fifty feet of woodland between the path and the golden place—a field? Tess glanced at her phone again. Plenty of time.

Picking her way through the woods, Tess pushed past brush and low-hanging branches until she emerged into the sunlight at the edge of a vast meadow. The long grasses shone green and gold, and the sun caught in the dry seed pods and spindly skeletons of Queen Anne's Lace. All around the field, the mountains rose in colorful slopes. It was perfect, like a painting, and Tess held up her cell phone to get a picture.

It was then that she noticed the cottage.

Nestled toward the end of the field, the cottage sat with its back against the forest that ran unbroken up the mountain. It was built of stone and its roof was shingled, and a fence stretched to a small shed that stood nearby. Tess was utterly charmed by it: surrounded by the picturesque meadow, the cottage looked like it had sprung from a fairy tale. If she could just get a little closer, it would make the most beautiful picture.

Tess strode through the tall grass, drawing in lungfuls of its fresh, hay-like scent. As she came closer to the cottage, she could see that a portion of the field surrounding it had been mown short, and other parts were bare dirt. A fenced-in garden sat on the far side, brimming with squash and other fall vegetables as well as herbs. The shingles on the roof were crowded with soft lumps of vibrant moss.

Tess's heartbeat sped up. She'd always wanted a little house of her own, far away from the city, where she could grow flowers and vegetables and let her rabbit roam around outside once in a while. It had been a childhood dream, nurtured by stories of young women who lived by themselves in the woods, talking to the birds and sewing dresses and baking apple pies. Growing up in a crowded duplex where she and her brother had to share the attic bedroom space and the carpets had holes worn in them, Tess had ardent fantasies of living somewhere peaceful and quaint. But she'd always thought houses like this only existed in England or where Heidi lived in the Swiss Alps.

As she got closer, she began to pick out details. A large glass jar sat on the sill inside one of the windows, filled with a yellow-orange liquid and numerous lemon slices. *Sun tea*, Tess thought happily. She hadn't made any of that in years, but her grandmother used to put tea bags in jars of water and steep them in the sun all the time when she was little. At the side of the house, where the ground was bare, there was a workbench with planks of wood, various tools, and some partially constructed furniture. The dirt below was littered with sawdust and shavings. Tess crossed the patch of bare ground to peer at the carved curlicues on what might become the top of a wooden chest.

Just as Tess moved her gaze to the ivy that climbed the cottage's stone wall, a sudden, irate bleat sounded so close behind her that she jumped forward and tripped over a bucket she hadn't seen lying near the workbench. Tess landed heavily on her elbows in the dirt and rolled over to find an indignant-looking goat looming over her.

The goat bleated again and Tess got the impression that it was giving her a thorough scolding. She winced; her elbows stung where she'd scraped them.

"Geez, what are you trying to do? Give me a heart attack?" She blew a flyaway curl out of her face and struggled to sit upright. Goats could be kind of mean sometimes, right? All she knew about them were that the videos she'd seen online of baby goats leaping around were freaking adorable, but this goat looked more like a grumpy old lady. "You're going to let me up, right?" Tess asked hopefully. The goat regarded her with skepticism.

"Excuse me," said a low, chocolatey voice some distance behind Tess. "Why are you scaring my goat?"

Tess craned her neck to see behind her and her heart gave a startlingly energetic flutter. A woman stood there leaning nonchalantly against the cottage's doorframe, her eyebrows raised and a slight smirk on her lips. For a moment, there was nothing Tess could do but sit and stare—the woman struck her dumb.

She was tall and long-legged, and her sleek muscles struck Tess as having been developed from manual labor rather than at the gym. The jeans she wore looked as if they'd seen many days of hard use, and her dark blue and gray plaid shirt—rolled up to reveal forearms that made Tess's knees feel mushy—matched the deep indigo of her eyes. Those eyes regarded Tess now with a hint of a smile in them, as if she already knew exactly what Tess would do in response to her question.

Tess opened her mouth and closed it again, equally staggered by the woman's charisma and by her sudden appearance. "Your goat's the one who scared *me*," she heard herself reply. The woman gave a brief snort of a laugh and looked away, then pushed herself off the wall. Her sharp jawbone gave her the look of a sculpture, highlighted by chestnut hair buzzed on the sides and back but long enough on top to swoop rakishly up in a subtle pompadour. One corner of her mouth quirked as she gave Tess a long look.

"Well, *one* of the two of you lives here, so you can see why I might've made that assumption." A chuckle was hidden beneath her voice, and Tess blushed. Just the sound of that voice made her feel like heat was moving beneath her skin in a disconcerting dance of desire and embarrassment.

Tess cast a quick, nervous look back at the goat and then scrambled up onto her knees. Suddenly there was a hand in front of her face, stretched out casually toward her in a gesture of assistance. Tess blinked up at the woman, who was no longer leaning against the cottage wall but was now offering Tess a hand up. The woman's eyes sparkled with amusement.

The blush on Tess's cheeks deepened as she clasped the woman's hand and allowed her to help her up. There was strength in that grip, a tempered strength so great that Tess felt like the woman could've lifted her onto her feet without Tess having to move a muscle.

"Um," Tess began, fighting through the embarrassment and her racing pulse to locate her usual cheerful friendliness. "Do you...live here?"

The woman bit back a smile. "No, I'm just here to keep people from harassing the goat." For a moment, Tess was too distracted by the woman's perfect jawline and the depth of her mischievous eyes to realize that she was being teased. Then she huffed a breath out through her nose.

The woman chuckled, her eyes narrowing merrily. "Sorry. Yes, I do live here."

"It's charming." Tess regarded the cottage's old stonework and the evergreen ivy waving gently in the breeze. When she stepped into the field and saw the cottage for the first time, she thought she'd never seen anything more beautiful. Whoever this woman was, she'd just proved Tess wrong.

Tess turned her gaze back to the woman and this time she put her own hand out, smiling a smile that lit up her round face. "I'm Tess."

With a little tilt of her head that put Tess in mind of the bow a knight might give to a lady, the woman took her hand again. "Remy." When their palms pressed together, Tess felt the same strength, but this time she noticed more: a warm grip and delightfully rough calluses. Her heart skipped a beat, fascination blossoming within her. It wasn't until Remy's eyes raked blatantly up and down her form that Tess came back to reality. She cleared her throat, the smile still spread goofily across her face in spite of the self-consciousness that prickled up her back. *Get a grip, girl. You're acting like a fourteen-year-old smitten with some stranger.*

But Remy's eyes still roved over her as if she were evaluating an art piece, and that made it considerably harder for Tess to "get a grip." She felt like a whole swarm of butterflies had been let loose in her middle. Attention like this would've normally made Tess apt to trip over her feet, but strangely, Remy's gaze brought out a feeling of confidence in her that she hadn't felt in a long time. *If someone* this *beautiful thinks I'm worth looking at...* Tess lifted her chin and put her shoulders back, posture straightening as the thrill of this encounter made her whole body feel lighter.

"It must be like a dream to live here," she said. It would've been appropriate, at that point, for Tess to admire the cottage and the garden again, but she couldn't tear her eyes away from Remy. "I've always..." Remy thrust her hands into her pockets with an easy grace, and Tess took in the lines of her form, from her strong shoulders down to the curve of her hips, and forgot what she'd been about to say.

The corners of Remy's lips curled up, that knowing twinkle returning to her eyes. "You've always...?"

Tess shook her head, returning her focus to Remy's face. "Always wanted to live somewhere like this. You must feel like a long-lost princess from a fairy tale."

At that, Remy snorted and then began to laugh outright. She tucked one arm beneath the other elbow and leaned her cheek in her hand, looking at Tess as if she were too precious for reality. "I have to admit that I've never felt much like a princess, lost or otherwise."

Tess felt heat flood her face. Sometimes when she got caught up in the moment, things came out of her mouth before she thought about whether they'd make her look foolish or not.

"I just meant...that's how I'd feel," she amended, determined to match this debonair woman in confidence.

"I bet you would," Remy murmured, her mouth still hooked in a suggestive smile. Tess was befuddled: she couldn't decide whether she should be flattered or flustered by the way Remy looked at her and spoke to her. "So," Remy continued, dropping her hands and placing them on her hips. "Were you just meandering through the forest and singing to the birds, then, Princess?"

Tess cocked her head with a little admonishing grin, as if a gorgeous women teasing her was something she experienced every day. "No. I'm with a hiking group that'll be heading up to the Rising Star Yoga Resort in a half hour or so, and I decided to take a little walk. Your home is so lovely that I couldn't help but come take a closer look. I am sorry I startled your goat, though."

She expected Remy to make another quip about the goat, but her face fell when Remy rolled her eyes, the flirtatiousness gone so completely that it was as if it had never existed.

"You're one of *those*, then," she said, angling her body away from Tess. Tess frowned, her brows furrowing in somewhat offended confusion.

"One of who?"

Remy didn't meet her eyes. With a scoff, she bent and picked up the bucket Tess had tripped over. "One of the rich, vapid idiots who pay to traipse up a mountain and get fed bullshit they think will make them skinnier and more spiritual." Tess opened her mouth to object, but before she could, Remy continued. "You'd better scurry back to your little group. If you don't take your time going up the mountain, you might break a nail, and then what *will* the other girls at the spa think?" The vitriol in her voice was masked beneath light sarcasm, but Tess detected it nonetheless.

Her shoulders fell. How had the atmosphere changed so suddenly? Thinking back, her stomach started to clench. Maybe what she'd taken for provocative banter had just been condescension. Had she made even more of an idiot of herself than she'd thought? Maybe Remy had been making fun of her this whole time.

The burn of humiliation transformed to a more comfortable anger. Tightening her ponytail with finality, Tess turned on her heel and stalked away from the cottage. "Sorry to have *bothered* you," she shot over her shoulder. Remy still wasn't looking at her.

"Watch where you're going the next time you trespass," Tess heard Remy mutter, but she was already across the mown area and into the long grass.

"The nerve of that woman!" Tess fumed. Nobody was listening but the winged grasshoppers that flickered out of her way. "Talk about presumptuous! Like I'm some empty-headed bimbo who's climbing a mountain because it's fashionable! Since when has eight hours of sweaty hiking been fashionable? And someone like her who apparently makes furniture for fun should know that breaking your fingernail *hurts*." She balled her hands into fists, shame settling like a lump of clay in her stomach. *And here I'd thought she was attractive. This is why my standards have to be so damn high. I can't just let my body rule my mind when a pretty face comes my way.* A pretty face, gorgeous hips, and strong arms... Tess shook her head forcefully. So what if Remy had made her feel beautiful and confident? There was always something hiding underneath that would ruin things.

Chapter Two

Tess tried to put the whole encounter behind her as she emerged from the Whitethorn Loop trail and saw that the other hikers were all gathered in a cluster around Paul the guide. He was grinning, and when he saw Tess, he waved her over.

"We've been given the all-clear," he announced. "The storm's apparently moving off west and shouldn't bother us at all. Now that everybody's here, let's get our gear collected and move out!"

"Apparently he thinks he's leading a wagon train," Emily, coming up beside Tess, whispered with a grin. Tess chuckled and shouldered her backpack. Today was a perfect day for hiking and they had an adventure ahead of them. She'd forget all about Remy in a matter of moments—it had been a mere ten minutes of her life and it only served to remind her how she had to be careful of falling fast and hard. Just looking at Remy had made it hard to breathe, and Tess resented that she could feel that physically attracted to someone within seconds of laying eyes on them. It wasn't as if it had been an unpleasant feeling—far from it—but she knew it clouded her judgement.

Oh, well. No more thinking about Remy. It would be easy to forget her, remember?

A chilly, refreshing wind blew down off the mountain as the group tramped forward. Brief introductions were made while they walked, and conversations started up here and there. Tess raised her eyes to the treetops, admiring the brilliant colors against the blue sky. Days like this, with phenomenal weather and foliage at its peak, came only a handful of times each fall. She was here to enjoy it, to let it soak into her and break free from chronic doldrums her old job had put her in.

Emily and Stefan were talking animatedly and laughing with each other, and as much as Tess wanted to join in, she kept her distance. They didn't need her barging in on their anniversary vacation. She'd have plenty of time to talk to Emily later, and chances were they'd be in some of the yoga classes together. Maybe she could steal Emily for a little bit of girl time at the spa, too.

Up ahead of her, the rest of the group was walking in clusters as well. Tess took the opportunity as they were covering some of the flatter ground near the bottom of the trail to look them all over. The more she did, the more she got the sinking feeling that Remy had been right—they *were* a bunch of rich, vapid idiots.

First, there was the gaggle of women who were maybe five or ten years younger than Tess, the ones who all had the same hair style—shades of dark blonde or light brown, worn in straight ponytails with a headband to keep flyaways back. She couldn't remember any of their names. Each one wore a variation of the same white or light khaki shorts and thin-soled Keds. Tess stared at them with fascination: not only was it late October in New England, but mountainsides weren't known to be the cleanest of places. One of them had her smartphone out and was apparently videoing her friends as they professed to each other how very spiritual they were, and how yoga made them feel so in touch with their truer selves. Tess got the impression that there was some sort of contest going on that involved being more spiritual than your friends.

When Paul asked them if they'd remembered to bring bug spray, not one of them knew what a tick was.

Next, Tess spent a little while walking behind a pair of college students, a guy and a girl. Both of them carried huge, spotless hiker's backpacks kitted out with everything Tess could imagine, from compasses and water pouches clipped to the outside to a fancy camping stove and two lightweight tents. She sped up her pace to catch up with them.

"Hey, guys," she said brightly. "You look like you're ready to conquer the wilderness."

They laughed. "Awesome, huh?" the boy said, shrugging his shoulders so that the backpack bobbed up and down. "After the retreat, we're going to spend a couple of days camping up here. I think my old man just wanted to get me out of the house, but he sure has good taste in equipment!" Tess eyed the four overflowing backpacks and thought that the kid's father must have good taste in stock options, too.

As they hiked on and the trail began gradually to climb, Tess hung back to walk near the middle-aged couple and see if she could get a read on them. The woman looked positively rapturous to be out here, but her husband plodded along with a look of sour resignation on his face. Overhearing their conversation, Tess learned that the woman had discovered yoga because "all her daughter's friends did it and swore it helped them drop twenty pounds in two months." When Tess caught a clipped mention of their couples therapist in response to the man's grumbling, she speed-walked ahead so she didn't overhear anything even more personal.

Paul was a bit off-putting himself, although he was extremely friendly, and that was usually enough to win Tess over. He wove through the hikers, correcting their technique (Tess hadn't even realized that walking up trails *had* a technique) and encouraging them to drink more water. When Tess told him, eyebrow raised, that at this rate she was going to be out of water before lunchtime, he opened his mouth and then closed it again, looking disappointed. Tess shook her head as she watched him hurry off to tell the hikers not to drink too quickly.

The morning wore on, and while Tess felt the fatigue beginning to seep into her muscles, she was still relaxed. There was something comforting and fulfilling about mindless physical activity, especially when contrasted with sitting in a cubicle all day. They had only just resumed their walk after stopping for lunch (did the ponytailed ladies seriously bring canned *soup?*) when clouds began to steal over the formerly crystal-clear blue sky.

When Tess felt the first raindrop, she sighed lightly and paused to unpack her windbreaker. A little sprinkling was no big deal, although she knew it was going to make her hair puff up like a dandelion. Still, the pattering amongst the leaves was soothing, and the rain heightened the autumn scent of fallen foliage. As the rain began to fall faster, cries of dismay went up from the group of young women. They hadn't brought raincoats. Annoying as Tess found them, their insulted expressions when Paul offered them trash-bag ponchos were worth it.

Hiking in the rain was a little uncomfortable, but Tess liked how the rain turned the tree-trunks black, resulting in an even more beautiful contrast between them and the vivid oranges and yellows of the leaves. Even when it became a downpour and then a deluge, she smiled when she heard the middle-aged lady comment to her husband about how much more "real" this made their vacation. The college kids were equally excited about this addition to their adventure— although they joined the rest of the group in cheering when the deluge finally let up.

No one was applauding, though, when the sky turned from pale uniform gray to a heavy, darker blanket overhead and the rain began to sting their skin. Tess had her eyes on the trail in front of her so that she wouldn't slip on any wet rocks or roots, but when she saw the little white speckles collecting in the hollows, apprehension and dismay squirmed inside her stomach.

Sleet.

She looked up at the group ahead of her, watching Paul squint at the sky and the young women hunching in their thin sweatshirts. The college kids, of course, had all the rain gear they could have needed for a walk in the Amazon rainforest.

Lunchtime should have been around the halfway point, right? Tess could tell that the trail was a pretty easy one, so it likely crisscrossed the side of the mountain to keep the grade low. But surely they were over halfway there? She glanced over her shoulder at the trail behind them. It hadn't seemed all that steep coming up, but now that she looked back, the prospect of walking down over all those sleet-covered rocks was somewhat more chilling than the rain itself.

Even though there were a few complaints here

and there, as well as a few general remarks about discomfort, nobody questioned Paul as he soldiered on up the mountain. Tess was too busy focusing on where she was walking to notice when the hikers clustered in front of her, and she nearly walked straight into Stefan.

"What's going on?" Tess asked Emily, an uncharacteristic grouchiness stirring in her. She just wanted to get to the lodge, where warm fireplaces and fluffy towels and saunas were waiting for her. Emily shrugged, her brow pinching together with worry. Tess moved around the taller people so she could see what Paul was doing.

He stood at the edge of a wide, wet furrow in the earth. Tess could see rocks and roots jumbled in the dirt, mixed with the gravel that paved the trail. Rivulets of water dragged the gravel down the mountainside and disappeared amongst the trees.

Paul put his hands on his hips and stared hard at the washout, as if he could somehow put the trail back together with his mind. He chewed on his lip as Tess skirted the group and came up to his side.

"What happened to the trail?"

"That downpour we had a little while ago must've washed it away." He looked up ahead of them, where water was still rushing down the steep section of the trail they were approaching. "There's a stream up there, and the banks have been a little unstable this year. I guess they crumbled and the stream flooded down here."

Tess pulled her windbreaker more tightly around her shoulders. "Can we get past it?"

Pointing up the trail with a flat look that Tess found somewhat insulting, Paul replied, "Does it look like it?"

"Well, what are we supposed to do, then?" one of the college kids asked. "We can't go back down now! We've come all this way!" The pair looked like a disappointment like this might utterly crush them. Paul fidgeted.

"Look, we should still have cell service. It doesn't usually cut out until a bit higher than this. I'll call down to the ranger station and ask them what they think we should do."

Tess waited nervously while Paul dialed the number. Sheer luck had allowed her to attend this retreat, and if a fluke storm ruined it now, she'd know the universe had it out for her. Hopefully her encounter with Remy—which, like this hike, had started out so pleasant—wasn't a harbinger of things to come.

The pang of disappointment that Tess felt when she thought about Remy only grew sharper when she considered the potential letdown of turning around. The memory of Remy's deep-ocean eyes caressing her body still made her heart speed and her skin tingle in spite of herself. Within seconds, Remy had stopped Tess's breath with how beautiful she was, how charismatically she spoke and carried herself, and that made it sting all the more when Remy turned cold. The feel of Remy's hand in hers as she pulled Tess to her feet, the ease with which she lifted her, was so at odds with that sudden callous dismissal. That was a hard enough blow for one day.

When Paul got off the phone, though, he looked a bit more hopeful. "Hey, folks," he said, and everyone crowded around to hear him (and likely to warm up a little). "The rangers say there's an alternate trail that branches off this one a little way back the way we came. The sleet's supposed to stop. They said it's up to us whether we want to continue. Personally..." Paul's attitude shifted away from uncertain and back to the conviction he'd shown earlier when he gave the middle-aged couple tips about how to bend their knees while climbing. "I think we should keep going. We're definitely more than halfway there, and it'll take us a lot longer to go downhill, even if we hurry. I'm sure we're close enough to the lodge that it makes more sense to just continue on."

A murmur of assent went through the group, and Tess was heartened that her vacation wasn't going to end before it really began. They picked their way carefully back down until they came upon the split where the alternate trail broke off. It was narrower and somewhat steeper. The hikers started gamely up it, using their hands to steady themselves on rocks and tree branches as necessary. *No more disappointment,* Tess vowed, but then the sardonic curve of Remy's mouth flashed in her imagination and she clenched her jaw, trying to ignore the fierce yearning that had begun to smolder like an ember in her chest.

✍

"Alternate" was a kind term for this trail. "Use only in case of emergency" might have been more apt. Yes, it did feel like it was more straightforward than the main trail's gentle slopes and winding curves. But by the time Tess's hands were brown with mud and nearly numb from holding onto cold rocks, roots, and whatever else she could grasp to keep her from slipping, she missed those gentle slopes fiercely. *This is a welcome challenge,* she kept reminding herself. *If I can do this, I'll know I haven't lost my edge.*

That worry had been growing in Tess's mind ever since she was accepted as a teacher at Sunflower Preschool and started to seriously reevaluate where her life was going. It had been dismal indeed to realize that "College Tess" probably wouldn't even recognize the Tess of today. College Tess had been a go-getter in the extreme: she was the president of several student orgs, she volunteered weekly at an animal shelter, and she was the star jammer in her local roller derby league. The Tess that was dragging herself doggedly up a trail that rivaled a Stairmaster in leg exhaustion hadn't so much as put on her skates in ten years. These days, elbowing somebody to get past them was a daunting prospect.

Tess was scared that she'd lost her fire. In college, when she'd finally escaped her small-town high school and discovered the magic of the GLBTQA student alliance, that fire had burned so brightly every day that it could've powered a small planet. Tess was lucky now if she could dredge up the motivation to go to the gym. Her life was comfortable enough, but she felt like it was so...small. The world had been wide open to her in college, but once she graduated, she took up residence in a tiny corner of it and hadn't even noticed as it narrowed down to a single lane.

The trail ahead of them wouldn't have been so bad if it were just steep. But after an hour of nothing but the sounds of sneakers thumping on dirt and labored breathing, Tess began to notice that while the early stretch of this trail had been maintained recently, the section climbed now looked more like a mountain obstacle course.

Fallen branches and brush now lay in the path, punctuated by large stones that had fallen and lodged themselves in the middle of the trail. When they reached the first downed tree, the entire group halted, trying to judge how one might climb over the trunk on an incline such as this. The tree, a fir, had fallen down the slope and so its branches were pointing at the hikers, making it even harder to climb over.

Tess felt frustration bubbling in her veins; her toes were numb and her jeans were soaked up to the knees, her hands were so dirty she didn't think she'd ever get them clean, and now, the sleet had transformed into big, fluffy snowflakes that made the rocks even slipperier. Fantasies of a hot drink laced with brandy taunted her. She just wanted to get to the damned lodge.

As Tess watched the college kids help the middle-aged man slowly over the trunk, she gritted her teeth with determination. There had to be an easier, safer way around this tree than having everybody clamber one at a time through sharp, unstable branches. Nothing ventured, nothing gained.

On the downhill side of the trail, the crown of the fallen tree hung a short way into the brush. Maybe climbing through that part might be easier. Tess noticed a faint track of mud that led up onto the trail's bank and through the tree's top branches. They were thin enough that it looked easier to step through them there. Then it was merely a small hop back down onto the trail and off they'd go.

Tess stared at that muddy track with narrowed eyes. Okay, it *was* on the downhill side. But it'd be easy. Much easier than poking holes in her clothes and getting splinters trying to climb over the thick trunk like the others were doing. Besides, this was the first day of the rest of her life, wasn't it? College Tess was still somewhere inside her, and there was no better way to tempt her out than this.

The bank was about at thigh height, but it was irregular enough that Tess found a way up it without having to use her hands. This part of the mountain was thick with trees and undergrowth, and Tess grasped at the flexible branches to keep her balance as she straightened up on top of the bank. The muddy little path looked a bit more slick from up here, but Tess was wearing hiking boots with good treads. It was a matter of a half dozen steps to reach the fir boughs, and then she could hang onto them while she stepped over them. Even if none of the other hikers wanted to come this way, at least she'd be on the far side and able to help people over the trunk more quickly.

She set one foot onto the muddy patch and it stayed put, gripped by her boot's treads. All right. This was where she proved to herself that she still had the gumption that drove her in her younger years.

Tess closed her eyes, her stomach twisting. Back in college, she'd had all the gumption she needed—except when it really mattered.

She'd been so happy, at the end of her senior year, when she received the letter announcing her acceptance to teach English in South Korea. It would be the first step toward her dream: she'd get experience relating to kids and helping them learn to love something unfamiliar to them. Then, she'd come back to the U.S. and teach girls how fun math can be and how they can excel at it as much as boys. Already she'd exchanged e-mails with the family she'd be staying with.

But then the doubts she thought she'd left behind at her small-town high school came rushing back like a rockslide. What if all of her friends had moved on by the time she got back? What if the people she met in Korea found out she was a lesbian and hated her for it? What if she failed miserably at teaching in a foreign setting and could get no good references, which would doom her chances of getting hired when she returned?

Staying here and looking for a local job would be safer. Easier. She wouldn't risk getting her heart broken or destroying her career before it started. So, on the day of the deadline to confirm her plans, Tess backed out.

It took less than a month for her to utterly regret that decision, and it was stuck like a poison thorn in her heart ever since.

Now, Tess looked down at the red-brown mud beneath her feet and chewed on her upper lip. She'd been so cowardly. Well, no more.

Tess took another step forward. Her boots slid an inch or so, but since she was expecting it, she kept her balance. Only a few more feet to the fir tree, and then she could hold onto those branches as well as the flimsy ones she was clinging to now.

"Tess!" Emily's shout came to her from the other side of the tree. "What are you doing? Just wait with the others!"

"I'm fine!" Tess called back. Emily could be really bossy sometimes, as if she always knew better than anybody else. *I'm not some reckless kid. I'm a grown-ass woman who knows when to take risks.* "This way is going to be—"

Then her foot slipped, and her knee bashed into a rock, and the branch she was holding onto bent much farther than expected, and she rolled onto her thigh and off the bank and down the slope.

Brown and orange and black blurred around her

as she tumbled, and the only thing she felt was pounding adrenaline and hard things battering her body. She squeezed her eyes shut, reaching for anything within her grasp that would slow her fall, but she was sliding too fast and her hands scraped past anything solid that they touched. There was nothing in her world but pain and fear—there wasn't even time to think how stupid she'd been.

Then Tess's body thudded into something soft, something firm with no rocks to bruise her or branches to claw her skin. For a moment, her head spun so badly she had no idea she'd halted in her fall. She felt cradled, curled protectively against this warm thing.

Her heart thudding loudly enough to eclipse all other sounds, Tess opened her eyes and looked up into Remy's alarmed face.

Chapter Three

I'm hallucinating.

She'd hit her head. That had to be it. Tess certainly remembered hitting her head a bunch of times as she toppled down the mountain slope, but she hadn't thought any of them had been hard enough to make her see things (aside from stars). Hallucination-Remy still stared down at her with wide blue eyes, breathing heavily.

"Good God. You don't screw up by halves, do you, Princess?"

Tess frowned, though it was really more of a wince. She would've hoped her hallucinations would be a little more chivalrous. Or at least polite.

Has she been knocked out? Was she still rolling down that hill in real life, probably toward a cliff with a rocky bottom where she'd bash her skull to pieces? But then she heard a clamor from above, shouting voices and scrambling feet, and she peered up through the trees to see the blurs of familiar-looking rain jackets heading toward them.

Tess blinked up at Remy, coming to the sudden realization that she was pressed close against Remy's chest in a standard bride-over-the-threshold carry while Remy half-knelt and half-sat in the underbrush.

Wait, this was *real?*

"Wh...what are you doing here?" Tess breathed.

If she thought she'd been dizzy before, that was nothing compared to the way Remy's concerned face—and, oh, God, her scent, like fresh herbs and wood shavings and pine trees—made her feel. Every limb trembled with spent adrenaline and relief, but she couldn't differentiate that from the parts of her that trembled at Remy's touch.

"Saving you from a broken neck, apparently," Remy replied with a raised eyebrow. Then the slightest of smiles appeared. "I don't know whether you have terrible luck or fantastic luck."

Tess watched her face, taking in the sculpted cheekbones, dark eyelashes, and lips that were a perfect shade of dusky rose but had probably never even seen a tube of lipstick. "Both."

Remy lifted her eyebrows in an expression that might have been surprise if it had been at all unguarded; as it was, it almost approached impressed. Tess had no idea what that was supposed to mean, but she felt the same confidence begin to unfold within her that she'd experienced when Remy first looked her up and down. It was conflicting and confounding—how could this woman make her feel powerful and like an idiot at the same time?

The sound of branches snapping and leaves crunching came to them then, and Paul scrambled through the woods from a lower part of the trail.

"Jesus Christ, Tammie! You can't do stupid things like that! If you get hurt, I'll be fired!"

Tess stared at him for a second until she realized he was talking to her. "Tess," she corrected. Everything else he'd said had yet to sink in.

Remy shifted, placing Tess's legs on the ground and sitting down beside her. She left her arm snug around Tess's waist. "Maybe you should, I dunno, ask her if she's okay?" Remy suggested with subtle venom in her tone. By then, Tess had had enough time to be appalled by her guide's priorities.

"You should thank *her* that your job is safe," Tess snapped. She tried to get her feet under her but the pain of smashing against so many things during her fall still reverberated through her body. Remy's arm tightened around her.

"You're not going anywhere until I make sure you still have all your parts," Remy ordered, her eyes flashing, and Tess sat back down. Obeying Remy was like a reflex; resentment and excitement stirred in equal portions in Tess's chest.

While Paul trudged back up to tell the other hikers that the excitement was over, Remy positioned herself downhill, in front of Tess. Her dark red-brown hair was not quite as effortlessly styled as the last time Tess had seen her, but tousled strands now hung down over one eye, making Tess's mouth go dry. Seeing Remy's eyes rove over her with concern made Tess remember parts of her body she'd almost forgotten she had.

And when Remy laid her hands on Tess's thigh, Tess's heart could've powered a small building. Tess watched with astonished fascination as Remy ran firm hands around her thigh and down her knee, lightly massaging and glancing up to gauge Tess's expression every so often. When she'd finished with that leg and ankle, she moved onto the other.

"Does any of this hurt?" Remy asked, and then one corner of her mouth hooked up when she noticed Tess's stunned, red face. Tess shook her head, unable to get words out. "Good," Remy said softly, and then her hands were smoothing down Tess's arms, gently bending her elbows and circling her wrists for her. Tess felt as limp as a wet sock, and she wasn't sure whether that was due to the loss of adrenaline or Remy's expert touch.

With the examination of her other arm complete, Tess expected that Remy would move away now, stand up, maybe offer her a hand like she had back at the cottage. But instead Remy leaned forward on her knees, her body pressing against Tess's shins as she sat on the hillside.

Tess's breath caught in her lungs. Remy's stomach was warm, solid, comforting against the bruises and her cold, wet jeans. She looked up into Remy's eyes, getting lost in their deep blue, frozen by the raw sensuality that surrounded this woman. Remy lifted her hands and cupped Tess's face with both palms. The callouses that Tess had found so pleasant when they shook hands made her shiver.

Something about Remy made Tess lose all capacity for rational thought. It was as if she were under a spell, entranced, and all she could do was feel. That face, those eyes, Remy's strong shoulders and the curve of her breasts just barely visible in the lines of her fitted hiking jacket—they captivated her.

Then Remy tilted Tess's head to one side and then the other, and Tess broke free of her reverie. Neck injuries. Remy was checking for neck injuries.

Tess's blush deepened and she frowned, humiliation darkening her eyes. Remy's hands slipped away from her face and she stood up in front of Tess, dusting off her knees. When her eyes met Tess's, there was a wry smile in them.

"Looks like you're all there."

Tess scrambled up, holding back a groan at the aches that protested. She didn't look to see if Remy had offered her a hand.

What's wrong with me? This woman treated me like garbage a few hours ago. She pulled a few sticks and leaves out of her hair and glanced tentatively over at Remy, who was watching her with her hands in her pockets. *And now she just saved my life.*

"Thanks," Tess said, her voice quiet. Remy gave a nod as if it were no big deal. "How... How did you even end up out here?"

With a grin, Remy tossed her head and cocked one hip. "Didn't I tell you? I'm a forest ranger with the U.S. Forest Service. I work in the park next to the resort property. I'm off today, but when your guide called down to the ranger station, they asked if I could go up and make sure you guys weren't getting yourselves into trouble." Her grin widened, and Tess knew she was about to make a smartass comment. Tess cut her off.

"Well, I appreciate it. Though I'm not sure why you'd bother yourself with 'one of *those.*'" She hadn't meant to sound quite so snippy, but Remy's earlier treatment of her had cut deep. She was surprised to see chagrin pass over Remy's face.

"I rescue hikers here all the time," Remy replied with a wave of her hand. "A lot of them are going up to Rising Star, but there are plenty of dumb ones who aren't." Tess wasn't sure if that was supposed to be some sort of apology. It didn't really sound like one. But hadn't Remy said she was off today, and wasn't this private property anyway? Did she regularly set out to rescue hikers she wasn't paid to help?

Remy started toward the trail, glancing at Tess

over her shoulder. "I'll walk with you up to where your group is." Tess followed her with furrowed brows, trying not to admire the view as Remy hiked up the hill several paces in front of her, her rear at convenient eye-level.

It was even harder climbing up the steep trail now that Tess was covered in bangs and bruises. Remy kept pace with her, though, and in several minutes they reached the fallen tree where the rest of the group waited. They had all managed to climb over.

Feeling chastened, Tess struggled over the trunk of the tree, but she at least did it without any assistance. Emily rushed over to her the moment she lowered herself down on the other side.

"Oh, my God, Tess, when I saw you go over the bank I almost passed out. You can't do stuff like that! You could've broken something!" Emily took Tess carefully by the shoulders and looked her over, brushing dirt off her jacket. Then her eyes moved beyond Tess's shoulder to Remy. "Who's that?"

"Uh..." Tess mentally groped for an appropriate way to describe Remy. Since everything that came to mind was too complicated, she settled with the bare minimum. "She's a forest ranger. She stopped me from falling."

"She saved your *life?*" Emily gasped, and Tess chewed on her lip, glancing over at Remy. She had to admit, that might not be an exaggeration. Emily raised both eyebrows with an impressed smile and mouthed *What a hottie!* Tess glared at her.

Meanwhile, Remy was heatedly discussing something with Paul. "These are dangerous climbing conditions, and the weather is taking a turn for the worse," she told him, her hands on her hips. "You need to turn around and come back down before someone really gets hurt. It's a miracle I was there to catch *her* as it was," she added, flicking her hand at Tess. Irritation appeared on Tess's face as she wondered whether that was supposed to be a dig.

A general murmur rippled through the group of hikers, and Paul folded his arms with a patronizing grimace. "We're almost to the lodge. It would be much more dangerous for us all to try to hike downhill in this slippery weather."

"Have you hiked this trail before?" Remy asked, although by her tone it wasn't much of a question. Paul looked guarded.

"Well, no, but I know this mountain like the back of my hand."

Remy cocked her head. "You've been a guide at the resort for, what...four months?"

"What's your point?" Paul demanded.

"My point is," Remy said, stepping closer to the tree trunk that separated the two of them, "you're not as close to the lodge as you think. This trail gets there eventually, but you've still got a good four hours of hiking left to go. And that's assuming you're going fast." She swept her gaze over the assembled group, and it came to rest on Tess. "I think I can safely say that you won't be."

Embarrassment welled up in Tess's chest like scalding steam. Did Remy exist to insult her? But then she caught a flicker of worry in Remy's eyes, and she wondered if it was possible to misinterpret what Remy had just said. Every moment they spent together, Tess felt more confused.

"*You* don't work for the resort, do you?" Paul asked pointedly. Tess was surprised to see Remy's face harden. She looked away from Paul, and he chuckled. "I thought not. I know for a fact that we're less than two hours from the lodge. Thank you for your assistance, but we're going to continue on." He looked over his shoulder at the group. "As long as that's what everyone wants?"

The wet, exhausted hikers exchanged glances. Six hours of slipping and sliding back down the mountain, or two more hours of arduous climbing before they got to change into warm clothes and sit in front of a fire? Everybody nodded, including Tess—her eyes on Remy, she gritted her teeth and tried to convince herself that her aches weren't *that* bad. She'd show Remy how tough she could be.

Remy rolled her eyes and shrugged, her jaw tight. "Fine. I can't make you do the smart thing. But if anyone wants to come back down with me, you're welcome to." She looked at Tess again, her blue eyes intent. Tess lifted her chin defiantly. She wasn't going to back out this time.

"Come on, folks," Paul said, turning and going to the front of the group. "Only a little bit longer." One by one, they all followed, and Emily put her arm around Tess's shoulder.

"I'll help you if you need it, okay?" Emily said, and Tess nodded. But when she looked back to watch Remy leave, she saw her instead climb spryly over the trunk with a frustrated frown on her face.

"Actually, I'm... I'm okay," Tess told Emily. She motioned with her thumb to where Stefan was leaning against a tree, stretching his lower back. "This is your romantic vacation. You don't need to be babysitting me the whole time. Besides, Stefan looks like he could use your help." She offered Emily a small, encouraging smile. Emily snorted, smiling too.

"He acts so macho, but I'd like to see *him* run a 10-K and a 5-K back-to-back." Emily had almost won the Women's Cross-Country Championship back when she and Tess were in college. She headed up the trail to help her boyfriend, and Tess hung back, trying to look casual. Moments later, Remy came up beside her.

"I thought you were going back down," Tess commented lightly. Remy let out a growly sigh.

"I'd never live it down with the other rangers if one of you falls off a cliff and smashes your brains out all over our mountain's picturesque granite."

Tess wrinkled her nose. "That image is a little too vivid."

"And that's leaving out what the bears could do to you," Remy added with a teasing grin. Tess shot her a flat look.

"You're not going to scare me, you know."

"Wouldn't dream of trying."

They hiked in silence for a while, and as much as Tess wanted to get to the resort, she was grateful to find that the other hikers were starting to slow their pace. Thankfully her ankles and knees were holding up, but the bruises on her hips and arms were making the hike through sleety snow even more uncomfortable.

"So what do you have against yoga?" she asked Remy during a relatively flat stretch of trail.

"I don't have anything against it," Remy replied, shrugging. "It's great for your body and people tell me it's very relaxing."

Tess narrowed her eyes. "Then why were you such a jerk when I said I was going up to Rising Star?"

Remy shrugged again, exhaling through her nose. "It's not the yoga. It's the resort. And the people who usually go there." She cast a glance at Tess, her eyes once again running up and down Tess's body. A warm, conflicting surge of pride and self-consciousness flooded through Tess. "It's possible I might have jumped to conclusions. But most of the time, the people who come here are rich, entitled morons who don't know the first thing about spending even a few hours in the wilderness."

Tess's mouth pulled to the side and she gazed dolefully up at the group ahead of them. One of the college kids was scrambling to pick up a pile of camping gadgets he'd spilled out of his backpack while trying to get his water bottle out, and the middle-aged man was putting a Band-Aid on a blister his loafers had given him. One of the ladies wearing white shorts had her phone out again and was taking a picture of herself. "I'd be lying if I said you were all wrong. But I'm certainly not rich, and I try not to be entitled." She shot a brief sardonic smile at Remy. "I guess you'll have to decide whether I'm a moron or not."

"There's a thin line between moronicy and bravery," Remy said, her eyes meeting Tess's as if they were sharing a secret. "And I'll admit I've crossed over once or twice."

Not for the first time, Tess wondered if she should interpret Remy's words as a compliment or an insult. But the way Remy looked at her, with appraising eyes and a perceptive, amused smile on her lips, made her feel worth looking at...and that deserved the benefit of the doubt, just this once.

The snow was an inch deep when Tess's

dogged cheerfulness finally ran out. Climbing a path with this many steep sections and fallen branches and trees to climb over was bad enough, but now she could see her breath in the swirling snow and blond curls were sticking to her face beneath the soaked hood of her windbreaker. Her ankles and knees ached.

Ahead, even the college students no longer seemed to be enjoying themselves. Paul had a determined scowl on his face, as if he wouldn't allow even himself to question his decision. Tess glanced over at Remy; the two of them had fallen silent some time ago, and Remy looked tense. She noticed Tess looking at her and shook her head slowly.

"I don't like this."

Nervousness flipped Tess's stomach over. She was pretty sure that wasn't just a general comment about how miserable the climb was.

"What do you mean?" Tess asked.

"We're moving a lot more slowly even than I anticipated." Remy pushed her knitted beanie up off her forehead and frowned at the sky. When she'd put the hat on a little while ago, Tess had to look away lest little heart bubbles appear over her head—she loved a short-haired woman in a winter hat. But now, Remy's grim expression was more important than how sexy she looked. "Best estimate, we're still at least two hours away. And night falls fast in the snow."

Now it was Tess's turn to look up at the sky. It was the heavy, blank white of a snowfall, and she watched the pale gray silhouettes of snowflakes float down over them. Now that Remy mentioned it, the shadows beneath the trees were a lot deeper than they were a little while ago. Tension crept into Tess's shoulders, making her bruises even more painful.

"What are we going to do if we don't get there by then?"

Remy shrugged her eyebrows, giving Tess a look that said "I think you already know." Tess moaned quietly.

About twenty minutes later, when everyone stopped for a breather, Remy approached Paul with Tess trailing behind.

"Listen," Remy said. "Anybody can misjudge distance, especially in bad weather. I think even you can agree that we're not going to make it to the lodge tonight." Paul's eyes shifted nervously to the hikers around them as everyone fell silent.

"Of course we'll make it to the lodge," he scoffed, but even he didn't sound convinced.

"Do you really want to hike this group up an unfamiliar high-intensity trail, in the snow, in the *dark?*"

"Um..." Paul glanced behind himself at the others again. There were undeniably a bedraggled group.

"Are you saying we're going to sleep out *here?*" asked one of the white-shorts ladies. She looked around as if she expected a Sheraton Hotel to pop up out of the mountainside. "Where?"

Remy responded with a serious stare. "There's a maintenance shed I know of that's just a little ways away. It's not ideal, but it'll give us shelter and keep us relatively warm. Did anyone bring emergency blankets?"

"Yeah!" piped up one college student. "Jackson's dad made sure we're prepared for any hiking emergency!" She swung her backpack off her shoulder before Remy could say anything and began digging through it. "Along with plenty of emergency blankets, we have extra socks, a first aid kit, head lamps, foil-packet meals, a GPS that can run on water power and solar power and is synchronized with the atomic clock, signal flares, a water filtration straw—"

"Okay, okay," Remy cut in with an amused glance at Tess, who was glaring at the students with disgusted disbelief. "I have a couple of blankets in my pack too. We can build a campfire to warm up and hopefully dry out a little, stay the night in the shed, and get to the resort in the morning."

The white-shorts ladies looked dubious, but the college students and the middle-aged woman were starting to perk up. The latter turned to her husband with an excited (though tired) grin, and he scowled. Tess exhaled, relieved that an end was in sight.

"But... But..." Paul shoulders drooped. "I'm going to get in so much trouble."

Remy threw him a sideways glance. "I think your priority right now should be the safety of your hikers. The trail up to the shed is just a few minutes ahead of us. Let's get going before darkness falls completely."

The mood had been less than enthusiastic since they found the washout in the trail and started this alternate route, but now a tentative relief seemed to fall over the hikers. Just as Remy predicted, they continued on for another ten minutes and came to a narrow track that led off to their left. The track didn't ascend much and so was easier to navigate in the fleeting twilight.

Tess looked up through the trees ahead and saw power lines swooping through the darkening sky. A handful of minutes later, they emerged into a grassy swath cut into the forest, following the lines and poles all the way up and down the mountain. A small cinderblock building sat beneath one of the poles, its heavy metal door fastened with a lock.

"Um," Tess whispered to Remy as they approached. "How are we going to get in?"

"Leave that to me," Remy replied with a sideways smirk that made Tess's breath hitch momentarily. While the group gathered by the door and the college kids began unpacking their ten thousand hiking gizmos, Remy went around the back of the shed and reappeared moments later brandishing a key.

Tess came to stand beside her as she fiddled with the lock. "How did you know where that was?"

"I have my ways," said Remy airily, then shot Tess a mysterious smile. Tess shook her head.

"What is it, a state secret?" Being kept in the dark for no reason was something that Tess found particularly irksome. With a flourish, Remy removed the padlock and pushed the door open.

"Are you going to be okay sleeping rough, Princess?" she asked, and Tess glared at her for changing the subject.

"I've been camping plenty of times, I'll have you know. Not that I can say I've ever owned a water filtration straw," she added with a chilly glare at the college students. Remy chuckled.

"You're not the sort of person I expected to see on a retreat like this," she mused, her eyes straying down to Tess's lips. Tess tried to look offended, but she couldn't keep a bewildered smile from creeping onto her face.

"I don't make my confetti out of dollar bills, if that's what you're implying." It was hard enough to keep her cool around Remy without the woman constantly checking her out. "I wouldn't even be on this trip if I hadn't been given the ticket as a gift—from somebody who won it in a raffle, no less."

"Ah." Remy nodded as if that answered a question.

"What, do you think this sort of thing isn't worth the money?"

Remy shrugged one shoulder. "Maybe. The Rising Star's clientele doesn't strike me as particularly sincere, is all."

"Because you've gotten to know so many of them," Tess scoffed. To her shock, a red blush spread up Remy's neck.

"Hey, everyone—the door's open," she called tersely, brushing past Tess to head toward the college students and their pile of gear. "We've got to clear everything out that's removable so there's enough space for all of us." Tess watched her go, mouth open. *She looks at me as if she knows everything about me, but she won't give up a single thing about herself.*

Sighing, Tess dug a flashlight out of her backpack and flicked it on, shining it into the storage shed. It wasn't, as she feared, overrun with spiders and hornets, but there was stuff piled everywhere and it smelled strongly of mildew and motor oil. She and Emily ended up carrying most of the junk out, aided somewhat by the middle-aged couple; Stefan had done something to his back while hiking and was out of commission, the white-shorts ladies just stood near the doorway looking horrified, and Paul had elected himself overseer of the college kids and Remy as they started the campfire.

After about twenty minutes, a heap of toolboxes, buckets, tarps, and other equipment lay against the outer wall of the shed and Tess had located a broom to sweep out the dust and dead insects. Then she and Emily shook out a couple of the tarps and laid them down on the floor so they'd have at least something between them and the cold concrete. By this time, Remy had set up the campfire on a handful of fist-sized rocks she'd instructed the college students to gather, ensuring that any melted snow from the flames would run off without dousing the fire. Tess watched as Remy helped the kids secure an emergency blanket against the cinderblock wall nearest the fire to provide more heat reflection.

"She really knows what she's doing, huh?" Emily commented, stopping beside Tess.

"Yeah, she's a real jack-of-all-trades," Tess responded acidly. Emily turned to her with a slow, sly smile.

"I don't know what you're so sore about. You've been getting pretty cozy with your rescuer."

"Who, Remy?" Tess snorted. "She's...weird. She's got a chip on her shoulder about the yoga resort, for some reason."

"Yeah, but she's smokin'."

Tess huffed a breath out her nose and glowered at her friend. "Smokingness aside," she pointed out, "I can't tell whether she thinks I'm a complete loser or..." She stopped, a blush coming to her cheeks.

"Or what?" Emily asked, starting to sound legitimately curious.

"Well, she keeps...looking at me. Like I'm... I dunno. Pretty."

"You *are* pretty, dummy!" Emily laughed incredulously. "If someone that hot has noticed, you better take advantage of it."

"I'm not going to have a fling, Emily," Tess

said. "You know me. And especially not one with...her." Remy stood a dozen feet away, her hands on her hips, examining the fire setup. The way she stood, like she wouldn't tolerate anyone encroaching on her space, made Tess's heartbeat speed up even as she scowled. She couldn't even explain it—she'd never felt this much raw attraction for anyone. And it wasn't just physical attraction (although there was certainly plenty of that). Tess was attracted to Remy's voice, her attitude, the way Remy made her feel seen. Even Remy's capacity to fill her with conflicting emotions was compelling.

But she could be *such* a pain in the ass.

Chapter Four

Tess had to admit, the food that the college kids brought was pretty delicious. They had, of course, packed a cooking pot, and there was enough snow piled up by the windward side of the shed to melt for water so nobody had to use up their hiking supply. The little foil packets of dry ingredients transformed into gourmet dinners such as salmon pasta with cream sauce, chana masala, and twelve-spice shepherd's pie. Unfortunately there weren't enough utensils to go around, and Tess spent a gleeful half hour watching the white-shorts ladies trying to eat chana masala with their fingers.

After they ate, the group huddled around the campfire trying to soak up as much warmth as possible before they had to go inside to sleep. Tess would have normally made herself a big part of the conversation, but with this particular group, she felt a little bit like an island. She didn't share life experiences or values with most of these people, and Emily wasn't much of a talker in group situations. It seemed that Remy was the same.

When the conversation turned to yoga, one of the white-shorts ladies took her phone out of a very expensive-looking handbag and started taking a video "for her personal development vlog." Silly as she thought that was, Tess perked up, hoping that the talk of yoga might give her a chance to chat a little. She was wrong.

"My guru told me," said the lady into her phone's camera, "that I should be able to reach a state of enlightenment in another three months or so. But just because I'm enlightened doesn't mean I won't need his guidance." The other two ladies nodded sagely, and Tess tried to keep her eyes from rolling all the way out of her head and down the mountain. "What are you hoping to accomplish this week?" The lady turned her phone to one of her friends.

"Well, my guru told me that this retreat will be especially beneficial for my spiritual development," she replied. "He said the reason my son is so fussy is because I was badly parented in a past life, and once I work through that, Zebulonne will sleep through every night as quiet as a mouse!"

"*My* guru told *me* to give up sugar, and now my aura is twice as bright and I'm able to levitate." The words were out of Tess's mouth before she even thought about whether that level of sarcasm was appropriate for a complete stranger. She heard a stifled snort from Remy, but the rest of the hikers fell silent.

Even the flickering light of the campfire couldn't hide the blush on Tess's face. The white-shorts ladies glared daggers at her, and Paul coughed. He leveled a look at Tess as if she were a second-grader who burped in class and he was her teacher.

"It's impolite to make fun of other people's spiritual beliefs, Tammie."

"*Tess,*" she said, closing her eyes in momentary frustration. Then she looked over at Zebulonne's mother and grimaced. "I'm sorry. That was mean." Her skin burned all over with embarrassment and she was highly aware that the lady with the fancy handbag was still filming on her phone. Tess should've been used to her big mouth getting her into trouble, but every time it happened, she felt just as flustered as if she were in junior high again.

"Well, *Tess*," Zebulonne's mother said snidely, looking down her nose, "I hope that in your next life you learn to be a little more tolerant."

Tess stared at her for a moment and then got up off the tarp she'd been sitting on. "I'm going to bed," she said flatly and went into the shed before anyone could respond.

"Bed" was an exaggeration. At Remy's suggestion, they had brought in armfuls of leaves and pine boughs to lay on the floor before replacing the tarps, and that made a slightly softer mattress than concrete would, but only slightly. Tess picked up one of the emergency blankets that the college kids had left near the door and wrapped herself in it, then went and sat in one of the corners.

Despondency settled on her like a cloud. She'd just doomed herself to a retreat with no friends except Emily—and since Emily ought to be spending almost all of her time with her boyfriend, that essentially meant no friends. Yeah, okay, the other hikers were annoying, entitled, or incompetent (or all three). But nobody liked being mocked, and if she didn't do something about her tendency to run off at the mouth, this would be a pretty miserable week. She'd be at an unfamiliar place doing things she'd only started to learn about, and she was starting to feel like even annoying friends would be better than none.

Tess's heart leapt into her throat when the door opened again. But it wasn't Paul coming to give her a talking-to or the white-shorts ladies ganging up on her like mean girls in a lunchroom.

It was Remy.

Tess kept a wary eye on her as Remy approached, her boots making crinkling sounds on the tarp-covered leaves. She sat down next to Tess against the wall.

"Hey."

"Hi," Tess replied in a low voice. They sat together for a while in silence, and Tess felt like she might either explode or faint with the tension, the anticipation of finding out why Remy had joined her. Then Remy leaned her head back against the cinderblock wall and shot Tess a sidelong smirk.

"That was fuckin' hilarious."

Tess began to smile tentatively. "You think?"

Laughing through her nose, Remy turned an amused grin on Tess. "She thinks going on a yoga retreat is going to make her newborn sleep through the night? I pity that kid!"

"I pity anyone unfortunate enough to be named 'Zebulonne,' personally," Tess added, chuckling. Remy shook her head.

"And that other one. Clearly her 'guru' is scamming her. I can't say I know much about enlightenment, but I'm pretty sure you can't mark down in your day planner the time when you're going to achieve it."

Tess started to feel more at ease. "I *tried* to be patient with them, really. I haven't said anything all day, and they've all been asking for it. Did you know that those two college students don't know the first thing about using any of that fancy equipment? Paul had to show them how to turn their electronic hand-warmers on. And that one woman kept saying to her husband: 'It's not miserable, it's authentic!' I think I can fairly say that our hike today was both."

"If by 'authentic' you mean that you were authentically trudging up a mountain through sleet and mud, then yes," Remy agreed, her eyes sparkling with laughter. "Do you see now how right I was?"

Tess rolled her eyes but gave Remy and indulgent smile. "Fine, yes. But I'm still mad at you for jumping to conclusions about me. And I still think you were a jerk. But so was I out there, so I guess we can be jerks together." Tess watched how the laughter smoothed some of the hardness away from Remy's face, how her eyes crinkled at the corners. Remy had gorgeous features when she wore a tough expression, like a warrior archangel carved from stone, but when she smiled, there was so much life there. Tess wanted to draw more smiles from her—ones that were happy and unguarded instead of the sly, discerning smiles she had so often graced Tess with today.

"I've given all of them nicknames, you know," Tess told her. "Because I can't remember any of their real names. That's not their fault—I've just got a terrible memory. But it kept me occupied while we were hiking." She smiled impishly, leaving that piece of information out there.

"Well?" Remy prodded after a moment. "You can't just say that and not tell me what the nicknames are!"

"Okay," Tess said, holding up her hands and scooting around so she and Remy were facing each other, knees to knees. "First, those three ladies with the white shorts. You've noticed that one of them is wearing all these loose bracelets? They kept getting caught in branches and stuff. I call her 'Way Too Many Bangles Betty.' Then there's the one who's been carrying that ridiculous pocketbook over her arm, even though she's got a backpack like the rest of us. She's 'Thousand-Dollar Handbag Hannah.' And the third one's been stopping every mile or so to touch up her lipstick."

Remy, who was trying to catch her breath in between bouts of laughter, flapped her hand at Tess. "She's the one who looks like a raccoon now after all this rain!"

"That's right," Tess replied, grinning. "I see you've noticed 'Overly Made-Up Millie.'"

"Oh, you've got to keep going," Remy urged as she leaned back against the wall, weak with laughter.

"Right, so those college kids? I call the boy 'I Only Eat Organic Oliver.' His daddy clearly buys him only the best of everything. And the girl keeps talking about how she—" Tess put on a snobby, mimicking voice. "'avoids the consumption of all popular media,' so she's 'I Don't Watch TV Tina.'"

"Ha! And the older couple?" Remy wiped tears of mirth from her eyes.

"I'd lost my creative kick by then," Tess admitted with a lopsided smile. "They're just 'Reinvented Middle-Aged Woman' and 'Reluctant Husband.'"

"Short and to the point," Remy chortled. "Okay, what about Paul? He seems ripe for it."

"Well, I actually managed to remember his name, but I just kept cracking up at his hair...so I've been calling him 'Paul Bun-yan.'" Remy gave a shout of laughter and covered her mouth with one hand.

"Wow, nobody ever gets me to laugh at puns,

but that one was just too good. What about those other two? The tall girl with the really long legs and the guy who threw out his back?"

"Well..." Tess scratched the back of her head sheepishly. "They're actually friends of mine, so I didn't give them nicknames. I guess I should be calling myself 'Snarky McJudgypants.'"

"I dunno, I think we could come up with a better nickname for you than that." Remy's grin widened slowly and her hooded eyes flashed with innuendo. Heat sparked on Tess's skin and her cheeks tingled with a blush. Remy had that look again—that knowing, calculating look that made Tess feel like Remy was sizing her up and finding her entirely satisfactory. Remy's whole attitude changed at those times, from her posture to the energy she exuded. It went from aloof, short-tempered, even callous to alert and predatory, focused on Tess as if she were the only thing in the world. For Tess, this was an exhilarating ego-boost at the same time as it overwhelmed her.

"Like what?" Tess murmured, her heart thudding in her ears, reverberating in every fingertip. Remy leaned forward over her folded legs, her knees pressing into Tess's. She rested her forearms on her knees and ran a finger lightly along the top of Tess's thigh. This close, Tess could smell the wood smoke from the fire on her and the sharp scent of snow.

Remy's lips quirked in a suggestive smile. "I guess I'll have to get to know you better to find out."

The air that filled Tess's lungs seemed to grow thicker now, and she fought to draw a breath. Every particle of her being was focused on Remy, like a telescope through which she could see nothing besides the single star filling its lens. For a moment, Tess was so completely taken with Remy's face, with her deep-sea eyes and the confident curve of her lips and the perfect angle of her jaw, that she forgot her body even existed. But then she felt Remy's hand rest on her thigh, light and questioning, at odds with Remy's commanding expression. That touch made sensation ripple through her body like she'd been lit on fire.

This is a bad idea. This is a bad, bad, bad idea. Whoever that little voice in her mind was, they weren't nearly loud enough to drown out the attraction thrumming through Tess's veins. She wanted to know what Remy's lips tasted like. She wanted to know if kissing Remy would be as utterly confusing as interacting with Remy was otherwise, or if it would suddenly make everything she was feeling clear.

Sometimes Tess felt like she had no idea what Remy was thinking—right now, it couldn't be more obvious. Remy's deep blue eyes were dark, her lips parted, an expression of undeniable desire playing like light over her face. Tess's body answered that look by tilting her chest forward and lifting her chin, in spite of the rational part of her that warned her away from this unpredictable woman.

Remy's lips drifted closer and her breath whispered across Tess's mouth. Tess forced her mind to go blank, to stop the fretting and the chiding for just one moment. She saw Remy close her eyes, and Tess closed her eyes too. A brush, an electric spark, a caress of skin that sent goosebumps thrilling down Tess's arms—Remy's lips were soft but white-hot, and the desire to grasp Remy's shoulders and drag her into a passionate, powerful kiss was almost too much for Tess to resist.

Then, with a bone-rattling bang, someone flung

open the shelter's metal door. Tess jumped about five inches off the ground, and when she opened her eyes, Remy had scooted away and was glaring at the crowd of hikers that streamed into the room.

"Remy!" Paul shouted from outside. "Can you come help take this heat reflector thing down? I can't figure out how you rigged it up!"

With a sigh that was more like a growl, Remy got to her feet and shouldered through the group to get to the door. Tess remained seated, stock-still, every muscle trembling.

What *was* that? What had she almost done? She'd almost abandoned all reason, that's what. Tess's shoulders curled inward and she pressed her hands to her chest. It scared her how good abandoning her reason had felt.

The other hikers moved around her, putting down their backpacks and unfolding emergency blankets. Tess felt like her senses were too heightened even to move; if she did, she might fly apart. Her lips felt swollen, burnt. The faint taste of Remy still tingled there. She pulled in one careful breath after another, and after a few minutes she felt settled enough to arrange her own sleeping space.

As much as Tess considered herself a people person, personal space was important. Sleeping with nine other people in a room barely larger than her kitchen was about as comfortable as a sitting on a cactus. Speaking of which, the layer of leaves and pine boughs they'd laid on the floor only made the hard concrete lumpy and pokey. Tess pressed herself as closely as she could against the wall, since that seemed better than being sardined between two other people. She had nothing but her backpack for a pillow, and although she put on an extra sweatshirt and wrapped herself in the emergency blanket, she still felt chilly. Sleeping in a cinderblock shack wrapped up in tin foil like a burrito was pretty much the opposite of what Tess had been expecting on this vacation.

A solitary, bare light bulb hung from the ceiling and providing the only light. When Remy came back inside, she flicked it off. The room was plunged into darkness with the exception of a few dim spots of light from cellphone screens (no matter that they couldn't make any calls—some of them needed a soothing game of Candy Crush after the day they'd had). Tess huddled inside her blanket and wondered how on earth she'd get any sleep. She was exhausted and everything hurt, but her blood was vibrating through her veins and she couldn't see sleep anywhere on the horizon.

Amidst the coughs and shifting clothes, Tess heard light footsteps crunching toward her. Then, there was a sound that made her heart ricochet around in her chest like a pinball: someone lay down next to her. The smell of forests and wood smoke identified Remy.

Tess stayed still, hardly daring to breath. This had to be the only place left in the room to sleep, right? Considering how Remy had acted earlier, though, maybe she had more in mind. Confusion knotted in Tess's stomach. If Remy made another move, would she resist her, as she knew she should? Or would her body take over again?

The barest whisper reached her ears then. "Sorry about earlier." Remy's voice was almost inaudible, and in the darkness, Tess couldn't see her expression even when she peeked out of her blanket. Remy didn't seem the type to apologize, though, and Tess bit her lip.

"What for?" she asked, matching Remy's volume.

"I came on a little strong," Tess heard Remy say. There was a pause, and a gravely quality crept into Remy's voice. "I don't want you to get the wrong impression."

Tess's heart thumped against her ribs. What impression was that? That Remy was the type of person who'd put the moves on a woman she'd only just met? Or that Remy was interested in Tess at all? She stayed silent, hoping that Remy would clarify.

"I..." Remy trailed off, and Tess wished she could see her face. Her voice sounded tentative, unsure, and that was the opposite of everything Tess had seen in her since the moment they met. "I got carried away."

But what did that *mean*? Tess couldn't bring herself to ask. Exploring these feelings was a bad idea; any encouragement she gave would only make it worse. Her heart squeezed like a wrung-out sponge, but she knew that was the right decision. Remy made her feel too many conflicting things, and Tess needed to be absolutely sure before she even considered someone to be date material. And nothing was sure about Remy...except the fact that Tess couldn't stop thinking about her.

All Tess could think to say was "Okay." She murmured it softly, wincing as she did. What a feeble answer.

In the darkness, she could hear Remy's breath but she couldn't discern what Remy might be thinking or feeling. If only she could see her face... The tarp crinkled and Tess felt Remy roll onto her back. That was that, then.

Tess pulled the emergency blanket back up

around her ears and huddled against the wall. It was cold but not unbearably so, and the room had already gotten stuffy with the presence of so many people. There was so much going on in her mind that she had to concentrate to keep it quiet enough to doze; but gradually, she realized that she felt a tiny bit more comfortable. With Remy beside her, there was a barrier between her and the rest of the group. It wasn't like being alone by any means, but somehow, she felt almost...protected.

A flood of aches and pains came creeping back with the rising of the sun. Tess thought she'd been sore yesterday—she'd been in perfect health compared with how she felt this morning. Sometime after day broke, one of the hikers got up and propped the shed door open. The breeze that came in actually felt good, although it was chilly, because the room had become so stifling in the night. Tess had alternated between exhausted sleep and vaguely conscious dozing, but now that others were moving around, she found herself quite awake. Able to move without pain was an entirely different matter.

Groaning, Tess climbed to her feet and started to fold up her blanket. Her knees and hips hurt the most, since they'd been worn out by hiking as well as battered when she fell. She struggled to put her backpack on, and then gave up and just carried it outside where the college students were passing out granola bars.

"Hey." Remy appeared beside Tess, who nearly jumped out of her skin. With a small sideways smile,

Remy continued softly, "'I Only Eat Organic Oliver' has a first aid kit, and I bet if you asked he'd give you some Advil or something. In fact, the kid probably has hospital-grade painkillers in there."

"I dunno, do you think he approves of pharmaceuticals like that? Won't he just give me arnica salve or something? Anyway, I have my own first aid kit." Tess's ability to make a snarky comment seemed intact, at least. She was grateful that it came automatically and saved her from her inner awkwardness toward Remy.

Remy just chuckled and continued past her to start hauling the shed's equipment back inside. Tess watched her go, her mouth pulling to one side. How did she get herself into this conundrum?

She took a double dose of Advil from her kit with her nearly-empty bottle of water and then filled the bottle back up with fresh snow. After about twenty minutes of sweeping their makeshift mattress material out of the shed and moving the buckets and toolboxes back inside, they were ready to go.

"I'd say we're about two hours from the resort," Remy told Paul, and this time he didn't argue with her. He looked wilted and mussed. They all shouldered their packs and headed away from the maintenance shed, toward their trail.

The storm had dissipated overnight and two inches of fresh snow lay over the woods like a thin, cold blanket. The sun was out brightly now in a deep blue sky, and as the morning began to warm, snow pattered off the trees. As tired as she was, the sight made Tess smile. It wasn't every day that she got to walk in the deep woods after a snowfall. There were animal footprints crisscrossing the ground everywhere she looked, from ones large enough to be deer to the tiny scratches of mice feet.

Tess watched Remy's back as the woman hiked in front of her, staying near the head of the group. Remy had taken off her hat and somehow, the longer hair on the top of her head was a perfect wave over her crown. Tess was pretty sure that in contrast, she looked like she'd stuck a fork into an electrical outlet. Her blonde curls were frizzy enough as it was without sleeping in a humid room with her hood up all night. She'd never get them untangled.

Last night had thrown her self-assuredness and optimism into the gutter. When Remy touched her thigh as they sat together, her vibe had been pretty clear—Tess had been positive that Remy initiated their brief kiss. But after they were interrupted and Remy backed off so quickly, now Tess wasn't so sure.

She couldn't deny that she'd felt lonely lately. Discovering that Emily and Stefan were on an anniversary trip and then making the white-shorts ladies and Paul mad at her had only exacerbated that loneliness. And Remy was undeniably hot. Tess's cheeks prickled as the blood rushed to her face. Was it possible that she was just projecting her hopes onto Remy? She remembered those eyes, the darkening of their deep blue to indigo in an expression she'd taken at the time to be desire. Tess couldn't imagine what else that could have been. But it wasn't as if she'd been exactly thinking clearly.

As they hiked, the trail gradually began to flatten out. The melting snow made the going muddy, though; when mid-morning approached, they were liberally spattered in mud and grime up to their shins. This was the final insult to the white-shorts ladies, and although they had only periodically complained yesterday, they had reached their limit and a constant stream of whining could be heard from them. Tess was just glad that the trail was a little more even now. Mud might not be slipperier than snow, but it was definitely grosser to fall into.

To block out the aggrieved conversations of the rest of the hikers, Tess started to mentally plan what she'd do once they arrived at the lodge. They'd have to check in, of course, but the first order of business after that was a long, hot shower. Between the sweat, the mud, and having slept in a dusty, moldy shack all night, she'd never felt so dirty in her life.

And this (she remembered her brother's words with a smile) was a fancy-pants resort. It was bound to have the most luxurious of amenities. The bed would be huge and so soft you'd sink right down into it. And the shower, she was sure, would be one of those huge tiled rooms where soft lights streamed down on you while you stood under the multi-spray showerhead. She'd turn on the regular spray first, and then the massage spray...

Something warm and pleasant began to swirl in Tess's abdomen. A shower like that would be the perfect place for two bodies to press together, curve fitting into curve, water sluicing down over fingers that dug into backs. The perfect place to taste someone's lips, to feel the hot water mingling in your mouths. The water would tickle in delightful places and provide a contrast to the smoothing of hands over skin and the gentle rake of nails. The sensation of the falling droplets would be an incredible addition to the feeling of your breasts against hers, your hips rocking with hers...

Tess tripped on a rock and stumbled, heat

crawling all over her skin with mortified awareness. She recognized those hands, those lips. She'd kissed them last night.

With a dismayed moan, Tess covered her face with both hands. How had her body and her feelings gotten so out of control? This needed to stop, and now.

"Problem?" Remy was suddenly there at her side, regarding her with that I-know-too-much-about-you smirk. Tess flushed crimson and glared at her.

"You've got to stop sneaking up on me like that."

Remy grinned, running her fingers through the short locks falling over her forehead. "And *you* should be a little more aware of your surroundings. You might fall down another hill."

Tess stuck out her tongue before thinking better of it, and then she felt like a child. She sighed, giving Remy a hard eye. "How soon until we get there?"

"It's not far now," Remy replied, still smiling as if the joke were on Tess. "Probably twenty minutes or so."

"Thank all the gods," Tess huffed. "I'm going to be so damn happy to see that place."

Remy grunted, and Tess glanced at her with surprise. The smile was no longer on her face—instead, there was a reluctance just short of nausea. Tess raised her eyebrows, but Remy refused to look at her and quickened her pace so that she moved to the start of the group once more.

Tess wanted to throw up her arms in frustration, but she ached too much for that. Remy was confusing and unpredictable enough all on her own, regardless of what she made Tess feel. Throw in this befuddling mix of attraction and irritation and the sense that she should know better, and it was a recipe for disaster.

Chapter Five

The trail widened less than a mile later into a gravelly road, and then, over the tops of the snow-frosted evergreens, Tess saw the Rising Star Resort. The snow had melted from the paved circular drive in front of the main doors and the sunlight shone into the lodge's numerous windows.

The Rising Star Resort's chalet-style lodge was built from warm honey-colored wood and sprawled over a few acres of land in the high mountain valley. The main building consisted of clapboard-covered walls, peaked roofs, and numerous gables, all paneled with windows. Rising above the entrance patio was a high wall of glass panes topped with a triangular roof. This wall was split in two by a towering stone chimney that emerged from the peak of the roof; a welcoming cloud of smoke drifted from the chimney's mouth. Lights sparkled in every window.

Paul led the group up to the entrance and held the door open for them as they streamed in with grateful exhaustion. The moment they came through the door, a young woman came out from behind the desk and dashed over to them, a look of immense relief on her face. She had very straight mouse-brown hair that fell to her shoulders and her bangs were swept to the side and held with two barrettes. Her white dress shirt and black skirt were impeccably pressed.

"Paul! Oh, thank God. Did the search team find you?"

Paul looked happier to see her than he had looked since it started to rain the day before, but then his brows drew together. "Search team?"

"Yeah, we sent one out early this morning for you. Everybody was so worried—the weather report said the storm wasn't supposed to come this way." She looked over Paul's shoulder at the guests. "They didn't find you, then?"

"Nope," Remy replied, coming forward. The girl's face lit up when she caught sight of her. "We stayed the night in one of the maintenance sheds down by the power lines. But we're all here in once piece."

"Remy! No wonder they were okay if you were there." The girl, whose nametag read "Martha," relaxed visibly. "I'll radio the team and say you're safe. Then the second I'm done, I'll check you guys all in, okay?" She smiled and nodded at the hikers and then scurried back to the desk.

"Thanks, Marti," Remy called. Her eyes roved over the large common room and she grimaced; seeing this, Tess looked around too, hoping to figure out what Remy found so distasteful.

Like the outside, the inside of the lodge was built of warm wood. Hand-hewn rafters in the Scandinavian style held up the ceilings and the bare log beams were shiny with lacquer. The floor (on which the hikers currently stood dripping water and mud) was made of irregularly shaped flagstones, and in places there were thick area rugs in dark greens, reds, and browns. Furniture was scattered throughout the area past the reception desk: leather couches and easy chairs made up most of the seating and there were a few tables and coffee tables, all hand-made out of honey-yellow wood. The walls were hung with festive fall garlands and horns of plenty. A fire flickered and snapped in the fireplace behind them and another crackled at the other end of the room.

It short, it was the most welcoming, comfortable-looking place Tess had ever seen. She thought she might cry with gratitude.

After Marti got off the radio with the search team, she turned her bright smile on the bedraggled hikers. "All right! Let's get you to your rooms so you can relax and recover!"

"Recover!" one of the white-shorts ladies scoffed ("Thousand-Dollar Handbag Hannah," if Tess recalled correctly). "I'll never recover from that! We want our money back. Don't we, girls?" The other two nodded but looked as if they were too wiped out to add their indignation.

"After you've come all this way?" Marti looked distressed. "Don't you want to rest and get cleaned up? I'm going to have to talk to my manager—we did receive your waivers for the hike that came with your tickets..."

Remy sidled smoothly up to the three young ladies. "You may not feel like it now, but I promise you, the Rising Star is worth a hike even as grueling as that one. And besides, maybe that was the test of your spirituality. You made it through and worked off some of the troubles of your past lives... You should celebrate."

The three of them gaped at her with wide, wonder-filled eyes. "Wow," one said. "That is so deep."

They turned back to the desk and checked themselves in, and Tess gave Remy an incredulous stare. Remy sauntered over.

"Yeah, hip-wader deep," Tess muttered. "How come they don't get mad at *you* when you mock their spirituality?" And since when did Remy think so much of this resort?

Remy responded with a smirk and a shrug. "What can I say? Ladies find me irresistible."

Tess pressed her lips together, both annoyed and turned on by Remy's blasé confidence. At least that confirmed that Remy was interested in women (as if last night hadn't been a good indication).

There was the click of a door opening in the quiet of the common room and then a woman emerged from behind the reception desk. A movement at Tess's side—Remy stepping back—caught Tess's attention and shock zipped down her spine as she watched Remy's face go white, then flush a mottled red. Tess turned her eyes back to the woman who had just appeared; Remy's gaze was pinned on this woman too, and her face was as hard and stiff as if she'd been carved out of the same wood that the lodge was built from.

The woman's high-heeled shoes tapped on the stone floor as she came toward the group of hikers. Her eyes skated over them, but when they came to rest on Remy, her crimson lips turned up in a slow, surprised, calculating smile. Then she turned back to the hikers and clapped her hands together.

"Folks, I am *so sorry* for the ordeal you went through. I'm Melissa Hart, the owner of this resort, and I want to officially apologize on behalf of everyone here." In her charcoal gray pencil skirt and dress jacket combination, complete with a pressed white shirt underneath showing the barest of feminine ruffles on the placket, Melissa looked the height of elegant businesswoman. She brushed a few strands of her ash-blonde, chin-length hair away from her cheek in a practiced motion. "Please allow me to make this up to you. You're all going to receive special complimentary gift baskets in your rooms and I will personally lead your first yoga class. We'll start in two hours, after you've had time to freshen up."

The hikers remained silent, as if they expected her to go on. When she didn't, Tess raised an eyebrow. This lady looked like she'd be more at home in a corporate high-rise than on a yoga mat. How was her teaching their class supposed to make up for anything? And more importantly...

Tess glanced at Remy again out of the corner of her eye. Remy stood stiffly back, her jaw clenched, staring with an intense, blank expression at the other side of the room. Tess chanced a look; there was nothing over there worth seeing, as far as she could tell. Tess had already learned that look, though, that stance—Remy was ignoring something, and ignoring it hard.

Melissa's confusing speech apparently over, Marti went on checking the guests in. As Tess moved closer in the line, she kept an eye on Remy, but the woman hadn't budged. Then Melissa clicked over, her arms folded, a smile on her face like that practically screamed *Well, look who the cat dragged in.*

"Remy Labelle," Melissa purred, her voice low enough to sound intimate but loud enough to be heard by those surrounding her. "I see you came to the hikers' rescue once again."

Remy, her shoulders tight, cast the barest of glances at Melissa. Her gaze otherwise rested on the floor. "I'm not heartless," she murmured. "But the other park rangers think we ought to just leave your guests' safety to your own guides. Interfering on your land could get us into trouble someday."

"Oh, but you wouldn't do that, would you?" Melissa suddenly looked vulnerable, her blue-gray eyes large. "I know you want to protect the resort's guests...for me."

Remy exhaled through her nose, her eyes widening. Her hands curled into fists at her sides, and Tess saw with unease that Remy's breathing had started to speed.

"I'm leaving," Remy ground out.

Tess's heart flew into her throat. She wanted to jump out of line, push Melissa out of the way, and grab Remy's arm before she could make it out of the door. But what would she do then? Ask her to stay? Say she wanted to spend more time together? Kiss her?

Even now, Remy was turning and walking away. Tess chewed on her lip, her pulse racing. Everything she felt toward Remy was so utterly confusing, and every rational part of her urged not to give in. But when she thought about that smirk, the way Remy's dark eyes roved up and down her body and made her feel beautiful, Remy's strong arms around her when she stopped Tess's fall...

Just as Tess opened her mouth to call out, she was interrupted by a man's voice shouting Remy's name across the room. An older guy with curly gray hair loped toward them, and, with surprise, Tess noted the dog trotting after him.

"Remy!" the man said again, breathless. He stopped between Remy and Melissa, and the latter shot him a sour look. "What luck that you happened to be up here today! I really need your help."

With a wary glance at Melissa, Remy turned back. "What's going on, Glen?"

"The flue in one of the guestroom chimneys is stuck closed. Brian's on vacation and I've got nobody else to help me unstick it. Do you think you could give me a hand?"

Remy opened her mouth as if she would refuse, but then her shoulders dropped and she tilted her head. "Yeah, sure. I can help. What room?"

"Two-eleven," Glen told her. The dog, which looked like some kind of extra-furry beagle mix, trotted up to Tess and nosed her. Tess put her palm out for the dog to sniff in greeting and then scratched his ears. She found she loved every dog she set eyes on.

"Glen," Melissa said with an edge in her voice. "What have I told you about bringing that thing inside?"

Tess glanced up to see Melissa sneering at the dog, and Tess glared back, putting her arm around the dog's chest. He licked her chin.

"Cedar's never done any harm to this place," Glen responded mildly. "I clean off his feet every time we go out and he's never tracked in a speck of mud."

Remy gazed at the door as if she were plotting her escape. "Glen, I'll meet you in the room, okay?"

"I'm going to the other wing to pick up a few tools first," Glen said, then whistled for his dog. Tess smiled as Cedar pranced away and they hurried off together.

"You'll never know how grateful I am that you're staying to help us out," Melissa said to Remy, her voice overly sincere, like a bad movie actress. With her index finger, Melissa traced up the shoulder seam of

Remy's jacket, and Tess gave her a look of disbelief. Melissa couldn't seriously be flirting with Remy so audaciously. Melissa looked like she was a well put together person. Nobody like that would overdo it that much by accident.

"Save your gratitude," Remy replied. She brushed past Melissa, and all of Tess's senses sprang to attention when she realized that Remy was headed her way.

Remy stopped when she was a scant few inches away from Tess. Tess felt frozen, captured, all thought suddenly blown away by Remy's closeness. How could the woman do this to her? Tess had no control over it at all.

"I'll probably be done in an hour or two," Remy said, keeping her voice so low that nobody else could hear her words. "If you're not...in a class or something..." She faltered, which again took Tess by surprise. "You could come see me off if you want."

"Yes!" The reply flew out of Tess's mouth so quickly that she wondered how it even got there—it obviously hadn't traveled down from her brain. But all she knew right then was a desire to see Remy again, to make sure this wasn't the last time they spoke. The way Remy leaned toward her, not towering but almost enfolding, and Remy's intense gaze, and the hardness of her jaw contrasted with the softness of her lips... Tess was infatuated. She knew the doubts and second thoughts would come tumbling over her soon enough, but right now, all she wanted to do was stand here and look at Remy and let Remy look at her.

A smile pulled at Remy's lips. It wasn't the usual knowing smirk, but a smile of true pleasure. "All right, then. See you at one o'clock?"

"Okay," Tess agreed breathlessly, and with a wink, Remy moved past her and headed off in the direction Glen had come.

That wink made her positively dizzy. Tess watched Remy cross the room, and when she turned back toward the reception desk, a still figure nearby caught her eye. Tess looked up to see Melissa watching her with narrowed eyes and a very slight frown between her brows. Tess offered her one of the awkward, obligatory smiles you gives someone when you accidentally make eye contact with them (and this one was even more awkward than usual). Melissa, on the other hand, put on a saccharine expression that felt wholly unfit for the situation and swept off to the door behind the desk.

Something told Tess that might be a bad sign.

As predicted, Tess's room was the fanciest she'd ever stayed in. She dropped her backpack on the plush carpet and saw that her modest suitcase had been brought up with everyone's luggage and placed by the closet. The room was larger than the first floor of Tess's house—there was an entryway with a glass-topped table displaying a vase of freshly cut flowers, a huge, circular (circular!) bed farther in, a stone fireplace, and a sitting area with not one but two couches and a desk. She had no idea what she was going to do with all this space, especially during a retreat where she'd be in sessions or enjoying the spa for a lot of the day.

When Tess saw the bathroom, her plans for unpacking before she showered went out the window. There were separate mini-rooms for the toilet and the sink, and the shower was a huge Jacuzzi tub surrounded with pale blue tile and the fanciest-looking showerhead Tess had ever seen. She'd been rolling her suitcase toward the bed, but she just dropped it where it was and started peeling off her stiff, dirt-encrusted clothes. That shower was going to be heaven.

She wasn't disappointed.

The moment Tess stepped beneath the stream of hot water, she let out a moan of relief. The sweat and grime of hours upon hours of hiking started to sluice off her, and she held her hands out to catch the shining droplets that reflected the soft overhead light. Being clean was a luxury she normally took for granted. Never again.

She put her head directly underneath the stream of water. As she ran her fingers through her hair, attempting to loosen the matted, windblown rat's nest that her hair had become, Tess's mind kept returning to Remy. That fantasy she'd had earlier today... God, it had been good, but she felt humiliated that it sprang so easily to mind. And it would be too easy to continue it now, to imagine that the pulsing of the water was Remy's fingers massaging her skin, Remy's kisses moving along the arc of her neck...

No. Tess purposefully yanked on a snarl in her hair, dragging herself back to reality. She couldn't fantasize about Remy. Remy was unpredictable, confusing. And that wasn't what Tess wanted.

Her friends, the tightly knit group of mostly lesbians who Tess had known since college, always told her that her standards were too high. That she was looking for an impossibly perfect woman who couldn't exist. But Tess didn't see it that way.

For as long as she could remember, she'd been

a hopeless romantic. It was in high school that she realized she was gay; Tess would sit in history class, ignoring the teacher to write pages of pencil-scribbled stories in which she was a young woman in Regency-era England, wandering wistfully on a green hillside, and a dashing lady wearing men's breeches, tailcoat, and cravat would ride up to her and sweep her into her arms. Caught up in these fantastical worlds, Tess didn't date an actual flesh-and-blood woman until her senior year of college.

That year, suddenly afraid she'd miss out on the college dating experience that everyone seemed to find so important, Tess dated three different girls. None of the relationships worked out, in no small part due to Tess's lofty expectations (which even she couldn't quite pin down or describe). In the time since, Tess had gone on dates here and there, a handful a year. Only a few ladies made it to a second date, and none to a third. Some were too tight-laced, some too reckless. Some pushed Tess past her limits and some bored her. Whenever Tess thought a woman might be right for her, some flaw or incompatibility would show itself and Tess would bail. Her friends told her to give her dates more of a chance or at least be willing to compromise, but Tess was sure that the more of a chance she gave them, the greater the disappointment would be.

Tess had never had her heart broken. She watched her friends have relationships, falling in love and breaking up, marrying and divorcing, and she vowed that she'd never let that happen to her. It was torture, seeing the pain that those dearest to her went through for love.

Her curls successfully untangled, Tess massaged shampoo into her scalp, determined to get all the sweat and dirt off her skin. She breathed in the steam, just happy to be warm and comfortable again. This was supposed to be a vacation of renewal, and so far it had done nothing but make her feel lost and exhausted.

Except for those moments with Remy. Those made her feel exhilarated, alive—conflicted, yeah, and way out of her depth, but the emotions and sensations that Remy's gaze and touch made her feel were exciting. And now Tess had the uncomfortable realization that she wasn't sure where being cautious ended and lying to herself began.

She was in her thirties and she'd never been in a serious, long-term relationship. If she'd actually been one of those Regency ladies, she'd be racing towards spinsterhood by now. Was it time to face reality and lighten up on her precious standards? She hated the term "settling," because that belittled both her and the person she might end up with. But maybe the time when she'd been able to be so picky was over. She rinsed the shampoo out of her hair and reached for the fancy conditioner.

She'd spent so much time lately worrying that the chance to follow her career dreams had passed; maybe she should be worrying about losing her chance at love as well. Tess dreamed of finding a love right out of her high-school fantasies; but she didn't want to spend the rest of her life without any romance at all.

And then she remembered the blind fear of falling helplessly down the mountainside and the sensation of thumping into a warm body, into arms that caught her and cradled her and literally plucked her from the jaws of certain death (well, certain bone breakage at the very least). She remembered looking up into those concerned, twilight-blue eyes and feeling her heart crack open and unfurl. Maybe...

Tess made a sound of frustration and rinsed her hair clean. Shutting the water off, she stood dripping in the shower as steam billowed around her and fogged the full-wall mirror. Then she stepped out and wrapped one of the impossibly fluffy white towels around herself. She wiped a porthole in the fogged mirror. Her own round face and uncertain brown eyes stared back at her.

Maybe it was time to try again?

With unfocused eyes, Tess squeezed the water out of her hair and unzipped her suitcase. There would be no harm in asking if she and Remy could see each other again sometime, right? They'd just exchange phone numbers, that's all. No commitments. She put on a pair of bright turquoise yoga pants that hugged her hips and a black tank top, then braided her damp hair. It was almost one o'clock. Slipping on a pair of flats she'd packed in her suitcase, Tess put her room key in her pocket and went out into the hallway that led to the lobby.

"Reinvented Middle-Aged Woman" and "Reluctant Husband" were nestled on one of the sofas near the fire and the desk girl from before was on the phone in the reception area, but Tess didn't see Remy anywhere. She wandered toward the desk and tried not to look like she was searching too desperately. A few people came and went as she waited, checking in or chatting or heading toward the wing of the resort where the spa was located. Minutes ticked by, and still no Remy.

Tess felt like the knot in her stomach was pulled tight enough to snap when Marti got off the phone and called over to her.

"Hey, you're Tess, right?"

"Yeah," Tess replied hopefully, jogging over.

"Remy was here a little while ago. The problem with that chimney flue is taking longer than they expected and she thinks she'll be here for another hour or two. She's planning to leave at three now. Can you come back then?" Marti smiled at her and tilted her head forward as if she were sharing a secret. Tess leaned toward her over the desk in response. "I think Remy would really like that," Marti added.

Tess's heart cartwheeled in her chest. "Yeah! Sure, I can do that!" She felt a goofy grin appear on her face, but then the sparkle dimmed somewhat. "But I have my first yoga session at two... How long do they last?"

"Oh, they're only an hour," Marti assured her. Tess sighed out in relief, but she remained leaning over the desk, looking at Marti and chewing her lip.

"You seem to know Remy pretty well," Tess ventured. "In fact, everybody here does."

"Yeah," Marti said with a nod. "That's because Remy used to work here. She was the site manager before Glen."

"Oh..." Tess's eyebrows drew together. That would explain how Remy knew where the key to the maintenance shed was, but why hadn't she mentioned that? It seemed like a relevant thing to bring up. "She never told me that."

"Well..." Marti gave an uncomfortable shrug that roused Tess's curiosity even further, but when Marti didn't elaborate, something about it made her reluctant to ask.

"Um... Tell Remy I'll be there, okay?" Tess tapped the marble surface of the desk and, with a smile, headed back to her room. This was okay. She could wait. Then she'd get more time to plan exactly what she'd say. And maybe doing yoga first would calm her down a little.

❧

When Tess arrived at the yoga studio with her rolled-up mat under her arm, she was gratified to feel a sense of peace come over her. Yoga was a practice that satisfied her need to be active while and gave her the silence and focus that she needed to recharge. And this studio space was pretty breathtaking: the polished hardwood floors were bordered by mirrors on three sides and a huge curve of windows on the fourth that displayed a perfect, unobstructed view of the deep green and brilliant orange of the fall leaves that swept up to the snowy white peaks above. The mountains were reflected in the mirrors, making it look like they were doing yoga surrounded by the grandeur outside.

Tess spotted Emily and spread her mat out beside her friend. Emily wore a headband to keep her short, messy red hair out of her eyes.

"How's Stefan?" Tess asked, settling on her mat and folding her legs in front of her.

"Eh, he's getting a massage," Emily told her, waving her hand in a dismissive gesture. "He really did mess up his back, the dumbass. I told him he ought to stretch before the hike."

"Too bad he's missing the class." Tess glanced around the room, noting the white-shorts ladies in the front. One caught her eye and turned away with a lifted chin and a toss of her hair. Tess grimaced.

"Those three women are never going to forgive

me for snarking at them."

"Oh, forget them," Emily said. "You have better things to think about." With a sly grin, she leaned over and actually nudged Tess with her elbow. "I noticed that Remy the Sexy Park Ranger went into the shed after you last night. *And* you slept right next to each other." Emily rocked on her mat with excitement. "Tell me what happened!"

"Nothing happened," Tess insisted. What a lie.

"You can't fool me. You're blushing now."

With a frown, Tess turned toward the front of the studio and put her legs out straight in front of her, making a show of stretching. "Look, it's... This isn't the right place to talk about this. Yes, she's hot. But I don't want to blow things out of proportion."

"Ooh, so there *is* something to blow out of proportion, then." Emily waggled her eyebrows at Tess.

Tess rolled her eyes. "I just want to be careful."

Emily regarded her with a gentle, bemused expression. "You could stand to be a little less careful sometimes."

"Yeah, and where did that get me?" Tess asked with a wry smile. "Down a hill, that's where."

Emily chuckled and nodded in acquiescence. "True."

Another yoga mat flopped down next to Tess and the female half of the pair of college students sat down. She smiled brightly at Tess.

"It's so amazing that we get to have Melissa Hart teaching us! She's, like, my yoga idol."

"I didn't know she did yoga..." Tess said. "I Don't Watch TV Tina" stared at her as if she had suddenly sprouted antlers, but then her face lit up with excitement.

"She's amazing! I'm too free-spirited for corporations, but Melissa pretty much single-handedly made yoga at the office a common practice. She's led all sorts of seminars on how it's good for productivity and focus. It's the only reason my parents are okay with how serious my practice is. They thought it was all 'pointless New Age garbage' until their company brought Melissa in," she said, making a face. Tess raised an eyebrow, feeling a bit more sympathy for "Tina."

At that moment, Melissa strode into the room and crossed the floor to the front. Tess couldn't help but stare at her. She was dressed in the most fashionable Lululemon yoga wear: patterned black and white cropped pants with mesh panels and a sea-foam green sports bra top with multiple crisscrossing straps in the back. The severe cut of her hair—it was almost as short as her hairline in the back and angled down to her chin in the front—looked somehow just as appropriate for yoga as it had for her business suit. Melissa's body was as magazine-perfect as her fashion sense: she had long, lithe legs, a completely flat stomach, and well-proportioned hips and breasts. Tess slouched on her mat and looked down at her thick hips and thighs and her small bust and felt a grumpy sense of inferiority.

"Let's get right to it, ladies and gentlemen!" Melissa said with a clap of her hands, sounding like she was kicking off a teleconference. She motioned them all to their feet and the yoga class started.

Tess was sort of a yoga beginner. She'd been going to classes for about three months, and she loved the instructor—he was a short, elderly man who urged everyone to go at their own pace and reminded them that while he might be able touch his head with the bottoms of his feet, everybody's body was built differently and they shouldn't compare themselves to each other. As a result, Tess had gotten a lot more flexible and had built up some stamina and muscle, but she wasn't by any means ready for the big leagues.

This session was starting to feel like the World Series of yoga. Melissa led them in a rapid series of breath-and-flow movements that the rest of the class seemed to already know. Tess tried to follow along, but with no verbal instruction, she wasn't sure what she was doing half the time. Melissa had them hold poses far longer than Tess was used to, and every limb was shaking by the time half an hour had passed. The moment that Melissa called for the group to find a comfortable place on their backs, Tess collapsed onto her mat, her muscles feeling like noodles. She almost fell asleep during shavasana.

At the end of the session, Tess limped to her mat with the antibacterial spray they used to clean them. She groaned as she rolled the mat up. This "relaxing" retreat had involved an awful lot of pain so far.

Tess slipped on her flats and hurried toward the door, glancing at her watch. Three o'clock on the nose. She smiled a little, imagining the comment Remy would make when she saw her all wobbly and spent. Then Tess felt a touch on her arm.

She turned to see Melissa smiling at her. Her matte, bright red lipstick set off the pale ash blonde of her hair and the blue-gray of her eyes, which didn't seem to be smiling quite as much as her mouth.

"Tess, right?"

"Um. Yeah!" Tess replied brightly. She didn't want to seem rude, even though this woman had already given a somewhat odd impression of herself. This was the lady who ran the resort, after all. She couldn't just brush her off.

"Well, Tess, I saw you...struggling," Melissa said, her lips pursing in a frown of pity. It was the expression more than the words that stung Tess (even though she knew perfectly well that Melissa was right). "Was this class a bit too advanced for you?"

Tess shrugged, averting her eyes uncomfortably. It rankled her to admit she'd been having a hard time. "I kept up as best I could," she replied, trying to sound cheerful. Melissa nodded sympathetically.

"You just need some remedial training. Come on over to my mat." She gestured elegantly at the mat on the far side of the room, where she'd been instructing the class. Tess balked. It was already three o'clock... Remy would be waiting for her.

"I... I can't right now. I've really got to—"

"If you want to keep up in all of the other sessions, you really need some help," Melissa cut in, pressing her hand into the small of Tess's back and guiding her insistently away from the door. "It'll just take a minute or two."

"But I..."

"Now, now." Melissa jabbed her finger at the mat and flicked it down in a "sit" motion. "I want you to get the best experience possible out of this retreat, and you won't do that without some pointers."

Tess glanced helplessly over her shoulder at the door. Remy would wait, right? And from what she'd seen so far, getting on Melissa's bad side might be foolish. It would be a mistake to snub her by leaving now.

Nevertheless, Tess's stomach churned when she

thought of Remy standing in the lobby, waiting (probably impatiently) for Tess to show up. It was then that Melissa took her shoulders from behind and steered her over to the mat, pressing her down with a force that brooked no objection.

"All right, now. I want you to show me your best downward dog."

Something in her tone made Tess immediately obey, and as she stood in the pose with her toes pressing into the mat and her head hanging between her arms, she felt intensely disconcerted. She wasn't usually the sort of person who just took orders like that. But Melissa had a way of putting things—and, frankly, a way of just existing in a room—that made it hard to argue.

Several series of positions and stretches later, Tess felt no better at yoga. Instead, she felt harassed and anxious. Finally, with a satisfied smile, Melissa backed off a few steps and regarded her with one manicured nail tapping her lips.

"Quite an improvement," she said. Tess collapsed into a sitting position, her muscles quivering with exhaustion. "I trust I'll see you at the next class?"

"Yeah, yeah, of course," Tess panted, stumbling to her feet. If she just grabbed her shoes and water bottle and ran, she still might be able to catch Remy.

"And, Tess..." Melissa called as Tess practically dashed for the door. Tess paused to look over her shoulder with a desperately impatient expression. Melissa paused, her mouth curling in a smile. "Remember not to let anything distract you from your practice."

Tess narrowed her eyes, but she was too preoccupied with getting to the lobby to have enough time to really wonder what Melissa meant by that. As her bare feet slapped on the hall's hardwood floor, Tess looked at her watch and whimpered. Three forty.

The lobby echoed with her quick footsteps when she rounded the corner, and her eyes flitted across the room. The middle-aged couple was still there, and a group of guys were lounging near the far fireplace and drinking coffee. Marti was at the reception desk.

But no Remy.

Tess came up to the desk, her pulse thumping in her ears and her breathing labored from running so soon after the draining yoga session. When Marti looked up and saw her, her lips flattened with regret.

"Remy left about ten minutes ago... I'm sorry."

Struggling for breath, Tess stared at her. For a moment she felt nothing but shock, but then piercing disappointment grasped at her heart and turned her stomach to lead. Her last chance, missed. She'd be far too humiliated to show up at Remy's cottage again, and it would be intrusive to ask Marti for her phone number. Images of Remy walking away filled her mind, and the pain in her heart made her chest feel tight. But then she frowned. That image brought up a question.

"Did she get a ride down or something?" Surely Remy didn't keep a car up here.

"Oh, no, she's hiking down," Marti said, offering a little exasperated smile. Tess's mouth dropped open.

"At three in the afternoon? After yesterday? We hiked for like...ten hours! And then more this morning!"

Marti shrugged and leaned her elbows on the desk, her mouth pulling to the side sympathetically.

"Remy's pretty intense. And she really, *really* doesn't like being here." Tess felt herself pale, and Marti lifted her hands. "Oh, no, not because of you! Just because... Well, it's complicated. But I packed her a lunch. She'll be fine. It's faster going downhill anyway."

Tess stood with her arms at her sides, her mind reeling with disbelief. She missed her. God, she shouldn't have stayed behind for that stupid extra help...

Frustration kick-started Tess's brain and she slapped both palms on the desk, leaning toward Marti. "Which trail did she take?"

Marti blinked, sitting back. "Well, I imagine the one you guys came up this morning... The main one is washed out, right?"

Without responding, Tess whirled away from the desk and raced down the hall toward her room.

Chapter Six

Room key, jacket, hiking boots. That was all Tess needed and that was all she grabbed before jogging back down the hall, tying her boots on haphazardly as she went. She pulled her jacket on as she ran through the lobby and ignored Marti, who called after her with a quiet "Um...!"

Remy was only ten minutes ahead. Okay, maybe fifteen now. But that was enough to catch up if Tess moved quickly, right? *Nothing ventured, nothing gained.* This was what College Tess would've done—she would've gone after the woman she wanted to see, the woman she wanted to try to build something with. For the moment, all of the conflict and doubt evaporated from Tess's heart. She knew she'd see Remy again, and then she'd find the courage somewhere to ask for another chance to spend time with her.

That spark between them, that electricity— Remy had felt it too, right? She certainly seemed to, but then every time something was about to begin, she would turn cold or aloof. Tess didn't understand it, but that didn't matter right now. Understanding each other took time, and they'd never get that time if Tess didn't catch up.

Predictably, the path was still muddy as hell. In fact, the bright mid-afternoon sun had melted even more snow, and now Tess had to splash through puddles. She winced at the dirty water that splattered her nice clean turquoise yoga pants, but gritted her teeth and put the state of her clothing out of her mind. College Tess wouldn't have let a little mud stop her.

This path wasn't conducive to running, though. It dipped down through the trees, winding through hollows and over roots. Even though whoever carved the path out had attempted to weave around the bigger rocks that liberally dotted the landscape in New England, the path was still studded with rocks of all shapes that had to be carefully navigated, especially on a wet day like this. Going down would have been easier if it were dry; Tess had to choose her footing very carefully.

Her confidence began to slip as she jogged farther and farther down the path and still caught no sight of Remy. She hadn't really been paying attention to how far she'd gone. How long would it take to get back up? Her knees were reminding her of the previous day's injuries and her ankles felt jarred to bits from the impact of scrambling down the hill.

Maybe Remy had gone down a different trail entirely? Tess hadn't thought to check for signs of her, like footprints. Not that she'd probably be able to recognize the treads of Remy's shoes in the first place.

The air hurt her lungs as she pulled in breaths, her eyes scanning the trees below for any glimpse of color. Remy's jacket had been mulberry-colored, right? It was better than brown or green, but it wouldn't be the most obvious splash of color in the forest. Tess huffed with frustration. It was almost hunting season, after all—Remy should've been wearing bright orange. That'd certainly make her easier to find.

Tess felt the chill before she realized that the

sun had gone behind a cloud. Her ears ached a bit with cold, but her footsteps continued in a steady thump down the path. How fast was Remy going, anyway?

Finally Tess came to the edge of a sudden descent in the trail. She slowed to catch her breath and gazed down; the trail trickled down the hillside in a fairly straight line. There was nobody anywhere in sight.

By now, Tess's lungs were sore and everything below the hips hurt. Gloom seeped its way into her heart and settled there to become misery. She was so tired and so disappointed that she wanted to cry. She'd been stupid—spinelessness had kept her from refusing Melissa's help and made her miss Remy, and now she was who-knows-how-far into the wilderness without so much as a hat or a water bottle. *This is where recklessness gets me*, Tess thought bitterly.

Remy was gone. Tess was too exhausted to keep going and too heartsick to keep up the hope that Remy might be just around the next corner. At least back at the lodge she'd be able to take a hot shower again. And maybe stuff herself with gourmet mashed potatoes from the resort's kitchen, laden with butter and sour cream and fresh chives and bacon. Her stomach growled and she realized all she'd had to eat today had been that granola bar at the maintenance shed.

She turned, whimpering at the sight of the trail stretching up ahead of her, but then she straightened her shoulders. Every step would take her closer to a seat beside the fire, to hot cocoa (hopefully spiked with cinnamon liqueur). But every step would also take her farther from Remy.

Tess pushed the heel of one hand into her eye, wiping away tears. This awful heartache was exactly what she wanted to prevent. And it wouldn't have worked out anyway. It never did.

She placed her boot onto a rock in the path, and when she shifted her weight to take another step, the wet mud made a squeal between her sole and the rock and her foot went out from under her. For a split second, time seemed to stand still, and then Tess felt herself falling.

As she flailed to try to catch herself, Tess's other foot snagged on a root and she went over backwards with a yelp, tipping down the slope she'd so glumly surveyed only moments ago. She fell on her side and rolled over once, twice, then slid to a bumpy halt on her back in the mud and sticks.

For a minute or two Tess just lay there, feeling the world spinning around her and the moisture seeping into the back of her clothes. This was so fitting. Such a perfect endcap to her day. Maybe she'd just lay there until the sun went down and she froze to death.

With a groaning sigh, Tess opened her eyes.

And, upside-down, she saw Remy's head and shoulders bobbing quickly up the path.

Tess's eyes flew wide. Yes, it really was—it was Remy, hurrying up the hillside toward her, a look of disbelief and alarm on her face. Tess was so stunned that she couldn't even turn over. She just lay there on her back, staring.

"Tess, what...?" Remy came to a halt a few feet away, peering down at Tess, who still gaped at her. "Did you fall down the hill *again?*"

"No. Gravity is increasing on my body." When Remy merely cocked an eyebrow, Tess's sarcasm gave way. "I was coming to find you," she explained tremulously. With an exasperated chuckle, Remy came to her side and slipped her arm under Tess's back, helping her sit up.

"Good lord, girl. You must be nuts to come all this way just for me." Remy lifted Tess to her feet, keeping one arm around Tess's waist and bracing her elbow with the other. Tess fully expected the chiding tone in Remy's voice, but she was surprised to hear a hard edge there as well. Self-consciousness made her skin prickle.

"Well, you didn't wait," Tess muttered, unsure whether to feel insulted by Remy's brusqueness.

Remy let go of Tess's waist and transferred Tess's elbow to her other hand, walking beside her for the first few steps up the hill. Unexpectedly, Tess felt a fierce wave of loss for the broken contact. Remy's arm had felt so good around her waist, so *right*. That simple touch made her feel supported and protected and encouraged all at once. She glanced up at Remy's face, but Remy had turned her eyes to the sky, leaving Tess only able to see the strong curve of her cheekbone and jaw. Something about it made Tess's stomach clench with apprehension.

"I didn't think you were coming," Remy replied after a moment. Her voice was serious and she still didn't meet Tess's eyes, instead focusing on the ground in front of their feet. Her hand hovered lightly beneath Tess's elbow.

Tess opened her mouth and then closed it again. "I'm sorry," she said softly. "I got held up in yoga class." With a little smile, she tilted her head at Remy. "I ran through the halls barefoot trying to get to the lobby in time."

"And then you came dashing down the mountain so fast you almost broke your ass, huh?" The chilly blankness on Remy's face was replaced by a sidelong smirk. "That's an awful lot to go through just to say goodbye."

A flush bled across Tess's cheeks. *She's right—so you'd better make this good. Now or never.* They walked on, the words tumbling through Tess's mind as she scrambled to put them together in a suave and attractive way. But she wasn't even sure what it was she'd meant to say in the first place.

"I just wanted to... I wondered if...we could maybe see each other again sometime." Tess bit her lips, chancing a look up at Remy. So much for suave.

Remy's blue eyes opened wide beneath arched brows for just a moment, and then a surprised grin broke out on her face. "Did you seriously fall down another hill just so you could ask me on a date?"

Tess's blush deepened and she sputtered. "That's—that's not what I meant! I didn't say 'date!' I just said...maybe we could *see* each other again. Like. Run into each other at the grocery store." She didn't even know what she was saying; the words just spilled out of her mouth in an attempt to hide her embarrassment. The fact that it had never worked before didn't stop her.

Remy was laughing. "Now you're just making it worse."

"I know!" Tess moaned. She glared up at Remy, unwilling to take her arm away even though she thought that would appropriately convey her irritation. Instead, she pulled her braid over her shoulder with the other hand and fiddled with the curl at the end. "You're going to make me say it, aren't you?" she grumbled.

Remy's mouth curved in a slow smile and her eyelids dropped, her gaze so smoldering that Tess felt a shock through the very core of her. "Yes," Remy purred.

Tess's knees turned to mush and she would've stumbled if Remy hadn't tightened her grip on her elbow. Good God, Remy could really turn it on, and Tess felt helpless against the feelings that just one look could create in her. Frustration slithered its way through the intense attraction, energizing her with its potent contradiction.

"I would like," she said, drawing her shoulders back, trying to salvage some kind of mud-covered dignity, "to see you again sometime in a date-like context."

Remy bit her lips to keep her from laughing at Tess's stiffness. "Let's get you back up to the lodge. If I don't come with you, I doubt you'll live to hear my answer."

As they moved together up the trail in silence, Tess hackles rose. *Is she not going to answer me until we get there?!* For a minute or two she could do nothing but fume, but then the path became a bit steeper and she felt Remy's palm against her back, soft and steadying. Remy's other hand flitted to her elbow again, ready to grab her if she started to fall.

Remy made her feel so many emotions at once: confidence and helplessness, irritation and desire, strength and indignation. Clearly, Remy got her rocks off by teasing her; but when Tess wished petulantly that Remy would stop, she thought about what it would be like for the two of them to spend time together without that part of the dynamic...and she realized she'd miss it.

I like her to tease me? I'm a grown woman, not a third-grader! Worse still, being teased should make her feel like she wasn't in control of the situation, and there was nothing Tess hated more than that. But for some reason, when Remy did it...

Tess clenched her jaw. She was worn out, impossibly sore, and still had plenty of climbing to do before the possibility of another hot shower and dinner would appear. She didn't have the energy to torture herself about this. So Tess put one foot in front of the other and allowed herself to relish the closeness between her body and Remy's.

The shadows of the mountains had thrown the resort deep into shade by the time they got back. Once they got to the more level end of the trail, Remy took Tess's arm and slipped it through hers, and as they walked through the door, Marti practically leapt at them from behind the desk.

"I thought I was going to have to send out another search party! I see you caught up with her, though. Geez, Tess, what got into you?"

The corner of Remy's mouth quirked and it looked as if she were about to say something, but Tess cut her off. "The stress of the last couple of days, I guess," she laughed weakly. "Do you have washing machines here?"

"Oh!" Marti grimaced in concern when she saw the state of Tess's clothes. "We have a laundry service. Just put whatever you want cleaned in one of the blue plastic bags in your room and set it outside the door, and we'll wash it for you."

"Thanks," Tess replied wearily.

"Remy..." Marti shook her head, fixing the other woman with a stern look. "It's too late for you to hike back down. That was crazy, anyway, after the day you had yesterday. If you need to get home tonight, I'll call you a cab."

Remy glanced at Tess, uncertainty flickering briefly in her eyes before it was hidden. Tess stood tensely, her arm still looped through Remy's, consciously keeping herself from tightening her grip. If Remy wanted to go home, Tess had no right to stop her. But Remy had to give her an answer first.

Then Remy's gaze crossed the room and lighted on the figure of Melissa, who stood by the little group of café tables near the opposite wall. She was talking to a couple of guests, her elbow in one hand and the other curled daintily in front of her mouth as she laughed. She didn't notice them, but when Remy saw her, the uncertainty in her eyes was replaced by stony displeasure.

"Yeah, call me a cab, will you, Marti?" She loosened her arm and Tess's dropped away, and with a clenched jaw, Remy headed toward the door. "I'll wait outside."

Tess's heart flipped over and she followed after Remy. On impulse, she reached out and caught the fabric of Remy's sleeve.

"You said you'd answer me," Tess told her in a low voice.

Remy paused and half-turned back. For a moment her expression was unreadable, then her eyes flickered over Tess's shoulder to the other end of the room. Wariness crossed her face and then she covered Tess's hand with her own, gently pulling Tess's fingers away from her jacket.

"Look, I don't know—"

"Remy! Oh, thank God, you're still here!" From

behind Tess, Glen came jogging through the lobby and stopped beside them. Tess stared at him with her mouth open, unable to think of anything to say that would allow them to continue their conversation. "The hot water's on the fritz again," Glen said, wiping his brow. "You know how much of a pain it is to get back there behind the heater—God knows why they installed it in such a stupid place—but if you're willing, I could really use your help." It was clear that "if you're willing" was code for "please, please, please say yes." A hopeful, apologetic smile that was really more of a wince appeared on Glen's face.

Remy dropped her head back in exasperation. "Are you for real?"

"Unfortunately."

Biting her lip, Tess watched Remy's face, hoping against hope that she'd say yes and that they would get just a little bit more time together. She hadn't been so sure she was going to like the answer Remy had almost given her.

Heaving a sigh, Remy set her hands on her hips. "*Fine*. But you owe me."

"I know I do," Glen said. "I'll make sure you get dinner and a room tonight. I think this might take a little while."

Remy opened her mouth to object, but then she caught Tess's eye. Tess held her breath. Then Remy's lips softened and a light came into her eyes.

"All right, fair deal." She shook her head. "How do things run around here without me, anyway?"

Glen grimaced and shot a look at Melissa. "Badly."

Remy shrugged her eyebrows in a gesture of agreement. "Okay, lead the way."

Glen motioned toward the corridor that led to the lodge's rooms and took Remy off, showering her with gratitude as they went. Tess's shoulders relaxed as she let her breath out.

What had Remy been about to say? She looked so unsure, conflicted...nothing like the Remy Tess knew, with her knowing smirk and her cocky confidence. It shook Tess to see her like that, particularly because it seemed to happen whenever they approached talking about what was beginning to happen between them. Tess recognized the signs: when that topic came up, Remy would close off.

With a sigh, Tess ran her hands back over her hair. Her blonde curls were coming out in a messy halo and there was dried mud caked into the braid. It was a good thing the shower in her room was so damn pleasant, since she'd be taking her second one in five hours.

With a wan smile at Marti, Tess took off her dirty boots and walked in her socks back toward her room. Darkness had fallen quickly outside the numerous glass windows in the hallway, and stars were beginning to appear in the deep purple-gray sky above the snow-capped mountains. This vacation was turning out to be much less relaxing than she'd hoped...but she couldn't deny the excitement that swirled in her belly whenever she thought of Remy.

Tess was so lost in thought remembering the strong, enfolding presence of Remy's arm around her waist that she almost ran into Emily coming from the other direction.

"Hey!" Emily said happily, a bright smile on her face. Then she noticed that Tess was carrying her shoes, and she looked Tess over and saw the mud covering her back. Her expression changed to shock. "What the heck happened to you? I just saw you like a couple of hours ago!"

Tess snorted. "It's a long story."

Emily folded her arms over the fluffy bathrobe she was wearing (pale green with big panda faces—she'd brought it from home). "Well, I'm on my way to the spa while Stefan puts heat on his back. And you're going to come with me and *dish*." She took Tess by the arm and swung her around to go the other way.

"But I'm filthy!" Tess protested. "I have to take another shower!"

"Okay, fine, but fast. We'll pick up some clean underwear at your room," Emily said, glancing down at Tess's muddy behind and the thin yoga pants she was wearing. "And you can hop in the shower. But don't worry about your hair—they'll wash it for you at the spa. Trust me, it'll be luxurious."

"I could use a little pampering, I guess," Tess conceded with a smile. Emily nodded with raised eyebrows, as if Tess were finally getting it.

One very quick shower (with Emily singing "Hurry up, hurry up, hurry up-up-up" to the tune of the Lone Ranger theme song) and some fresh underwear later, Tess joined Emily in a bath robe and they walked together to the other wing of the lodge where the spa was located.

Instead of a series of hallways like the guestroom wing, the spa was a huge circular chamber with sections split up by type of treatment. There were Jacuzzis, massage beds, tiled tubs equipped with chairs for pedicures, manicure desks, and lounges for just sitting and relaxing. Each one had an available bamboo curtain across the section's doorway that could be pulled for privacy. The whole spa was decorated with a Japanese garden in mind: there were bonsai and bamboo placed around the room in planters, gently tinkling water running down a rocky fountain by the entrance, and rice-paper partitions marking the sections. Chimes hanging from the ceiling stirred gently in a controlled breeze.

Tess stood in the doorway with her mouth open for a little longer than she would've felt was classy if she weren't so awestruck. She'd never been into a spa before; sure, she'd had her nails done a couple of times, but that was at the mall, nothing like this. She honestly felt a little uncomfortable imagining people catering to her like that, since she'd always felt so much derision toward those who expected that from others. But that's what she was here for, and that's what she (or whoever bought the ticket at her sister-in-law's job) had paid for.

Soon someone ushered them both in, and while Emily got a hot stone massage, a stylist washed Tess's hair and gave her a manicure. Tess and Emily settled down side-by-side in plush lounge chairs, Tess's hair wrapped up in a towel and both of them enjoying strawberry margaritas.

"All right," Emily said, turning to curl her legs up and face Tess. "Now that we're all relaxed and refreshed, you *have* to tell me what you got up to this afternoon." One corner of her mouth curled up knowingly. "I'm going to take a wild guess and say it had something to do with Remy the Sexy Park Ranger."

With a laugh, Tess covered her pinkening cheeks. "Okay, fine, you got me. I was supposed to see her before she left today, but I missed her, and so I went after her."

Emily looked at her for a long moment,

apparently trying to reconcile this with the state she found Tess in a little while ago. "You went after her *down the mountain?*"

Tess grimaced. "It wasn't my brightest idea."

"Yeah, but...that must mean you're really into her!" Emily bounced in her seat. "Wait, did you actually catch up to her?"

"Yeah," Tess replied with a dreamy little smile. "I didn't think I would and I was about to turn around, but then I slipped and fell—hence all that mud—and Remy heard me and came to help. And then she hiked back up with me." The smile faded from Tess's face then. "She was going to leave, though...until the site manager guy showed up again and said he needed more help with maintenance stuff."

"Well, that was good luck for you. But what do you mean, she was going to leave? Did you at least get her number?"

Tess dropped her head back against the chair. "No. I dunno, Em, I'm so confused."

Emily rested her chin on her fist. "I'm going to need more of an explanation than that."

It wasn't until this moment that Tess realized how much she'd wanted to talk to someone about this. Having so much jumbling around in her head only flustered her more.

"She's just bewildering. Remy, I mean. One second I feel like she'd readily put her hand up my shirt if I let her, and the next she's stalling about even answering me when I tell her I'd like to see her again. One minute she's making me feel like I'm sexy and desirable, and the next she makes me feel like a stupid kid. She just...doesn't make sense."

"Not many people do," Emily said with a

sardonic smile. Tess tilted her head in acknowledgement.

"I know. After yesterday and today... I've been thinking about how she makes me feel, and I think I want to give dating her a try. And I can't even get her to tell me whether she'd be up for that." With a long sigh, Tess held out her hand to examine her newly painted fingernails. They were a light, sparkly peach. "When I think about that part, about how uncertain and confused I am, I'm not so sure. I don't want to get crushed, you know?"

Emily pulled her mouth to the side. "I know I've said this before, but you're never going to find a relationship where there are no risks involved. It's literally impossible to be sure it'll turn out well."

Frowning, Tess passed a fingertip over each smoothly polished nail. "I don't believe that. I think sometimes people just *know*."

"Okay, maybe some people do," Emily said. "But have you ever considered that that might be more about the person doing the knowing rather than the person they're falling in love with?"

"Huh?" Tess raised an eyebrow, and Emily spread her hands.

"What I'm trying to say is that a person who 'just knows' that their partner is right for them might be better in tune with *themselves* and what they want than, say...you are." She paused as if she were unsure how Tess would take that. Tess was silent.

"Oh," she said after a moment. With another sigh, she glanced over at Emily, her brow furrowed. "I *do* know what I want, though. For myself."

"What's that?"

"I want to be like College Tess again."

Emily chuckled, sitting back in her chair. "College Tess? What do you mean?"

"Well, College Tess was brave and took chances and had this fire for life. She had the whole world at her feet and no doubts about how great her future would be." Putting it into words made a pang of loss throb through her heart. It seemed like all she had was doubts, and now that future was wasted.

"I think you're oversimplifying College Tess," Emily told her with a smile. "But for the sake of argument, what do you think College Tess would do in this situation?"

Tess matched her smile, feeling her cheeks redden. "She would've thrown herself at Remy with no questions asked."

"Well, all right then. Go for it. You've never been interested in a woman this way before," Emily said sincerely, gripping the arm of Tess's lounge chair. "Remember all those dates you were so picky about? You were certainly dedicated to finding somebody, but practically nobody met all of your criteria, and then something was always wrong with the ones who did. It's totally like you to be uncertain about Remy, but you've never had this light in your eyes before. You've never been this adamant about how a woman makes you *feel*. Besides..." Emily's grin grew wide and excited. "She saved you *twice*. Talk about romantic."

"Yeah, but..." Tess sat up straight, leaning toward Emily. Her heart was fluttering at the simple reminder of Remy's arms holding her, but she couldn't discount their conversations. "Sometimes she can be so cold..." Tess's thoughts returned to Remy's face when she saw Melissa. No matter what was going on, when Melissa was around, Remy acted strange. Something had to have happened between them, but judging by the way Remy closed down in those situations, Tess would probably never know.

"Tess," Emily insisted. "You've known her for two days. Less than two days. Don't make snap judgements—that's why you rarely have a second date with anybody." She reached for Tess's hands and took both of them. "Look, don't get me wrong—I *love* College Tess. But she did some pretty dumb shit sometimes. Remember when she tried to seduce the RA at our dorm and almost had to get reassigned to a different floor?"

Tess laughed, bowing her head. "Oh, God, don't remind me."

"All I'm saying is that College Tess was a little *too* impulsive at times. Not to mention that when she did hook up with girls that year, she was just as picky as you've been recently. You just need to give people a chance."

"I don't even know if I'll get that chance with Remy," Tess said, looking up at Emily with worry. "She still hasn't given me an answer about whether she wants to see me again. She keeps avoiding it, or we get interrupted."

"Well, she's not leaving tonight, is she?" Emily asked. "It's getting late, and I heard that we might get snow again."

"No, the maintenance guy told her he'd get her a room and dinner."

"Perfect!" Emily swung her legs over the side of the chair and stood up, pulling Tess to her feet. "You'll meet her for dinner, and when you do, you'll *demand* an answer. Now, it's time for both of us to have a facial. They have cucumber slices and everything."

Tess laughed. "People really use those?"

"Of course they do! I have no idea why, but I bet we'll find out."

By the end of their spa session, Tess felt like she maybe, *maybe* had the courage to ask Remy again for her answer.

Chapter Seven

Dinnertime at the Rising Star Yoga Resort was another unfamiliar occasion for Tess. She'd expected something along the lines of a cafeteria or a buffet; instead, she came into the resort's dining room to find tables covered in white cloths and little menu cards placed in front of each chair. Time to rethink how she would approach Remy, since sitting down beside her with a full plate had been the original plan.

Tess lingered by the door, her hands smoothing the knee-length navy blue skirt she was wearing. Except for jeans, Tess didn't really like wearing pants, and this soft skirt and the cloud-gray sweater she wore with it were like pajamas to her. She wondered if she was underdressed.

There were a few people already in the room. The three white-shorts ladies looked like they wore cocktail dresses everywhere they went, so Tess couldn't judge the implied dress code by their wardrobe. The middle-aged lady and her husband were there as well, the latter looking somewhat more comfortable than earlier. And Melissa stood over near the far windows, talking to a woman in a white chef's jacket.

Then Tess caught sight of Remy herself, sitting alone at one of the tables near the wall. She had one foot casually propped up against the leg of her chair and was leaning back and gazing pensively out the window. Images of James Dean flashed in Tess's mind, and the combination of that with Remy's curves made Tess feel a flush of warmth prickle all over her skin. Her heart woke at the sight (not to mention other parts of her body).

Tess was paralyzed by a whirlwind of indecision, and this didn't improve when she slowly realized that Remy wasn't looking out the window—she was watching Melissa.

Unobserved as she assumed she was, Remy didn't have the guarded, distant expression that Tess had come to associate with her reaction to Melissa. No; on her face now there was a mixture of hurt, resentment...and longing.

Cold fingers slipped around Tess's heart. Longing? She had to be imagining it. There was no way that someone like Remy and someone like Melissa...

Tess shook her head. The doubts were already threatening to crush her like an empty soda can; she didn't need to entertain any more. Whatever Remy's past was, whatever the tension between her and Melissa meant, if it had any bearing on her potential relationship with Tess they'd figure it out as they went along.

Balling her fists, Tess nodded to herself. *Quick, before somebody else comes to sit down with her.* Tess willed her feet to move and strode resolutely over to the table where Remy was sitting.

When she approached, Remy looked up, blinking as if she'd been shaken out of deep thought. A surprised, unaffected smile appeared on her lips.

"Hey," she said softly, sitting up straighter in her chair. Tess smiled back and unconsciously twirled a lock of drying hair around her fingers.

"Since you're holed up here for the night, I thought you might like some company."

"Yours is the only company here I'd like," Remy replied. She leaned her elbows on the table and presented Tess with a sultry lowering of her eyelids, then chuckled and cast a glance at the other people in the room. "Everybody else is...in a different class, let's say."

That look made Tess's knees weak, but she was immediately unsure whether Remy's comment had been meant as more of an insult to the others than a compliment to her. When Remy stretched her foot out under the table and pushed the other chair back, Tess felt encouraged. She sat down across from Remy.

"So… Um, how did your repairs go?" Tess asked awkwardly. So much for demanding an answer right off the bat. They should have a little pleasant conversation first, shouldn't they?

Remy groaned, rolling her eyes. "This place is falling apart. You'd never know it to see the brand-new furniture in the lobby and the polished hardwood floors and the state-of-the-art spa, but behind the scenes, this building is starting to show its age. Everything needs a little repair: the heating and ventilation systems, the plumbing... The maintenance is continually getting neglected and Glen's expected to slap a Band-Aid on it whenever something goes wrong instead of taking the little extra time and money he'd need to actually fix it."

Tess frowned and tapped her little menu card thoughtfully on the table. "That doesn't seem like an efficient way to run a resort."

"It's not," Remy agreed with a scoff. "Melissa doesn't want to fork out the money to get stuff like that fixed. She says she 'can't trust' outside maintenance people. And yet she had no problem trusting the company who came in to install that special tub for the mud bath."

Remy seemed intimately acquainted with the running of the Rising Star. Tess tried to think of something clever and biting to respond with, hoping to earn Remy's trust by commiserating with her about Melissa. With all of the ways Melissa had left Tess unimpressed, there was one in particular that rankled.

"You'd think she hated mud from the way she talked about Glen's dog." She shot a glare over at Melissa. Anyone who used "that thing" to refer to an animal was an asshole in her estimation.

Remy exhaled. "She's hated poor Cedar from the minute Glen adopted him. First she resented that Glen took time off to drive down to Georgia to the animal rescue, then she flipped out because Cedar isn't perfectly trained yet because of the way he was mistreated before he got rescued."

"How horrible," Tess said, appalled. The more she learned about Melissa, the less she liked her. And now she got the impression that Remy not only knew about how the resort worked...she knew about the history and personal lives of its employees, as well.

Tess watched her tentatively. "Marti mentioned that you used to work here?"

Remy's face hardened, but her posture remained as casual as before. "Yeah, I did." Tess waited for her to elaborate, but she said nothing else, only avoided Tess's eyes. Tess shifted in her seat. *There's got to be something we can talk about... This is like a first date, right? Kind of? People get to know each other on first dates. But how can I get to know her without some cliché icebreaker like "Read any good books lately?"* Not to mention the fact that I *might be the only one thinking of this as a first date.*

"Um..." Tess's eyes skimmed the menu but none of the words really sunk in. She was too busy trying to think of something to start a conversation. "How did you end up working in these parts?" she asked finally, hoping that would be a neutral question (and yet relevant enough not to seem like a non sequitur).

Remy leaned forward then, resting her elbows on the table. This time, she looked directly into Tess's eyes, and Tess felt the familiar pleasant dip in her stomach that eye contact with Remy brought.

"I apprenticed as a carpenter instead of going to a traditional university," she explained. Her smile had a slightly wicked edge, as if in doing so, she'd flipped the bird to some sort of authority. "There wasn't anything I loved as much as being outdoors, so when I finished my apprenticeship, I looked for a job that would allow me to get out of the city. The Rising Star needed a maintenance person, so." She shrugged one shoulder and said no more.

"Ah, so that's how you know so much about how things work around here." Tess drank in the information, eager for any glimpse of Remy's life. Remy nodded in response and her fingers played over the close-cropped hair at the back of her neck. It was somehow an unbelievably sexy gesture.

"And how about you?" Remy asked, her eyes seeming to come back from far away. "How do you fill up your time when you're not falling down mountains?"

Tess resisted the urge to stick out her tongue. "Well, I just quit a job I was in for ten years. I don't know how I lasted that long anyway. I'm going to teach pre-school now." Just the thought of it comforted her and pushed down some of the anxiety she felt.

Remy's smile was warm. "That sounds like a lot of fun, actually. When I was a teenager, I never thought I'd end up liking kids. They drove me batty. But these last few years, even though I'd never considered it before, I kind of thought maybe I'd want..." Her voice, which had drifted into a soft, dreamy tone that Tess hadn't heard before, suddenly cut itself off short. Remy shook her head, the smile gone. For a moment, her mouth was a hard line, and then she curled her fingers under her chin and peered attentively at Tess. "So how'd you get into yoga anyway?"

Tess blinked, taken off guard. There had been something so painful about Remy's expression... It made Tess's heart squeeze. She swallowed and gamely followed Remy's subject change.

"Honestly, yoga got me through the last few months of my previous job. I hated walking into that office every day, but on the days when I had yoga after work, it was a little easier." Encouraged by Remy's seeming interest—her deep blue eyes stared with perfect clarity and attention into Tess's—she continued. "Whenever I'm doing yoga, I feel alive. It gets you in your body rather than always in your mind, thinking about the next item to cross off on your to-do list. When I'm not doing yoga, half the time I forget I have a body at all."

At that, one corner of Remy's lips hooked up and her eyes roamed over Tess's chest and stomach, taking in all that was visible above the table. She tilted her head appreciatively.

"Dunno how you do *that*."

Tess's face turned as red as a tomato. There was no way to mistake that comment for anything but a come-on. And Remy still didn't want to answer Tess's question about whether she'd like to see her again?

With a cough and a pointed look, Tess went on. "It's just that I've felt...stagnant, lately. Yoga helps me pull out of that a little. I was hoping a whole week of it would rejuvenate me, give me a fresh start to go along with my new career."

"You've certainly had an exciting start to your vacation, I'll give you that."

Tess snorted. "And I suppose you rescue lost hikers every other day?"

"Oh, you'd be surprised." Remy leaned forward confidentially. "The stories I could tell you..."

"Well, don't just say that and leave me hanging," Tess replied with a laugh. Remy launched into a retelling of how she found a group of lost first-graders (who had actually gone back to the parking lot and were hiding in the restrooms). When a waiter came and took their dinner orders, Tess had to keep herself from being too irritated by the interruption. As they ate, Remy regaled Tess with story after story, sometimes about helping hikers who'd gotten hurt and sometimes about rescuing distressed animals (the one about the moose who'd gotten tangled in a clothesline was particularly thrilling).

Tess contributed a few stories of her own about camping trips and exploits she and her friends had gone on in college. She didn't really feel like she had done anything worth sharing since.

"And that's why I'm afraid of beavers," Tess concluded at the end of one story. Remy bit her lips as if she were trying not to say something. Then she leaned forward and leveled the most smoldering look Tess had ever seen.

"That really is a shame. Beavers are *wonderful.*"

Tess's mouth dropped open in an astonished, mock-scandalized grin. For a moment or two, she was so shocked that Remy would be this blatant that she couldn't get any words out at all. Then she shook her head at Remy with a scolding smile.

"You're unbelievable."

Remy smirked. "So I've been told."

By now, their dishes were cleared away and Tess was starting to suppress yawns. She took a deep breath and looked Remy square in the eyes, her expression gentle but serious.

"Are you going to give me my answer?" she asked with a little inquisitive smile. "I asked you something pretty important down there in the woods when you found me this afternoon."

Remy held her gaze for a long time, then reached into the back pocket of her jeans and pulled out a pen. With exquisite care, she slipped her fingers beneath Tess's hand on the table and drew it close.

Tess's heart performed aerial tricks as Remy touched the pen to the back of her hand and wrote a series of numbers there. The warm, dry firmness of Remy's fingers lightly grasping her own made a shiver skip through Tess's body; she hoped Remy couldn't tell.

"Call me anytime you think you're about to fall down a mountain, okay?" Remy said, her voice a low, husky murmur. The air caught in Tess's lungs. Then Remy turned Tess's hand over, bowed over it, and pressed a gentle, lingering kiss to her palm.

Tess couldn't breathe. With a wink, Remy got up and brushed past her, both hands now in her pockets as she walked away.

Finally, Tess drew in a shuddering breath and

pulled her hand close, cradling it against her chest. She felt dizzy with emotion and she trembled with the desire that poured through every inch of her veins.

That really just happened.

A silly smile wobbled its way onto her face. Remy couldn't have given her a better answer than that.

Tess had never felt a more comfortable bed. At first, she thought she'd feel weird in the wide expanse of sheets and fluffy blankets that could have easily fit four or five sleepers; but all it took was a few seconds of lying spread-eagled on the round bed and she felt like she was floating on a cloud.

After the past two days, Tess had never been happier to be in bed by eight thirty, and she slept until her cell phone alarm went off at eight the next morning. Although she still ached in about a hundred places, it wasn't as bad as yesterday, and she felt refreshed for the first time since she started the hike. Stretching her arms over her head and arching her back like a cat, Tess got up, found clean underwear, and slipped on a long t-shirt and a pair of yoga pants. She threw her hair into a messy ponytail. With a dinner as fancy as the one she had last night, breakfast was bound to be good.

As she was walking past the large window in her ground-floor room, Tess squinted at the brightness and then paused. Out her window, she could see...nothing.

At first glance, there was nothing outside her window but whiteness. Then, as she focused and stepped closer, she saw that the whiteness was actually millions of swirling snowflakes. The dim, barely discernable gray shapes of the mountains and other parts of the lodge were visible only if she concentrated.

Wow, Emily hadn't been kidding about getting more snow.

Tess thanked her lucky stars that she was safe at the lodge and didn't have any reason to make another ill-advised, unprepared sojourn into the woods today. As if to validate that feeling, the wind sent a gust against the building so strongly that she heard the window jiggling in the casement. It was certainly the right kind of morning to curl up in front of a fireplace with a mug of hot chocolate.

Tess closed the door to her room behind her and padded in her flats toward the lobby to find out whether breakfast was in the dining room or somewhere else. She'd been too tired (and, honestly, too preoccupied thinking about Remy) to check the schedule for today, but all of the classes were optional and were repeated throughout the day. She was just wondering if she'd be able to avoid any more sessions taught by Melissa when she heard footsteps coming up behind her and turned to see Remy hurrying to catch up.

"Hi," Tess greeted her, suddenly breathless. Remy was wearing a curve-hugging black tank top and pair of loose fabric pants with the resort's logo on them (probably a gift from Glen for letting him rope her into so many projects that she had to stay overnight). As much as Tess had admired Remy's figure in yesterday's plaid shirt and jeans, it was an unexpected pleasure to see her angles and curves in such bare display.

Remy's shoulders and arms were just as toned as Tess had imagined. The slope of her breasts gave Tess the impression that she was wearing a sports bra, an idea Tess found remarkably attractive. Her waist looked like the perfect shape for Tess to rest her arms around, and her hips and thighs curved in a deliciously smooth contrast to the angles of her arms and face. Tess couldn't tear her eyes away.

A slow smile crept across Remy's face as she watched Tess admiring her. She cocked one hip and folded her arms.

"I'd say good morning, but I get the impression you're not really paying attention."

A blush reddened Tess's neck and ears. She straightened her back. "Sorry! Good morning!" Remy chuckled.

"Actually, I retract that. I can't comment on the goodness of this morning until I make sure things are running okay in all this wind and snow." She glanced down the hall toward the lobby, concern tightening her features. "I doubt they were expecting weather like this so early in the year." She resumed striding down the hall and Tess followed beside her.

They could hear the noise in the lobby before they saw it. It seemed like every visitor in the entire resort was crowded there, talking nervously or demanding to use the phone. There were three people behind the reception desk, all trying to calm agitated guests.

Remy grabbed Marti as she hurried by toward the desk. "Hey, what's going on?"

"Oh, geez, what *isn't*? The road down is closed because of the snow." Marti looked harried. "Half of these people aren't even scheduled to check out today, but because we're essentially stuck here until the snow stops and they can plow, everybody's flipping their—" Paul, who was behind the reception desk, waved a piece of paper at Marti and she bounced with frustration.

"Sheesh, why don't they just use the phones in their rooms? Sorry, I've got to run!"

"Hoo, boy." Remy ran a hand back through her hair, raising her eyebrows at Tess. "I guess I'm not heading down the mountain any time today, huh?" Tess tried to hide the delighted smile that threatened to burst out on her face, but she was only partly successful. Remy's eyes sparkled as if they were sharing a secret. She clearly wasn't too put out.

Before Tess could say a word, the room was suddenly plunged into a dim, gray half-darkness. There was a split second of silence and then a clamor went up from the assembled guests. Tess looked up at the ceiling where all of the lobby's warm, cozy lights were now dark. The only illumination came from the snow-swept windows and the fireplaces at either end of the room.

"That's not good," Remy muttered, casting a dour glance at the crowd. "I've got to go find Glen. He's bound to need help firing up that clunker of a generator."

"I'll come with you," Tess blurted, eager to get out of the lobby, and she stayed at Remy's elbow as they threaded their way through. The corridors were even darker, but every hundred feet or so there would be a block of windows that let in snowy light.

"It's a good thing this place has so many windows," Tess commented.

"Good for the light, anyway," Remy said. "But the sooner we get that generator on, the better. Windows don't hold in much heat." They came to a break in the corridor with the elevators on one side and a staircase opposite. "Glen's office is upstairs. Let's check there first."

Tess opened the doorway into darkness and bit back a shriek as the pale light behind her fell on a dark shape at her feet. A string of expletives emerged, followed by a croaked question:

"Remy, is that you?"

Remy joined Tess in the doorway. "Glen?" She pushed the door wide. Glen was sitting in a heap on the floor below the bottom step, his glasses askew.

"I was coming down from my office when the lights went out and I fell down the godforsaken stairs." His face wrinkled in pain. "I think I did something to my ankle."

"Okay; don't worry, we've got you." Remy bounded over to him and knelt down to take a look at his ankle. "Well, it's already swelling up pretty badly, but there's nothing sticking out. That's a good sign, at least. Let's get you up." She reached for him and got one of his arms around her shoulder. Tess hurried over took Glen's other arm.

"I know there are a million people in the lobby," Tess said, "but those are the closest chairs." Remy nodded in agreement and they helped Glen hop slowly down the hall.

Much to Tess's dismay, the hubbub in the lobby had not diminished. In fact, it was even louder now, particularly because a fuming Melissa stood at the head of the crowd in front of the reception desk.

"I have an *extremely* important business meeting in Boston this afternoon! I can't afford to be late!"

"I'm sorry, Ms. Hart, but the road is closed until the storm's over. The governor declared a state of emergency." The unfortunate receptionist looked like he was trying to become a turtle who could crawl back into its shell. Paul had wisely made himself scarce.

"Does the governor cut your paycheck?" Melissa demanded, but then she caught sight of Remy and Tess helping Glen limp over to a couch. "Oh, Jesus, what now?"

Melissa elbowed her way through the crowd until she stood before the three of them (none of the guests seemed at all unhappy to get out of her way). She was silent for a moment, looking first and Remy and then at Tess, her eyes narrow. Then she turned her attention to Glen. "What happened?" Remy remained stonily silent, busy with taking off Glen's boot.

"Um," Tess spoke up. "Glen fell down the stairs when we lost electricity. He hurt his ankle."

"Hurt how bad?" Melissa asked Glen, not once looking at Tess. He raised his hands helplessly, sweat shining on his face.

"I can't walk, I'll tell you that. I don't know if it's broken or what." He flinched as Remy pulled his boot off and then rolled his sock down, revealing an already swelling ankle.

"Great!" Melissa cried, planting her hands on her hips. Tess made a face at her. *Some sympathy!*

Melissa took a step back and folded her arms. "Remy," she said in the same tone she'd use to tell a dog to "sit." "I need you to get out the four-wheeler and drive me down. I *must* make that meeting."

This time Remy did look at her, an expression of incredulousness on her face. "Are you insane? The roads are closed for a reason! Driving an ATV down would be just as dangerous as going in a car!"

"No, it wouldn't," Melissa countered impatiently. "As a park ranger—" She, for some reason Tess didn't understand, used finger quotes around "park ranger." "—You should already know that the

134

four-wheeler can make it through narrow trails and muddy spots that not even the hardiest truck could pass." She lifted her chin. "I'm getting down this mountain, and you're going to take me."

At this, Remy stood up. Her face darkened and Tess felt a chill down her spine at the restrained hatred in Remy's eyes.

"I'm not your employee anymore, Melissa." Remy's hands curled into fists as she faced the shorter woman, shoulders tight. Although Melissa had to look up in order to meet Remy's eyes, she stood with such poised confidence that she seemed no smaller.

"You owe me," Melissa replied simply, her words stated as irrefutable fact. "You know you owe me after what you did."

What she did? Tess was shocked to see an angry flush steal over Remy's cheeks. Remy gritted her teeth, her jaw working.

"You're delusional," Remy ground out. The strain of keeping her voice level was evident.

Melissa heaved a sigh, dropping her arms to her sides. Her eyebrows pulled together sadly and her body language immediately shifted from confident to vulnerable.

"You always turn it back on me, don't you?" she asked softly, her mouth turning down in a sorrowing little frown. Remy gave a wordless moan of frustration through clenched teeth. "You probably think my job takes precedence over everything else, don't you?" Melissa continued, tilting her head down to pierce Remy with doleful eyes. "You were always so insecure about that."

Tess looked back and forth between the two of them, her heart thudding. This stand-off had gotten seriously personal, and fast. Something big had gone on between Remy and Melissa. Remy's body was like a tightly coiled spring, and she shook her head slowly, her lips twisting as she held in words.

"Insecure?" Remy finally repeated. Her fists unclenched and her fingers flexed by her sides as if she longed to grab Melissa and shake her. "You're the one who saw betrayal everywhere! You fired *me*, remember?"

"Any good employer would dismiss an employee after a breach of trust like that," Melissa responded loftily. Remy looked as if she'd been kicked in the chest. Her eyes wide, eyebrows twisting, she stepped back from Melissa.

"I'll be billing your for six hours of labor."

Tess, who stood to the side with her mouth agape, felt somebody sidle up next to her. She glanced over to see Marti standing hesitantly by. Tess shared an astonished, questioning look with her.

"What the hell is going on here?" Tess whispered. Marti sighed, her eyes moving to Remy. A concerned frown pinched her face.

"It's not really my place to say, but..." She leaned closer to Tess, looking into her eyes. "You and Remy seem close, so I feel like it's not fair to keep it from you. The thing is—she and Melissa used to be together." Marti raised her eyebrows significantly.

For a moment, Tess felt like the floor was pitching beneath her feet. Together? Remy and Melissa? How was that even possible? But then she thought again about the way Remy looked at Melissa, the resentment and hurt in her face, and how Melissa seemed to go out of her way to needle Remy. Those were all clear signs of a bad breakup, but how Remy and Melissa ever began to have a relationship in the first place was a mystery she couldn't fathom.

Glen held his hands up, catching both Remy and Melissa's attention. "No one is driving down the mountain," he said firmly, "and that is that. The roads are all shut down, including the highway. Even if, somehow, you did survive the ride down to the bottom, you can't take the ATV all the way to Boston."

Melissa glared at him, but it was clear she knew he was right. She threw her hands in the air, turning away from Remy.

"Fine, Glen! You're right! Have you got that generator running yet?" Melissa glared at him, completely ignoring the swollen foot he had propped up on a coffee table.

Glen grimaced and gave a weary shake of his head. "That's what I was coming to tell you when I fell down the stairs. I thought we might lose power in this storm so I went to get the generator ready...and it's out of gas."

Silence fell among the four of them standing in a semicircle around Glen's couch. Tess looked worriedly over at Remy, who was standing with her arms folded, a grim frown on her face.

"Naturally," Melissa spat. "Martha!" Marti, who was still standing close to Tess, jumped. "Call down and make sure somebody knows we're stuck up here."

Marti shrunk back, fidgeting with the cuff of her white dress shirt. "That's what I came over to tell you, Ms. Hart. The phone lines dropped out just a few minutes ago."

"We have no phones?" Melissa asked dangerously, advancing toward Marti, who backed off and tried to hide behind Tess.

"Wait," Remy cut in. Her normal color had returned and she came up beside Melissa, steely determination in her eyes. "The four-wheeler gave me an idea."

"Right, there must be gas in its tank," Melissa said. "Figure out how to get it out and use that for the generator."

"That isn't what I meant," Remy told her flatly. "The four-wheeler runs on diesel. We need regular gasoline for the generator."

"So what *did* you mean?" Melissa turned to face Remy, the two of them standing nearly nose-to-nose again. Tess wanted to grab Remy by the arm and pull her back before a fistfight broke out.

Remy took a steadying breath and looked as if she might be counting to ten in her head. "Sweet Spring Resort is about ten miles away, in the next valley. I know of a road that cuts between the peaks. It's fairly flat and should be easy driving. I can take the four-wheeler over there, borrow some gasoline, and see if their phones are still working."

"Hmph. I suppose it'll have to do." Melissa rolled her eyes heavenward and turned her back on them, her heels clicking on the flagstones as she walked away.

"Remy, it's very valiant of you to do this," Glen said from his chair. "But you absolutely can't go alone. I would go if I could, but you're going to have to take somebody along with you for safety's sake."

Tess's heart leapt in her chest. This was her chance to show Remy that she wasn't just some silly girl who fell down mountains all the time. She was a dependable, self-reliant woman. She'd show Remy that she didn't need to be rescued every five minutes.

"I'll go," Tess said quickly. Remy glanced at her with upraised eyebrows, and for a moment it looked like she might object. But then the uncertainty in her face smoothed and the self-assured smirk that Tess was coming to know so well reappeared.

"All right, Princess. Get yourself into the warmest clothes you have and meet me by the lobby door in fifteen, okay?"

Tess nodded, excitement and nervousness bubbling in equal measure up through her chest. She'd never done anything like this before, but if ever there was a time for taking risks, now was it. Last night, she'd felt like she hadn't done anything exciting enough to tell Remy about in all the years since she graduated. Today was sure to make a good story—and Tess was even more excited that instead of telling Remy about it later, she'd be sharing it with her now.

Chapter Eight

Back in her room, Tess dressed swiftly. A sweater over her t-shirt and a pair of jeans over her yoga leggings made sure she'd have layers to keep warm. She stuffed a sweatshirt into her backpack along with an extra pair of socks and all of the granola bars and trail mix she'd brought for the hike. With her boots tied on, her jacket zipped, and a knitted hat on her head, Tess swung on her backpack (much lighter than it was on the hike up, thank goodness) and headed back to the lobby.

The crowd had dispersed and most of the people in the lobby now sat around the fireplaces at both ends. Since there were fireplaces in every room, too, the guests would have plenty of places to wait until either the generator was fixed or power was restored. With a little wry chuckle, Tess imagined all the hardcore yoga buffs trying to do their sessions in mittens and scarves.

As Tess passed the reception desk, Marti hurried out from behind it and placed a bag in Tess's hands.

"I made you both some lunch!" she said, smiling anxiously. Tess took the bag.

"Thank you, Marti! Do you just keep these on hand or something?" she joked.

"Ha, no," Marti replied. "But the folks in the

kitchen know me really well. There are always hikers who are planning to go out for the day and then forget to pack food until they're almost out the door." She tucked a strand of hair behind her ear. "Tell Remy to be careful, okay? You too."

"We will, I promise." Tess smiled. Marti was really sweet, and she seemed to care a lot about Remy. "Remy's a pretty good friend of yours, looks like?"

With a shy shrug, Marti combed her fingers through a length of her straight hair. "She's great. I was having a bad time last year and she really helped me out." A little secretive smile appeared on her face. "Remy gave me dating advice. I've dated both guys and girls, so she got it when other people didn't, you know?"

"Yeah, I know," Tess said. It made her feel warm inside to think that Remy had been so kind to Marti. It seemed like Marti might need someone to stand up for her once in a while. Though, as much as Remy teased and acted aloof, it was obvious from all those rescue stories that she was a very caring person after all. "We'll be back as soon as we can, okay?" Tess told Marti, waving as she headed for the door. "Try not to worry."

Outside, the snow was whipping across the patio so fast that Tess couldn't tell whether it was snowing heavily or the wind was just blowing around what had already fallen. Just as she approached the curb, Remy drove up on the resort's ATV. She wore ski goggles and the same jacket she'd worn on the hike up.

"Here, can you stuff this in your backpack?" Remy asked, handing Tess a canvas bag. "I didn't think we'd have room for my pack too." Tess fit Remy's bag and the lunch Marti had packed into her backpack and settled it on her shoulders. "Here, you get on first," Remy told her.

Remy left the ATV in neutral and dismounted it, allowing Tess to climb on using the footholds on each side. Then Tess scooted back as far as she could against the empty gas canisters tied down behind her, and Remy swung her leg over the seat and settled in front. "Ever ridden on one of these before?"

"No," Tess confided, "but it can't take that much skill just to be a passenger, right?"

Remy laughed. "True enough. Just hold on to me and you'll be fine."

A warm tingling over Tess's skin betrayed that she was blushing at the thought of sitting so close to Remy. There was no way around it, though—and frankly, Tess didn't want a way around it. She leaned forward and slipped her arms around Remy's waist, marveling at the firmness of her muscles. That woodsy scent filled Tess's senses, the smell of pine trees and sawdust and dusky herbs that seemed to define Remy. Clasping her hands together, Tess leaned against the warm solidity of Remy's back.

She felt like she could fall asleep here, cradled against Remy. But then the ATV lurched into motion and Tess tightened her grip with a little yelp. They crossed the parking lot speedily and then shifted to a slower, steady pace as they drove onto a wide trail opposite the one they'd hiked up two days ago.

The woods were utterly silent except for the buzz of the four-wheeler's engine. Snow already lay in a thick blanket on the ground, smoothing out the little mounds and dips in the forest landscape around them. Through the heavy snowfall, the shadowy trunks of trees rose like columns and large rocks and boulders pushed their way out of the snow, black spots in the whiteness.

Remy had been right about the road—it was fairly flat, with gentle ups and downs completely unlike the trail they'd hiked on the way up. Tess watched the snowy woods go by, and soon they were in the midst of trees that grew thickly enough that she could no longer see the peak of the mountain on their left. It seemed like they were traveling horizontally around the mountain's girth rather than up or down it.

"We have to hurry," Remy called over her shoulder. "This ATV won't run so well if the snow gets deeper than its undercarriage. I wish the Rising Star had a snowmobile, but they're a yoga resort, not a skiing one... They're usually closed for the season before we get any snow."

Tess didn't reply. She wasn't sure what she could add to the conversation. Remy was so familiar with the workings of the resort, and now she knew why... Not only had Remy worked there, but she had dated the owner.

Tess's stomach turned, and it didn't have anything to do with the dips in the trail. How on earth could someone like Remy ever date someone like Melissa? But then again, it's not like Tess knew either of them very well, especially not Melissa. But she always acted so...insincere. And Remy herself had said she hated people like that, hadn't she?

Tess wanted to ask Remy what had happened between the two of them. What could have been big to shake a confident woman like Remy? Tess watched the back of her head as they rode together through the snow, imagining what it might be like to trace her fingers across the buzzed hair over Remy's ears. What kind of person was Remy attracted to, anyway? Now that Tess had gotten past the first hurdle—getting Remy's number and confirming that she was interested in the spark between them—she needed to know what would make Remy like her.

But that wasn't something she could just ask about. Aside from being a totally clumsy way to kick off a potential romance, Remy had a habit of clamming up whenever the conversation took a personal turn. Could her breakup with Melissa be why?

Conjecture wasn't going to get Tess anywhere, and besides, whatever had gone on between Remy and Melissa was none of her business. But her heart ached when she saw that look on Remy's face, the stifled pain and regret in her expression whenever Melissa was in the room. When they were arguing, Melissa had thrown out something about a betrayal. Tess's first instinct was that Remy would never do anything like that...but how could she really know?

The truth was that Tess hardly knew Remy at all. They'd spent a little over two whole days together, and even though those days had been rather out of the ordinary, there was only so much you could learn about a person in such a short time. Tess tried to think up a list of everything she knew about Remy. It wasn't a long one.

That was exactly what she'd tried to tell Emily. How could she risk letting someone into her heart if she wasn't sure they'd treat it kindly?

Tess closed her eyes against Remy's back. All the things Remy made her feel fit nowhere in her plan. The attraction, the desire, the spontaneity...the way Remy pushed all her buttons, good and bad. It threw all of her carefully prepared assumptions and expectations out the window.

Emily was right: she needed to give Remy a chance. But Tess wanted reassurance. She needed to know that she wasn't going to get hurt for no reason. But where Remy was concerned, Tess was pretty sure no such reassurance existed.

Except for that kiss. Tess's palm tingled just remembering it. Had Remy been serious? Just like back at the maintenance shed when Remy put her hand on Tess's thigh and their lips brushed for the sweetest of moments, last night's flirtations could have been just that—a casual agreement to make out sometime if either of them felt like it. Is that what Remy thought Tess meant when she said she wanted to see her again? Or maybe Remy had been so hurt by whatever had gone on between her and Melissa that she didn't *want* a serious relationship...and maybe that was why she had stalled so much before giving Tess her answer.

And here Tess was, riding with her on the back of a four-wheeler with her arms wrapped tightly around Remy's waist, so tightly that she couldn't get any closer if she tried. This was time they could've spent getting to know each other, if it weren't nearly impossible to hold a conversation above the roar of the engine. Even though Tess was pressed so closely against Remy, she felt like she might as well be miles away.

They spent an eternity driving through the silent woods, the wind swirling snow around them. The trail cut through the forest like it had been carved with a knife. Tess was lost in thought and numb with the vibrations of the vehicle when Remy slowed the engine and gradually brought the ATV to a halt.

Remy pulled the ski goggles away from her eyes and set them on her forehead. Turning back to Tess, she grinned with pink, windburnt cheeks that sparkled with melted snow. Tess felt breathless, light-headed, captivated by her beauty and the incredible deepness of her dark blue eyes against her flushed skin and the snow.

"I figure we ought to stop for a snack," Remy said. "I don't think either of us managed to eat any breakfast before we headed out."

Tess agreed—her stomach had been rumbling for the past hour or so. They both turned sideways on the four-wheeler's seat and began to unpack the lunch Marti had given them.

"She's such a thoughtful kid," Remy commented, taking half of a ham and cheese sandwich from the foil packet it had been wrapped in.

"She's pretty fond of you, too," Tess said, smiling. "She told me you gave her dating advice."

"Oh, lord!" Remy leaned back, chuckling. "For somebody so sensible otherwise, she has more relationship drama than anyone I've ever known."

"And you're a master, I take it?" Tess bantered. She shut her mouth tight as soon as she heard the words come out. *Oh, God, I hope that didn't sound like a jab at her relationship with Melissa. But she doesn't know that I know.*

Remy just tilted her head and angled a small, cynical smile at Tess. "I'm not twenty-two, is all I'm saying."

"Man, I miss being twenty-two," Tess said quickly, hurrying the conversation along. "Right out of college, my whole life before me." She opened up a packet of potato chips that Marti had stored in their lunch bag. "Back then, I was much more—"

"Shh," Remy hissed suddenly, putting her finger

to Tess's lips. Tess's heart skipped a beat. For a split second, she almost didn't care why Remy had quieted her. Remy's finger against her lips was such a soft, sensual gesture that a shiver of desire worked its way out from under her ribs and down deep into her belly.

Then she looked where Remy was pointing. The snowfall had lessened but the wind was still briskly rolling sparkly wisps across the ground, and seated in between two trees about thirty feet away was a snowshoe hare.

It was almost impossible to see against the white, snowy slope, but the dark tips of its ears and the black beads of its eyes and nose betrayed it. Tess drew in a breath and held it, as if breathing might scare the creature away. It sat with the perfect stillness of an animal that's trying not to be seen, but then, after a few moments, its nose began to twitch and it hopped carefully a few feet closer.

Tess met Remy's gaze, a smile of utter delight on her face. Remy's eyes sparkled in recognition. As they watched, the hare hopped around the trees near them, taking the occasional bite out of a twig sticking up from the snow. The two of them sat and watched the hare until a shower of snow falling from a tree branch startled it and it sprang away, its long back feet making distinctive prints in the snow behind it.

"How about that, huh?" Remy said, grinning sidelong at Tess. She was clearly both amused and proud about how happy this had made Tess.

"That was *incredible*," Tess breathed. She gazed into the snowy tangle of undergrowth, wishing for another glimpse. "I love rabbits. I have one, you know," she continued. "A house rabbit." The happiness of the moment gave her the courage to cast Remy a sly, flirty smile. "Her name is Sappho."

Remy laughed aloud. "You named your bunny Sappho? That's priceless."

"What?" Tess asked, giggling. It was delightful to have this casual conversation, to share little bits of herself with Remy. "Don't you think that's the perfect name for a rabbit?"

"It's a great name for a rabbit!" Remy resumed eating her sandwich, still chuckling. "It's just a little...predictable, that's all."

"Predictable!" With mock-indignation, Tess threw her head back imperiously. "What are you saying?"

"I'm saying," Remy told her, eyes hooded and twinkling, as she leaned closer to Tess like she was about to share a secret, "that you might as well be advertising 'lesbian lives here' when you mention to people that you've got a rabbit named Sappho."

Tess's lips curved in a mischievous smile. "And that's a problem why...?"

"Well," Remy said airily, leaning back. "You might attract unwanted attention." Her blue eyes slid over to meet Tess's, a suggestion apparent, and one corner of her mouth hooked up.

Tess's heartbeat fluttered and began to thump double-time. Her mouth dry, she held Remy's deep ocean gaze.

"I'm very careful about who I reveal that particular piece of information to," she said, trying to sound flippant in spite of the blood rushing through her veins. "If someone undesirable asks me about my rabbit, I say her name is Whiskers."

"Is that so?" Remy lifted her eyebrows, her smile challenging the off-handedness of Tess's remark.

Tess blushed.

"Maybe," she shot back, unable to hide a grin. The banter between them felt like an electric current, energizing her.

"I never had a rabbit name named Sappho, or even one named Whiskers," Remy said. Tess perked up; maybe this meant she'd get to learn more about Remy's life. "But I did have a dog growing up. I named him White Fang, I'm ashamed to say."

Tess waved the last bit of her sandwich, dismissing Remy's concern. "There's nothing wrong with that. Did he look like a wolf?"

Remy's mouth twisted sheepishly. "He was a dachshund."

Tess burst out laughing. To cover it, she popped the end of her sandwich in her mouth and pressed her lips together tightly. Remy wasn't fooled.

"See, all I wanted when I was a teenager was to be a wildlife researcher. I was particularly passionate about saving wolves." Remy balled up the foil her sandwich had been in and gazed off into the woods with a wistful smile. "I was going to work at Yosemite. I had it all planned out."

Tess certainly knew that feeling. "What happened?"

Remy sighed and shrugged. "Rebellion ended up being more important," she said, her mouth pulling to the side. Tess waited for her to continue, her expression expectant. Remy ducked her head, and the shyness of the gesture charmed Tess. "My parents had a really tight grip, and I would've done anything to slip out of it. Ever since I was born they expected me to go to college—they'd decided where I was going to go and everything—so when the time came, I joined a carpentry apprenticeship program instead to piss them off." She glanced over at Tess. "Might not've been the best reason to make a decision like that. The past is the past, though, I guess."

A weight settled in Tess's stomach and her enthusiasm faded away. Remy'd had the chance to go to college, presumably paid by her parents, and she threw it away just to spite them? All those nights that neither of Tess's parents got home until after ten o'clock because of their second jobs, not to mention the immense school loans that still ate up a huge chunk of Tess's paycheck, seemed even more painful now.

"Wow," Tess said, unable to keep the heaviness from her voice. She couldn't think of anything else to say that wouldn't sound resentful. Remy chewed her lip, gazing pensively at her.

"I'm grateful for where the apprenticeship brought me," she said. "But with all the people out there who don't get the chance to go to college, I know it was a dumb move not to take that opportunity."

Tess felt the discomfort ease off, and she smiled slightly. It struck a chord within her that Remy seemed to understand her uneasiness and tried to rectify it. "Everybody should get to make their own choices." Tess did truly believe that, even though the odds people faced weren't always fair.

With a wry chuckle, Remy shrugged. "Yeah, you're right, but sometimes I think eighteen is a little too young to make a decision that big."

"I dunno," Tess replied contemplatively. She looked up at Remy with a hopeful smile. "I went to college hoping to be a teacher, and although I took a little detour, I'm going to be doing just that in a couple of weeks. When I was eighteen I wanted to teach middle school kids, but I'm just as excited to teach preschoolers now."

"Or..." Remy leaned across Tess's lap to stuff her lunch trash into the backpack, and Tess's mood lightened even more to feel such casual closeness. "It could just be that you're remarkable." Tess felt her face heat up, and happiness blossomed in her chest at such a compliment. Remy winked, almost sending Tess over backward with giddiness, and then she swung her leg over the four-wheeler's seat and snapped her goggles down over her eyes. "Ready to go?"

I'd go anywhere with you, Tess thought impulsively. To Remy, she just said: "Any time."

☙

Tess was sure her face was about to freeze solid when the wind, already biting as they spend along, began to blow even harder. Even shielding herself behind Remy, and even with her woolen hat pulled down over her ears, the exposed skin on her face and neck felt like it would be blue if she happened to look in a mirror.

There was so much snow in the air that Tess couldn't tell whether it was still snowing or whether the wind was whipping it up so much that it only looked like a whiteout. She didn't know how Remy managed to keep to the trail, because the few times she peeked up over Remy's shoulder, she could see no indication of what was the road and what was just a gap in the trees.

After what felt like hours of holding tightly to Remy's waist and willing her toes to warm up, Tess glanced around and saw that the trees were thicker on either side of them. She could at least tell where the trail was now, but the wind still cut her cheeks like razors.

Remy revved the ATV's engine as they began up a slope, and Tess tightened her grip around Remy's waist to prevent herself from slipping backward on the seat. Just as they came over the crest of the hill, a splintering crack resounded through the air and a tall shadow like a collapsing tower appeared out of the swirling whiteness above them.

Tess barely had time to think, let alone recognize what was falling toward them. Remy swerved the four-wheeler and braked, sending up a spray of snow and mud. Then Tess felt hands grasp her jacket and she was tumbling off the vehicle and into a drift of snow.

The sharp iciness of snow sliding down her collar jolted Tess out of her stunned daze, and she scrambled onto her knees. Through the windblown snow, the four-wheeler looked like a dark smudge with a longer, straight smudge lying on top of it. Ignoring the stinging snow that seeped into her socks, Tess stumbled up and dashed toward it.

The trunk of a limbless dead tree lay sprawled over the ATV, cracked in two. Beside the ATV in a heap was Remy.

Her body working on autopilot, Tess reached across the vehicle and turned off the ignition. Then, alarm shooting like fire through her veins, she bent down beside Remy and pulled off her own mittens so she could have the use of her fingers. Remy lay on her side, and as Tess touched her shoulder, she stirred.

Tess started to tremble when she saw the blood on Remy's face. It trickled down her cheek and stained the snow beneath them bright red in pea-sized circles. *Oh, God, oh, God, oh, God.* Tess tried to use her mitten to wipe the blood away, but the wet wool just smeared it around. Remy's eyelashes fluttered and a groan emerged from her throat. Then, blearily, her eyes opened and she focused on Tess's face.

Tess's breath rasped in and out of her lungs, painful in the cold air. "Oh, my God, Remy. Can you hear me? Can you move?"

"Yeah," Remy mumbled, closing her eyes again. Tess wasn't sure which question she was answering, but then Remy's muscles tightened and she got one arm under herself. Tess grasped her shoulder and put her arm around Remy's chest to help her upright. Once she was resting with her back against the ATV, Remy opened her eyes again and ran them over Tess's body.

"Are you hurt?" she asked faintly, wincing.

Tess shook her head. "No, I'm fine. You pushed me out of the way." She brushed Remy's tousled hair away from her forehead to get a better look at where the blood was coming from. It was smeared across her forehead and welled from a place above her eyebrow. As carefully as she could, Tess wiped the blood away. There was a two-inch cut there, scraped as if something had ripped the skin away rather than sliced it. "Jesus," Tess breathed. "Did the tree fall on you?" She couldn't see any splinters, but there was an awful lot of blood in the way.

"I don't think so," Remy replied in a gravelly voice. "I hit my head when I threw myself off the four-wheeler. I'm guessing I caught it on the handlebar." She peered up at Tess's anxious face through narrow eyes. "How bad is it?"

"It's not deep," Tess said shakily. "It just looks painful." Remy gave a half-hearted chuckle and Tess squeezed her shoulders comfortingly before standing up. "Stay right there, okay? I have a first-aid kit in my backpack."

She hurriedly collected her backpack from where she'd dropped it after climbing out of the snowdrift and came back to Remy. Tess's first-aid kit wasn't the most impressive, and she scowled at it.

"I wish I had a bigger one. But I think I at least have gauze." Her eyes darted up to Remy's, but to her relief, Remy seemed alert. Tess ripped open an alcohol wipe. "I'm going to clean your face off, okay? I'll just dab the cut for right now so I don't rip it open anymore. I'm sure we'll be able to get better help at the other resort." Remy nodded. Her hand moved to Tess's knee and gripped it, and a surge of worry and protectiveness filled Tess. She wished she had a free hand so she could clasp Remy's in her own.

"Don't worry," Tess told her firmly as she wiped the blood from Remy's cheek. "I'll take care of you. Shut your eyes so I can clean the blood around them." Remy complied and Tess finished wiping her face, then gently blotted the cut. Remy's grip on her knee tightened. "Sorry," Tess winced.

It wasn't easy to get the medical tape to stick to Remy's wet skin, but Tess was finally able to fix a pad of gauze over the cut. "Okay, we'll change it if it bleeds through," Tess said, snapping the first aid kit closed. "How do you feel?"

Remy swallowed. "The world's kind of spinny."

Tess chewed the inside of her cheek with concern. What if she had a concussion? They had to get to that other resort. It wouldn't be great for Remy to travel, but sitting here in the freezing snow was worse. "All right, um. Here's what we're going to do." She hunkered down in front of Remy. "I'll drive the ATV and you sit behind me. Just lean on me and hold tight. That's all you have to do."

Remy frowned, uncertainty clouding her face. "But you've never driven one before, have you?"

Tess mustered a smile. "How hard can it be?" With an exhaled chuckle, Remy shrugged her eyebrows and then winced at the pain it caused in her wound. Tess put her arm around Remy's ribs. "Let me just get you up onto the seat. You don't have to stand." It worried Tess even more that Remy, who she figured would be the last person to accept help, let her assist her onto the ATV without protest.

After trading her backpack with Remy for the ski goggles, Tess slid onto the seat in front of her and turned the ignition key. "It's a good thing you're not out cold," Tess joked nervously. "Tell me how this thing works?"

"Put it in drive," Remy told her, pointing to the gear shift. "Then you just twist the right handle to use the throttle. The break is the foot pedal down there." Tess did as she was told and the four-wheeler jerked forward. After a few spurts, she was able to smooth out the ride.

"See? Simple," Tess said over her shoulder. She was proud of how confident she sounded—she certainly didn't feel that way.

"Just follow this road," Remy said muzzily. "I'm not sure how far we are away, but it can't be much more."

"Hold tight," Tess told her in a small voice that much better conveyed how she really felt.

Driving the ATV across this trail wasn't as bad as it could've been, Tess convinced herself as they went along. It was at least fairly smooth—she suspected it was a dirt road underneath all this snow. The few times she did come upon rocky places and the front wheels of the ATV bucked and rolled beneath her, she wasn't so sure she'd have the courage to navigate a more difficult trail with this thing. But then she felt the warm weight of Remy against her back, Remy's arms around her waist and her body steadily rising and falling with her breathing, and she was certain she'd be able to do it if she had to.

A widening of the road and the glimpse of a dark brown building through the trees sent waves of knee-melting relief through Tess. It wasn't until then, after she could allow the urgency to ease from her mind, that she bothered to wonder what time it was. How long had she been driving? Although the snow had stopped, the sky was a flat gray-white with no visible sun. Not to mention that Remy's injury complicated their plan to get to this lodge, get a tank of gasoline, and drive back to the Rising Star.

Different scenarios played through Tess's head as she drove toward the lodge, trying to plan what she would say to the people there and how long that all would take. As the four-wheeler rumbled closer, Tess frowned through her goggles. Her first impression of the Rising Star lodge was that it had been fairly ablaze with lights in all of those windows, even in the middle of the day...but this place looked like it didn't have any windows at all.

A stone-hard fist of fear gripped Tess's heart as they pulled closer. It wasn't that there were no windows. It was that the windows had no lights.

Braking the ATV, Tess slowed to a halt. Remy lifted her head as if she'd zoned out while Tess was driving.

"Are we here?"

Tess didn't respond. She got down from the seat and walked a few steps toward the door, balling her hands into anxious fists by her sides.

The lodge was entirely dark inside.

"Stay right there, okay?" Tess called to Remy. *Maybe they lost power too*, she thought desperately as she ran toward the door. Before she even pulled on the handle, she knew it would be locked.

Cupping her hands around her eyes to shield them from the glare, Tess peered in through the glass door. There was a lobby much like the Rising Star's, with a reception desk and comfortable chairs. But no people were anywhere to be seen.

She tried to calm her racing heart. *Okay, it's fine. We can work with this. What would College Tess do?* Only silence responded. Tess shook her head and turned back toward the ATV. It seemed that summoning College Tess only worked in situations that called for guts, not resourcefulness.

Remy frowned questioningly at her as she approached. "What is it?" She wobbled a little bit on the four-wheeler's seat.

"There's no one there," Tess told her in a low voice. "But you're in no condition to ride all that way back. And I can't stand returning without gasoline when we're so close." She chewed her lip, staring hard at the dark lodge. "I'll find a way in."

Remy blinked at her and started to rise, but then she wavered and caught herself on the handlebars of the four-wheeler. "I don't think I can walk by myself," she growled in frustration. "I'm still too dizzy." She met Tess's eyes with a worried frown. "I guess I'll stay here and guard the ATV," she finished crossly.

"I'll be back soon," Tess said, offering her a smile. "Hopefully I'll be coming out through those doors, but if not, I'll come back anyway and we'll figure out what to do."

It felt surreal to leave Remy behind and tromp away across the snowy lot. The Sweet Spring Resort's lodge was built similarly to the Rising Star's, but instead of honey-colored wood, this was stained a dark brown. Following the outer wall, she made a lot of twists and turns, giving her the impression that the inside of this resort was just as labyrinthine as the one they'd left that morning.

With every corner she passed, Tess cursed the lodge for being so modern. None of the windows were the kind she had at home, where you could just pop the screen out and jiggle the glass pane to see if it was locked. Finally, she spied a low window that looked different from the others. Tess crouched and peered in. It was so dark inside that she couldn't make out much, but this one looked less fancy than the rooms she'd passed so far. She tapped on the glass—it even felt a little flimsier than the others, maybe a single sheet of glass instead of double. It would have to do.

Tess searched around for a big stick or a rock. The woods were fairly close to this side of the lodge, and by scuffing around in the snow for a moment or two, she was able to uncover some stones. As she knelt in the snow, using a stick to gouge the earth out from around one of them, Tess felt her head spin.

How had she gotten herself into a situation like this? It was like she'd canoed away from the wide, calm river of her life and found herself in white-water rapids. Riding with Remy on an ATV to another comfy lodge ten miles away had seemed like an adventure—a reasonably safe, predictable adventure. But she should've learned from the very first day that nothing was predictable on this mountain.

Tess blew out a breath as she finally pried the rock from the earth. She was marooned with an injured friend (hopefully more than a friend) at a closed resort that was at least ten miles away from anywhere, and even the only known "anywhere" was currently without heat and lights. She hadn't expected her week of renewal to require quite so many survival skills.

Well, you're here now, she told herself. *If this doesn't prove to Remy that you're not some incompetent fluff-brain who she'd never want to date, nothing will.*

Swinging the rock back between her legs like a kid learning to bowl, Tess cracked it into the window with all her might.

The spider-web fracture that resulted was small but encouraging. Tess continued to swing the rock into the window until it finally shattered, and then she kicked the glass at the edges inside with her boot. With a lucky flash of insight, she took off her jacket and laid it over the bottom of the sill so that she wouldn't get cut on the way in.

The room she found herself in looked like a basement office of some sort. Mentally apologizing to whoever worked there, Tess shook her jacket off and put it back on once she was sure it was free of glass shards. It hadn't occurred to her until she was inside, but no alarm had sounded when the window broke, which either meant that the resort wasn't alarmed or that there was no power. Flipping a switch by the door proved the latter.

Finding a stairwell up to the first floor was, somehow, more harrowing than breaking in had been.

The basement hallway had no windows and so Tess had to feel her way through the dark (if only she'd remembered to get the flashlight out of her backpack). Luckily, some of the rooms off the hallway did have windows, so she opened up every door she passed in order to let some light in, trying to see a "stairs" sign. She muttered "Oh, gosh, finally," when she spotted one, and it sounded strange and echoey in the silent building.

Upstairs, it was a lot easier to see. Tess followed the brightest hallway to the lobby and hurried across the carpeted floor to the door; she could see Remy sitting on the ATV and leaning on the handlebars.

"Ta-da!" Tess cried as she pushed the door wide, then dragged a cigarette butt receptacle closer to prop it open. Remy grinned with weary relief.

"I guess I'm the princess this time," she said as Tess jogged over. "And you're my knight in shining armor." Tess blushed, feeling a giddy rush of joy. She wrapped her arm around Remy's waist and helped her stand.

"Nobody says we can't be both," she said, looking up at Remy's face. She looked pale and the gauze pad taped to her head was soaking through, but her eyes were bright and she wore a good-humored expression.

"I'll drink to that," she said, leaning on Tess as they walked toward the open door. "You know, if we had anything to drink."

"I bet we can find something." Tess kicked the makeshift doorstop out of the way as they went through, letting the door swing shut behind them. "And a better first-aid kit, too."

"What do you mean?" Remy joked. "I've never

seen a better tape-and-bandage job in my life." Tess snorted.

"And you've rescued how many people? I think you're lying."

Tess helped Remy lower herself into the nearest chair and then went about searching the front desk for a first-aid kit and any other useful items. She came up with a briefcase-sized metal box with a red cross on the front, a bunch of keys, and a flashlight. "This'll be a start."

She dragged another chair over so it was facing Remy's and sat down, digging through the kit. Remy slumped in her chair, resting her head gingerly against the back cushion.

"The people here must've found out that the storm was coming and left last night before the roads closed," she mused. "Of course, the roads down from this part of the mountain are safer anyway, so they could've left more recently."

"How rude," Tess said with affected indignation. "Didn't they know we were coming?" Remy offered her a smile as if she appreciated the levity. After pulling out more alcohol wipes and tape, thicker gauze, and some antibiotic ointment, Tess leaned close and carefully pulled the makeshift bandage off Remy's forehead. Remy hissed in a breath when she did, and Tess bit her lip. "I'm sorry. It'll just be a second and I'll get the new bandage on. How are you feeling?"

"I'm okay," Remy said, and Tess paused in cleaning the cut to give her a pointed look.

"No, for real."

Remy huffed, petulant. "It hurts, and I'm still dizzy. When I try to move it makes me feel sick to my stomach."

"Okay," Tess said. "We're keeping you here, then, for the moment." Her mind raced, thinking back on how long it had taken them to get here. There was no way they'd make it back to the Rising Star before dark, even if Remy were in a condition to travel. With a sinking feeling, she realized they'd have to stay the night. *Well, this place is better than a maintenance shed, I guess.* She tried not to let her worry show on her face. "I'll go look for some blankets as soon as I finish this."

Tess dabbed antibiotic ointment on the cut and then pressed a fresh piece of gauze to it. As her hands hovered above Remy's cheeks, she wished she could take Remy's face in both hands and kiss her lingeringly on the lips instead.

It was the first time she'd actively imagined such a thing when she was this close to Remy. The other few times they'd touched, she'd been too startled or overwhelmed to really be in control. And, even more importantly, Remy had been the one who initiated it. Right now, Remy was sitting completely still, letting Tess's hands smooth the tape over her forehead. An image of Remy lying back and docilely letting Tess put her hands other places flashed through Tess's mind and made a wave of heat flow through her core, spreading to every bone.

Remy's eyes were fixed on her, her lips slightly open, her expression intent but unreadable. Tess swallowed. *Great job,* she chided herself. *Take advantage of an injured woman, why don't you?* Something flashed in Remy's eyes, a fire that darkened them, and a flush tingled over Tess's skin. With a wan, tense smile, Tess sat back and snapped the first-aid kit shut.

"You rest," she insisted quickly, banishing the

images from her mind and trying to calm the reaction in her body they caused. "I'll be back really soon with some blankets and things."

Exhaling a shaky breath, Tess hurried off, flashlight in hand, to the nearest corridor that displayed a sign with room numbers. Her legs trembled with the aftermath of those feelings, feelings that had come upon her much more suddenly and forcefully than she was ready for.

∅

The beam of Tess's flashlight swept over the doors that lined the hallway. She gripped the ring of keys tightly in her hand, scowling at each door as she went by—they were all key-card locks. Finally, she came upon one door that had a keyhole in the handle. A supply closet, maybe?

Tess's hands still shook as she fitted a key into the lock. Her body was moving faster than her mind, and it frightened her. Now that she knew Remy was open to seeing her romantically, it was time to prove herself. All she wanted was to show Remy that she was strong and resourceful and capable (and, okay, sexy too). And while the situation they'd found themselves in was pretty tense, she reminded herself to look on the bright side: it was the perfect opportunity to impress Remy.

That was the plan, anyway. But the feelings that crashed inside her like breaking waves demanded otherwise. It was a completely new sensation for her, and it was alarming. Never had passion this strong surged through her body; never had it been so insistent.

Okay, sure, that imaginary kiss wasn't the first

time she'd fantasized about Remy. But it was the first time she'd imagined such things when Remy was *right there* to do them with.

She had a chance with Remy, a good one. What would Remy think if Tess came on to her so early? Did Remy want to be the one to initiate things?

Tess drew in a long breath and then let it out again. *Come on,* she told herself. *Figuring out stuff like this is what dating is for. No one expects you to be psychic.* But still, her sudden flood of desire left an unsettling mix of anxiety and excitement in its wake. She had to do this right or else she might screw up her chances with Remy before they got started.

After trying several keys, one finally turned, and Tess swung the door open. With a sigh of relief, she saw that it was a linen closet, filled with neatly pressed sheets, wooly blankets, comforters, and pillows. A cleaning supply cart was parked inside the closet beneath the shelves. Tucking the flashlight under her arm, Tess pulled out masses of fabric and pillows. Then she kicked the door shut behind her and headed back to the lobby.

As her boots thudded down the silent hallway, Tess resolved to let things take their own course. Right now, the only thing she should be worried about was Remy's health and their safety. The cut on Remy's forehead seemed superficial, but who knew? She could have a concussion after all. Other than a vague idea about headaches and nausea and not letting the victim fall asleep, Tess knew nothing about concussions. She didn't have time to worry about how dating Remy was going to go.

But whenever Remy's face appeared in her mind, a glow sparked to life in her chest that she couldn't ignore. The glow suffused every corner of her and woke parts she didn't want to let run wild. Maybe she could keep it under wraps for now, but she had a suspicion that sooner or later, it would set her whole being alight. And that eventuality was both scary and exhilarating.

On the way back to the lobby, Tess noticed a side hallway that she'd passed over the first time she came that way. There was a little bit of light reflecting off the polished floor, and thinking that there might be other communal spaces down there with stuff they could use, Tess took a quick detour. What she found was sort of a miniature version of the front lobby. One bow window stood on the right-hand wall and let in the evening's pale light.

The other three walls were windowless, but the one opposite the window held a large brick fireplace. The floor was thickly carpeted and a variety of plush chairs and couches sat amidst some small tables. Games and books were scattered on these tables, giving Tess the impression that she'd found a den of some sort.

Taking a few steps in, Tess peered at the fireplace. There was fresh wood in an iron grate and a small stack nearby. Breathing out, Tess smiled and set her load of blankets and pillows down on one of the chairs. A place like this would conserve more heat than the large, drafty lobby.

Tess wiped her palms on the thighs of her jeans as she hurried back to get Remy. It was ridiculous how one little thought (one enormous thought, she amended) could kick-start her nervousness around Remy. She'd just started feeling comfortable with her, and now, all she could do was remember the desire that flashed through her veins when she imagined claiming

Remy's lips with her own. *Nothing has changed*, she told herself firmly. *Just because you're the responsible one now doesn't mean that you're any farther along in this potential relationship.*

She found Remy where she'd left her, sprawling in an easy chair near the reception desk. Remy's long legs were outstretched, her boots dripping muddy water on the floor, and her head was leaned limply back against the cushion.

"Hey," Tess greeted her, feeling uncomfortable about the way her voice reverberated in the empty room. Remy opened her eyes and smiled faintly. "I found a bunch of blankets and a little room with a fireplace. I think we should go there since it'll be easier to keep warm. We can light a fire and wrap you up until you feel better."

Tess held her hand out for Remy's and tried not to let it show when their touch sent a shiver of pleasure through her. Remy got to her feet woozily and Tess ducked underneath Remy's arm, giving her a solid place to lean.

"You're a regular Florence Nightingale, you know that?" Remy murmured, her voice low and gravelly. Even though Tess knew it sounded that way because Remy was hurt and exhausted, she still couldn't help but find it delicious.

"I'm not going to just drop you in the snow and let you freeze to death," Tess replied playfully. "I'm pretty sure you're the only one who knows the road back to our lodge." Remy chuckled in acknowledgement and took the flashlight from Tess while Tess picked up her backpack and the first-aid kit. Together, they went slowly through the darkened hallway until they came to the little den where Tess had left the blankets.

After helping Remy lower herself onto the couch, Tess dug through her backpack for matches. "Are you feeling any better?" she asked as she balled up some of the newspaper that was stacked by the fireplace for starter.

"It's better now that we're inside and sitting still." Remy tentatively touched the bandage on her forehead. "I still feel a little bit sick, but not as dizzy."

"Good." Tess struck a match and lit the newspaper, watching the flame as if staring hard enough would ensure that the logs lit. Then she glanced back over her shoulder at Remy, a thoughtful look on her face. "So where'd you grow up?" Remy furrowed her brows and chuckled at Tess's blatant conversation-starter. "Hey," Tess said, pointing a finger at her, "I'm just trying to distract you from the nausea. No judgement on how dumb my attempt is."

"No, no, I appreciate it." Remy held up her hands in acquiescence. "I grew up outside of Boston."

Tess waited, but the pause stretched on. Tongues of flame began to creep up the logs and she sat back, satisfied that the fire was strong enough to last. "And...?" Remy rolled her eyes and smiled. "What, is it a state secret or something?" Tess teased.

"No," Remy countered. "It's just... I'm kind of embarrassed by the way I grew up, that's all."

Tess's eyebrows lifted and she turned, settling on the floor and giving Remy her entire attention. "How so?"

With a slightly uncomfortable twitch of her mouth, Remy focused on prying one of her boots off with the other foot. "Remember how, at lunch, we were talking about the way I didn't really appreciate the opportunity my parents gave me to go to college? Well, there was a lot I didn't appreciate when I was a kid."

Tess was silent. She could tell that Remy was trying to be sensitive to her feelings, and she felt torn between her automatic resentment of wealthy people and her shame at being so judgmental. It touched her that amidst all the teasing and needling, when it came to something important, Remy cared about how her words affected Tess.

"I still want to know about it," Tess told her with a quiet smile. "I want to know about *you*."

Remy raised her eyes to Tess's and something strangely open and vulnerable flitted across her face. Then her casual, flippant mask slid back into place.

"My parents had a lot of money and a really bad attitude. I was supposed to be their perfect little spawn, a miniature mixture of the two of them who would do everything they wanted and make us look like the ideal family. They refused to send me to public school, so I went to private schools from kindergarten on up." Remy slid down in her seat and folded her hands over her stomach. She relayed the story like she'd thought about it a lot over the years.

"For a long time, I tried to be what they wanted. I swear they had my entire life planned out for me from birth, which just goes to show you that they had zero experience with raising children. Around the beginning of high school, I just stopped doing the work to get good grades. I'd already decided I didn't want to go to college, so I did just enough to graduate."

"They let you do that at a private school?" Tess asked with an incredulous smile. She'd always been under the impression that private schools were extra strict and students were required to excel.

"Pff, yeah." Remy rolled her eyes and chuckled. "Honestly, as long as your parents paid tuition, the teachers couldn't have cared less. Most of them, anyway. It was the couple of really good ones that kept me from failing entirely. There were a few times when I was so mad at my parents that I might've let myself bottom out just to make them realize how serious I was." She shrugged. "I don't think they ever really got me, though. Of course, at that time, *nobody* understood me," Remy added, putting the back of her hand to her forehead in a martyred gesture. "I was one of those dramatic, anti-establishment teenagers who would've died before admitting that they liked anything popular. I had a nose ring and only wore black and red—the whole nine yards."

Tess giggled. Teenage Remy actually seemed pretty hot to her. "Yeah, I can see that." Remy shrugged her eyebrows in a way that indicated she wasn't surprised. Then her expression turned pensive.

"I guess I'm lucky, though, that they didn't freak out when I told them I was a lesbian. In fact, they had already guessed, and they'd lined up a bunch of sappy, happy-sunny-bunnies-and-rainbows youth groups for me. You can guess how well *that* went over. It was a kind gesture, much better than it could've been, but it just proved that they had no clue who their own child was."

Tess pulled her knees to her chest and rested her back against the brick wall of the fireplace, warmth from the growing fire melting the chill from her bones. She didn't get along all that well with her parents when it came to certain subjects, but at least she felt like they knew her, even if they didn't like some of the things she did. And her big brother had always been on her side, no matter what. She wondered if Remy had been lonely as a child.

"They must've completely flipped when you didn't go to college," Tess guessed sympathetically.

"Hoo boy, did they ever." Remy grimaced. "I'm surprised there wasn't a mushroom cloud where our house used to be. They were both so selfish, and I guess I was selfish too...but I wasn't the one who'd decided to bring a life into the world." She shook her head, staring into the fire. "I don't see them much anymore."

Tess's heart clenched for her. "You don't owe them anything," she offered softly. Remy's eyes moved to catch Tess's and she smiled, a gentle gratitude lighting her face.

"Nah, I don't," she agreed. "Besides, the guy I apprenticed with ended up being kind of a surrogate father, I guess. I go have dinner with him every other weekend or so."

"Aww, that's wonderful." They lapsed into a comfortable silence broken only by the whistling of the wind outside and the crackle of the fire. In spite of the bizarreness of their situation, Tess felt quite cozy—the elements were outside and they, who could easily still be caught out there, were safely inside where it was warm and dry. She couldn't imagine finding a better place to shelter when you were stuck in a mountain storm.

Tess was so lulled by the warmth (and by her exhausted muscles after the trials of the day) that she nearly jumped out of her skin when she heard Remy's stomach rumble. Tess blinked at her as Remy looked down at her stomach with an equally surprised expression. Then Tess grinned.

"Feeling better?"

"Yeah," Remy replied, sounding both surprised and relieved. "I guess your distraction worked. I'm starting to get hungry."

Tess crawled over to where her backpack sat on the floor at the other side of the couch. "I know I've got some granola bars in here..."

"Bleh." Remy made a face. "This is a friggin' resort. They wouldn't have taken all their food with them when they left. There has to be *something* in the kitchens that's better than granola bars."

At first, Tess was merely amused by Remy's reaction to her snacks. Then she really thought about what kind of food they could find in a fancy resort's kitchen, and a slow grin grew on her face. She stood up and held out her hand.

"Want to go on an adventure?"

Remy matched her grin and slapped her hand into Tess's. The spark Tess felt when their skin touched sent delicious shivers racing over her skin and filled her with a heady exhilaration. She pulled Remy out of the chair and, boldly, slipped her arm around Remy's waist in case she was still wobbly.

For being trapped on a mountain, this was looking to be a pretty wonderful night.

Chapter Nine

The basement kitchen was windowless and therefore pitch black, but when Tess swept her flashlight across the room, she saw appliances and sinks and long, shiny counters that reminded her of a reality cooking show set. There were three refrigerators—the big, double-doored industrial kind—and several ovens set into the wall. One counter that lined a wall was entirely stovetop ranges.

"Good lord," Tess commented. "Is this what the Rising Star's kitchen looks like?"

"Pretty much," Remy said. "People who come to these places expect five-star food."

Tess began to poke around the cabinets, leaving Remy leaning against the island in the middle. "I'm sorry to break it to you, but my dinner last night wasn't anything special. It was fine and everything, but I wouldn't call it 'five star.'"

"You must have an undeveloped palate," Remy told her, affecting a snotty voice. "Clearly someone like you wouldn't notice the difference between a steak marinated in a 1984 merlot and the much superior *1987* merlot." Tess snorted.

"Oh, that's it, I'm sure." She opened up a refrigerator door and felt sheepish that she'd expected the light to come on. "Well, I don't think we can trust the fridges. If the power here has been out as long as it has back at the Rising Star, this stuff has been sitting without refrigeration for at least ten hours."

"Non-perishables it is, then," Remy said. She swung her own flashlight around the room, landing on a tall wooden door near the stovetops. "That looks promising. Pantry, you think?"

Tess headed over. "All I've found so far in the cabinets is dishes, so there's a good chance it is." She opened the door to find shelf upon shelf of cans and jars. "Jackpot," she said, smiling at Remy over her shoulder. "Come on over."

Remy was steadier now, and she joined Tess to peer into the pantry.

"Ooh, caviar!"

Tess laughed. "Seriously?"

"Yeah, why not?" Remy reached in and grabbed a couple of tins. "Have you ever had it before?"

Tess wrinkled her nose. "No. It sounds gross. Besides, caviar's like *the* pretentious rich person food."

Remy shook her head with a smile. "You don't know what you're missing." She took another tin for good measure.

"You don't strike me as a caviar sort of person," Tess replied.

"There's your problem," Remy said, setting the caviar down on the counter beside them. "There is no 'caviar sort of person.'"

Tess furrowed her brow, struck by how she'd always overlooked the logic of that, and resumed searching the pantry. "Hey, there's cheese here. Isn't cheese supposed to be refrigerated?"

"Depends on the cheese. This all looks like hard cheese, which should be fine." Remy reached over Tess's shoulder and picked up a paper-wrapped wedge.

Tess couldn't help but inhale her woodsy scent, and her stomach fluttered with attraction. She couldn't decide if being this close to Remy was heaven or if it was driving her crazy. Remy held her flashlight beam over the cheese's label. "Beaufort d'été. That sounds expensive."

Tess picked up another wedge and squinted at the name. "Makes me wish I spoke Spanish. This one is 'Dehesa De Los Llanos Gran Reserva.' Hey, I think I heard of this on the Food Network! It was on an artisan cheese show I watched one time."

"Well, that means we've got to try it, then." Remy reached for another. "Parmigiano-Reggiano."

Tess placed the Gran Reserva cheese on the counter beside the caviar. "I'm guessing that's not your average parmesan-in-a-canister?"

"I don't think so," Remy replied with a grin. "Let's try it."

"Here are some crackers," Tess added, pulling down a box. "Artisan flatbreads," she read. "Rosemary and lemon." Grabbing another two boxes, she tucked the first under her arm. "Garlic asiago. And this one is cranberry. Wow, who knew crackers came in varieties like this?"

"Everything has a super-expensive counterpart these days," Remy replied.

"I want the super-expensive counterpart to Cheetos," Tess said, and Remy laughed.

"I think you'll have to settle for whatever this is." Remy picked up a shrink-wrapped package from another shelf. "Alpaca jerky."

"*What?*" Tess crowed in disbelief. She took the package from Remy. "I love jerky! Seriously, though? Alpaca?"

"Alpacas are sort of like smaller llamas from

Peru—" Remy began, but Tess cut her off.

"I know what an alpaca is, Remy!"

"Sorry for assuming."

Tess refrained from sticking out her tongue and picked up a similar package. "Elk jerky. Oh, my god, I have to try this."

"Pâté for me," Remy said, reaching in for another couple of tins.

"Ew, can't you chose something that isn't made of fish eggs or liver?" Tess shot her a teasing grin.

"You can keep your exotic jerky and I'll have my fish eggs and liver," Remy replied loftily. "Now, there's got to be something good for dessert..."

They both examined the shelves with their flashlights, and Tess's hand shot out. "Ooh, chocolate bars! This one has chili powder."

"And bacon," Remy added, taking another one.

"That sounds awesome." Tess glanced over at their growing pile of food. "We're going to have too much to carry back pretty soon. We should look for something to drink; I'm almost out of water."

"Oh, I'm sure they have bottles of it somewhere," Remy said. "But I'm more interested in..." She moved away toward the back of the kitchen, swinging her flashlight across the lower cabinets. "Aha!" She grinned back at Tess as she illuminated a wine rack. "Here's what I was looking for." Remy bent and pulled out a bottle. "Dom Perignon 2004! I have no clue what the year means in terms of taste, but this seems like a good choice." Tess, meanwhile, had found some sealed bottles of spring water that had been put to chill in the fridge before the power went out.

"I think we're good." Tess regarded the pile of food on the counter. "This should do us," she said, satisfied.

They gathered the packages and cans into their arms, laughing at their eclectic "picnic," and made their way back upstairs to the warm, fire-lit glow of their den.

Remy sat back down on the couch after depositing her spoils on a blanket beside her. Then she looked over at Tess, who had grabbed one of the fluffy comforters and was wrapping it around herself. "You don't have to sit on the floor, you know," she said. "There's plenty of room on the couch."

Tess saw the warmth in her eyes and a flock of butterflies took flight in her chest. With a little smile, she came over and curled up on the opposite side of the couch, placing her food between them. She folded one leg beneath her and turned to face Remy.

"Okay, I'm going for the alpaca jerky first," Tess said, tearing into the package.

"Come on," Remy urged. "You *have* to try some caviar." She batted her eyelashes, a gesture far more feminine than Tess had expected from her—and one that Tess found intensely sexy. "For me?"

Tess was almost rendered speechless, and she could tell from Remy's pleased smirk that it was apparent. "Well, fine," Tess managed weakly. "For you."

With relish, Remy opened the tin of caviar and spread it on one of the artisan crackers. "If you don't like it, that's fine," she said, "but you can't pass it up without trying."

Tess reluctantly took the cracker topped with black, glistening beads. "What does it taste like?"

"Mostly it's salty," Remy said. "And it tastes like fish, too, naturally."

Tess liked seafood, but mostly the fried stuff.

She steeled herself and took a bite.

"Mmh!" Tess covered her mouth, her eyes widening in surprise. "They pop!"

Remy laughed. "Yeah, that's a sign of good caviar. They're supposed to pop gently or kind of melt on your tongue."

Tess blinked, chewing and swallowing. "Okay, yeah, that's kind of good."

"Ha!" Remy thrust a caviar-laden cracker triumphantly in her direction and then ate it herself.

"Open up that wine," Tess told her, pointing at the bottle. "I think this caviar is turning me into a snob." She put one hand on her chest, tilting her head and raising her shoulder like a black-and-white movie actress. "What do you say, Muffin?" she asked in a high, nasal voice. "After this, shall we take a stroll down to the yacht?"

Remy snorted and joined in. "Oh, dahling, the yacht is so tedious this time of year. Let's take the slave-powered dirigible instead."

Tess burst out laughing. She fumbled with one of the wedges of cheese, pulling off the paper, and continued the game. "I say, shall we try a bit of this cheese? It's made from the milk of one particular sheep that lives on the tallest mountain in France and bathes in stardust every second full moon."

"Yes, yes!" Remy handed her a knife, chortling. "And next, hand me that bag of jerky made from the last alpaca in the royal line of alpacas, who are all fed on gold-dusted quinoa."

Tess cut pieces for both of them but had to wait until her laughter subsided before she could put anything into her mouth. Then Remy continued: "Don't forget the pâté—it's made of the liver of a goose born under the sign of Scorpio and fed only crushed diamonds and rose petals." Then Tess had to wait through another bout of laughter.

"I'll never get anything eaten at this rate!" she gasped.

"Okay, on to safer topics," Remy replied, eyes dancing. "I told you all about my childhood, and now it's your turn."

"Oh, boy, talk about boring." Tess, still giggling, placed a slice of cheese on a rosemary and lemon cracker and rolled her eyes with pleasure when she put it into her mouth. "We lived in a kind of crappy part of this tiny town," she began as she laid out various pieces of her dinner on the blanket in front of her. "It was a development, no trees, just houses crammed together along this grid of streets and chain-link fences. Our house was one half of a duplex, and my older brother and I shared the upstairs, which was more like an attic. Good thing I liked him," she added, making a face. "Both my parents worked two jobs once my brother was old enough to look after me, so they had me in a lot of afterschool programs so I'd stay out of trouble. Our school sucked, though—there were about forty kids in my graduating class so everybody knew everybody else since birth and secrets were bound to get out if you shared them with even one person." Tess shrugged, opening up the elk jerky, which tasted pretty similar to the alpaca, she thought. "That's why I never came out until I found the LGBTQA student alliance in college. It wouldn't have ended well if people found out I was gay when I was in high school." Remy made a sympathetic noise, and Tess shrugged again, uncomfortable.

"Did your parents freak out?" Remy asked

hesitantly.

"They weren't happy," Tess said. She picked a piece of the jerky apart before eating it and turned her attention to the next wedge of cheese. "I guess I can kind of see where you were coming from, too," she added. "When I came out to my parents, it was obvious I wasn't conforming to how they wanted my life to go. It was worse, though, when I..." She paused, unsure whether she wanted to continue. Her parents had been even less pleased about her later failures.

For a few moments, they were both silent, and then Remy shifted, facing Tess fully. "When what?" she asked, her voice careful and gentle. Tess didn't look at her.

"After college, I was supposed to go teach English in Korea. They were really proud of me for getting into the program, but...I backed out. And they were even more disappointed in me than when they found out I was a lesbian."

Remy didn't ask why Tess had decided not to go. She just frowned in sympathy. "Their loss." Then the corner of her mouth turned up. "Don't they know lesbians have superpowers?"

Tess snorted softly. "Guess not. They just thought that without that on my resume, I'd end up having to struggle to survive like they did. I'm not saying things are totally okay between us—thank goodness my brother acts as a buffer at holidays and things—but we have a civil relationship, at least."

Remy balled up a piece of the cheese paper and threw it at her to lighten the mood. "Well, that explains the chip on your shoulder about rich people," she said with a wide smirk. Tess lifted an elbow and expertly blocked the paper, which bounced off her arm and behind the couch.

"I have a chip on *my* shoulder?" she asked, laughing. "Ever since the minute I met you, you've been all snotty about the Rising Star!"

As soon as Tess saw Remy's face, her stomach dropped. *Shit. Me and my big mouth.* Remy sat back against the couch's cushion, her eyes hooded, spreading some pâté on a cracker.

"I have good reason for that."

Tess bit her lip. She wanted to apologize, but she also wanted to know what really had gone on, and she thought there was a better chance of Remy explaining if Tess didn't break in. Most of all, she wanted Remy to confide in her.

Remy's eyes flickered up to Tess's. In their blue depths, Tess could see uncertainty and something else—a deliberation, a weighing. Remy ate the cracker before heaving a sigh.

"How much did Marti tell you?"

Tess was dismayed to feel her face heat. Remy knew she and Marti had been talking about her? "Not a lot. She just said you used to work there and that...you and Melissa were together for a while."

"I wish that's all there was to tell," Remy said cynically. She ripped the foil wrapping off the top of the wine bottle and frowned at the cork, then searched in her pocket for a jackknife. "We didn't grab any cups, so I guess we'll have to share this." She gestured toward Tess with the bottle. "I promise I don't have cooties."

Tess tried to smile, but she knew Remy was just stalling. Remy knew Tess had caught on to it, too. She popped the cork out and took a drink halfway between a sip and a swig.

"Did you know I make soap out of the herbs I

grow in my garden?" Remy asked. "Lotions, too."
Tess's brows pulled together. Was she still stalling?
Maybe she'd get nothing out of Remy after all. Then
Remy set the bottle between her thighs and gazed into
the fire.

"That's how I met Melissa. I was looking for a
job and selling my soap at a farmers' market, and she
had just arrived to take over the management of the
Rising Star from her uncle. We struck up a
conversation, one thing led to another...and soon I got
a job as a handywoman at the resort. They ended up
needing a new onsite manager after about a year, and
she hired me." Angling a look over at Tess, Remy raised
an eyebrow. "I don't know if you know this or not, but
dating your boss is never a great idea."

"Mm," Tess agreed compassionately. She
reached out for the wine and Remy passed it over.

"Melissa was always possessive and jealous, but
when we were first together, I liked that about her. Like
I was the only one good enough for her, you know?" A
small, tired smile passed over Remy's face. "She'd
throw these stupid tantrums when she thought I wasn't
paying enough attention to her. That should've been a
warning flag, but I thought it was cute. I thought it
meant that she..." Remy cut herself off, clenching her
jaw. "It doesn't matter what I thought," she continued,
looking down into her lap. "One day I was repairing a
thermostat in one of the guests' rooms, and Melissa
completely flipped out, saying that I'd slept with the
woman. Cheated on her. I don't even know how the
idea got into her head, but she was always reading
things into it when I'd even speak to other women she
didn't know personally. Melissa wouldn't believe me
that nothing happened between us. She threw the

woman out of the resort and fired me."

So that was what Melissa had meant when she talked about a betrayal. Tess pulled the comforter more tightly around her shoulders. From what she'd seen of Melissa, that didn't seem at all out of character. It must have destroyed Remy to have someone she trusted accuse her like that.

"It ended up looking like this ridiculous sitcom-style drama to the staff at the resort," Remy told her resentfully. "They were split as to who to believe. Marti was on my side, as I bet you could've guessed. Glen was hired as the onsite manager after that and I got a job at the with the national park."

"But you still helped them out with repairs?" Tess couldn't keep the surprise from her voice. After the way Melissa treated her, she wouldn't have expected Remy to want to step foot in the resort again. And clearly Remy hated doing just that...but she did it anyway.

"Yeah." Remy shrugged, taking the bottle back from Tess and swigging another gulp. "Melissa won't pay a reasonable price for maintenance workers to come in, and Glen was always desperate for help. The resort's typical clientele have always driven me crazy, but once my eyes were opened to how insincere Melissa really is, I couldn't stand the sight of the ones who remind me of her. But I got to care about a lot of the people who worked there and I didn't want the place to go under, not if my help could keep it afloat."

"That's so kind of you," Tess said, her voice soft and sincere. Remy met her eyes for a moment before grimacing.

It made sense now, Remy's constant attempts to sidestep any serious discussion of relationships.

Melissa had hurt her deeply, had given Remy cause to distrust people who said they loved her. Tess knew that if she were in that situation, she'd probably never want to date again. She didn't even know how long ago this was. It sounded like Remy and Melissa had been serious for some time, and who would blame Remy for being wary now? How had Remy even found the courage to give Tess her phone number?

Anxiety constricted Tess's stomach. A phone number might not mean anything. All Remy had agreed to was that she'd be interested in seeing Tess again. They hadn't established that a serious relationship was part of the offer. Maybe Remy didn't want one at all.

Tess thought back to the times that their interactions had become the most intense. They were all moments of physical closeness, of desire cut just short of being realized. From those indications, there was no reason to assume Remy wanted anything more than a casual lady-friend to tumble into bed with every so often.

And that was the polar opposite of everything Tess wanted. Or at least what she *thought* she wanted.

Would she be okay with a fling, if it was with Remy?

Looking at Remy's profile in the firelight made Tess's heart skip a beat. She was so stunning, the swoop of her short hair shining chestnut in the dim glow. Just gazing at her face, at its artfully beautiful angles and the curve of her nose and chin, Tess wanted to caress her and place kisses on every patch of skin. She knew that if she did that, she'd never want to stop.

Was that it, then? Was their relationship doomed to fail before it even started? *Get hold of yourself, woman,* Tess scolded fiercely. *You're not psychic, remember?*

You have to actually ask *Remy before you decide what she wants out of this.* But right now wasn't a good time for that. Tess watched the muffled sorrow on Remy's face and hugged herself. Bringing up whether Remy wanted a long-term relationship would only cause her more pain and make things unbearably awkward.

Remy noticed Tess looking at her and offered a bleak smile. "I think it's probably time we get some sleep, huh? After the day we had."

"Yeah—oh!" Tess sat bolt upright. "No, we can't do that! You might have a concussion! You can't go to sleep if you have a concussion, right?" All that stuff she learned about treating roller derby injuries seemed pretty fuzzy now, but there had been something about not falling asleep with a concussion, hadn't there? Remy cocked an eyebrow at her, skeptical.

"I think that's a myth..." For a moment, though, she looked unsure. "Isn't it?"

"I wouldn't want to risk it," Tess said worriedly.

"And you expect us both to stay up *all night?*" Remy shook her head. "I feel a lot better now, Tess, I promise. If we don't sleep, we'll be too exhausted to look for gasoline tomorrow and drive the ATV all the way back to the Rising Star."

Tess exhaled, pressing her lips together. "I guess you're right."

"I'm always right," Remy replied with a sly grin. Then her face softened. "But thank you for being so concerned."

The honesty in her eyes made Tess's insides melt. She swallowed, her heart beating inside her chest like the thrumming of violin strings. When they shared moments like that, real moments where they understood each other, Tess felt like anything was possible.

"Um," Tess floundered. "I guess I'll just...take my blankets to the other couch so you can have this one..." She tried to gather the remnants of their dinner and get up, but Remy stopped her with a hand on her wrist.

"You don't have to," Remy told her, and Tess's heart leapt into her throat. Remy smiled and shrugged one shoulder. "This couch has fold-out footrests on both sides." She released Tess's arm and pulled the lever beneath the armrest; the front panel beneath her legs popped up and the back of her section reclined.

Tess's smile was shaky, her heart still thundering at what she'd assumed was a suggestion that they share the couch in a—ahem—more horizontal fashion. "Oh, great!" she quavered. Together, they put the trash from their dinner into a neat pile by the door and then settled down onto their own ends of the couch. "Do you think we should put the coals out?" Tess asked.

"Nah, that'll keep any sparks in the hearth," Remy responded, flicking a hand at the bowed iron screen that Tess had set in front of the fireplace after the fire had begun to blaze. "We need to stay warm, anyway."

"True," Tess said sleepily. She gazed over at Remy, grateful more for the lovely play of light over Remy's face than for the heat the fire gave.

❧

When Tess opened her eyes to see sunlight cascading in and falling in a pool on the plush, pale blue rug, she didn't remember where she was. Sunlight seemed like a foreign concept for a few muddled moments. Then she wondered why the pillow she was lying against rose and fell gently beneath her, and she blinked to bring her eyes into focus.

She lay curled against Remy's hip, the other woman's legs hooked in front of her on the couch. Remy's head was cradled on her arms on the far armrest.

Tess shot up straight, her heart thundering. They'd fallen asleep on separate ends of the couch, hadn't they? And somehow they both moved in their sleep to be nestled together like this? Tess swallowed, trying to calm her breathing and remember if she woke up at any point in the night. Nothing came to mind.

She was grateful that she'd woken up first. Would Remy be okay with that kind of intimacy? Falling asleep on each other seemed awfully...relationshippy.

Tess gazed at Remy's sleeping face. She looked peaceful, all the sarcasm and cavalier confidence smoothed away. The sunlight hadn't reached them yet, but the ambient light from where it hit the carpet nearby made Remy's skin glow softly. She was radiant.

The way they'd fit together while sleeping... Tess only remembered a few seconds of it before she realized where she was, but it had felt so *right*. Not uncomfortable in any sense, emotionally or physically, until her embarrassment and insecurity took over. She was filled with longing for that unconscious ease.

It was then that their conversation last night about concussions came back to her and alarm shot through her limbs. Without thinking, she reached out and shook Remy's shoulder. She couldn't even remember what was supposed to happen if a person with a concussion fell asleep, just that they (maybe?) shouldn't be allowed to do so.

But Remy's eyelashes fluttered and then her eyes opened, deep and dark like the bluest iris bloom, and Tess breathed a sigh of relief. Remy's eyes focused on her and she smiled softly, and Tess's heart fluttered like a flag in the wind.

"Everything okay?" Remy mumbled. Tess nodded, feeling her cheeks redden.

"I was just...worried," she explained sheepishly. "In case you have a concussion."

Remy chuckled, and Tess could feel the rumble against her; she still sat with her knees curled beneath Remy's legs. At that point, Remy lifted her head and gazed down at said legs.

"Oh, sorry... Did I lay on you last night? I move around a lot in my sleep."

"Um, it's okay," Tess replied in a trembling voice. She cleared her throat. "Looks like the weather's improved." *Smooth, Tess.*

Remy watched her with one corner of her mouth curled in a smirk, and then she moved her gaze to the window. "Looks like you're right." Remy swung her legs down and stretched her arms up over her head, groaning. "Well, no rest for the weary. We'd better start looking for gasoline so we can get back."

"How are you feeling?" Tess asked anxiously as Remy stood up.

"Better. I'll just take some more Advil for my head, but I don't feel sick or dizzy anymore." Remy glanced around and then picked up a bottle of water and took a drink. "I guess it's cheese and jerky for breakfast," she added.

"I do have those granola bars in my backpack,"

Tess reminded her. "And some trail mix."

"Ah, they sound much better now!" Remy grinned at her and held out a hand. "Need a little help getting out of bed?"

Tess's mouth quirked to the side and she took Remy's hand. "Some 'bed,'" she said, getting to her feet and passing her hands over her hair. By now, more of her blonde curls were out of the ponytail than in it. "Ugh, another night sleeping in our clothes."

"There's a sink in the bathroom down the hall," Remy told her, handing her a fresh water bottle. "Go wash your face. You'll feel better."

Rubbing one fist into her eye, Tess yawned and did as Remy suggested. After splashing water on her face and scrubbing it with a convenient washcloth, she did feel more awake. She braided her hair (if only she had a comb!) and joined Remy in the hallway where she waited, fishing dried apricots out of a bag of trail mix.

"All right, where are we likely to find gasoline?" Remy mused.

"Not anywhere in the lodge, I would think." Tess pulled on her jacket and retrieved her backpack. "Maybe they have a garage outside or something."

"Sounds like a good place to start. Let's go get the gas containers from the ATV."

Outside the lodge, the air was warm and the snow was already starting to melt. "Classic New England weather," Tess commented, staring up at the strikingly blue sky. Remy chuckled as she unstrapped the bungee cords that held the empty red gasoline containers to the back of the four-wheeler. Tess took one and Remy took the other as they started a circuit of the building.

The outside of the lodge was full of corners and

turns, but none of them held a garage of any sort. There were a couple of cars parked at the edge of a wide, flat expanse that Tess guessed must be a parking lot. Even if there had been a garage, Tess thought morosely, the power was out so they most likely wouldn't have been able to get the doors up. A place like this wouldn't have manual garage doors anymore.

They continued around the building and as they turned a corner, a shed a few hundred yards away came into view. "That looks promising." Remy shot a smile at Tess.

The shed was, thankfully, unlocked. They had to wrench the door open through a drift of snow that had blown up against it, but inside there was the unmistakable smell of motor oil and gasoline.

"Even more promising!" Tess said, approaching a large riding lawnmower parked in the middle. "They've got to have spare gas for this thing somewhere." But a few moments of searching turned up nothing but empty containers. Tess moaned in frustration.

"Well," Remy began, placing her hands on her hips resolutely. "We do have one other option."

"What's that?"

Remy moved toward the wall and pulled a piece of tubing out of a bucket. "Do you know how to siphon?"

Tess raised a skeptical eyebrow. "In theory..." Remy grinned at her.

"Come on, you're not a real outdoorswoman until you've siphoned gasoline."

"Says who?" Tess shot back, smiling warily.

"Everybody. And regardless, that's our best bet at the moment." Remy went over to the riding mower and circled it, looking for the gas tank. When she found it, she motioned Tess over. "Bring that empty container, will you?"

Remy unscrewed the gas cap as Tess watched. "The trick," Remy continued, "is to make sure the gas tank you're siphoning out of is higher than the container you want to put the gas in." She regarded the lawnmower thoughtfully. "I think we should be fine here. If this were a standard push mower, we'd need to put it up on blocks or something."

Tess smiled, amused at the commentary. "Thank you, Tool Time Tim."

"Pff," Remy scoffed. "I could've gone the rest of my life without being reminded of that TV show, thank you very much." Peering down into the mower's gas tank, she inserted one end of the tube. "Now comes the tricky part. You watch the tube and tell me when the gas is getting close to my mouth, okay?"

Tess nodded. The tube wasn't entirely transparent, but it was hopefully translucent enough that she'd be able to see the liquid in it.

Remy knelt down on the ground near the empty container and wiped off the end of the tube with her sleeve, then put it in her mouth and sucked. Tess cried, "Ooh, I see it!" when yellowish liquid began to creep through the tube. When it neared Remy's mouth, Tess patted her shoulder. "Close, close!" she said, and Remy dropped the tube into the empty gas container. They heard the gasoline begin to pour in. "Woohoo!"

Tess and Remy gave each other a jubilant high-five. They watched with excitement as the gasoline flowed through the tube and slowly filled the red container. Finally, a few bubbles appeared in the tube and they heard a splutter.

"I guess all that's in there," Tess said as Remy pulled the tube out of the mower's gas tank and emptied the remaining contents into the container. "We filled it almost to the top, though!"

"Mission accomplished," Remy declared with a triumphant grin. She raised her fists in the air and Tess jumped up and down, clapping.

"You were right!" she cried. "Lesbians *do* have superpowers!" Remy began to do a victory dance that, if performed by anyone else, would have probably looked silly—but her swaying hips and bobbing shoulders only filled Tess with exuberant longing. She started to dance too, hopping around on the damp concrete floor, and then before she knew it she'd thrown herself into Remy's arms.

Remy clasped her tight around the waist, using Tess's momentum to swing her around. Laughter filled the little shed as they twirled, both of them dizzy, and Tess's feet connected with the ground at the same time as her mouth captured Remy's.

It was so sudden, so unplanned that Tess felt almost outside of her body and intensely inside it at the same time. Remy's lips were just as soft and hot and insistent as she imagined them, and she tasted like apricots and wood smoke and the sharp snap of snow. Tess tightened her arms around Remy's neck, finally indulging her desire to caress the buzzed hair above Remy's ears.

Remy pulled her close, their breasts pressed tightly together, holding Tess's ribs in a grip that was stone-strong and gentle at the same time. She drank Tess in, tilting her head back, kissing her passionately and desperately. Tess felt consumed, like every atom was on fire, every cell a spark that burst to life at

Remy's touch.

She kissed Remy again and again, biting at her lip until she felt Remy smile against her and heard a low growl of desire emerge from Remy's chest. Remy swung her around, devouring her lips, and Tess felt her back bump against the wooden wall of the shed.

Everything inside her was elation and thrumming desire. She was overtaken by it, her mind a blank, shut down in favor of the delicious sensations pouring through her body. Tess moved one hand to cup Remy's cheek, finally feeling that chiseled jaw for herself, holding it like it was made of porcelain. She drew back, her chest heaving as she pulled in a breath, and she looked into Remy's eyes.

Lust flamed there, darkening the sapphire shade nearly to black, desire and intense need transforming the lines of her face even more beautifully than the firelight had. Tess gazed up at her, her eyes narrowing with joy, ecstasy shining from her like the sun. She was filled with such pure happiness then that it even engulfed the desire.

Something flickered in Remy's eyes, something heavy and drowning, something almost like fear.

She loosened her arms around Tess's ribs, the strength and passion ebbing away. Tess felt like the breath had been torn from her lungs. What was going on? Desire still thumped inside her, but now it mixed with a tightening anxiety.

Remy's face was stony as she backed away, her hands still on Tess's hips but loose now. Tess's heart pounded, but not with ardor anymore. She searched Remy's expression for any indication of why she'd stopped. Did she find Tess unattractive? Were her kisses somehow repulsive?

Remy swallowed and finally met Tess's eyes again. Tess stared at her with wrinkled brows, questioning, fearful.

"Tess," Remy said roughly, then cleared her throat. "You're an incredibly, *incredibly* sexy woman and I would be more than glad to shag the everloving hell out of you." Something loosened in Tess's chest, but Remy's sudden change was even more befuddling now. "But you just need to know..." Remy licked her lips, her gaze flashing away and then back to Tess. "I'm not looking for anything more."

Tess felt like the earth was plummeting beneath her feet. She thumped back against the wall, her eyes wide. There wasn't enough air in the shed all of a sudden.

Without even asking, she'd gotten her answer.

Remy swallowed, watching her, and her hands dropped from Tess's hips. She took one step back. "I hope I didn't lead you on."

"No," Tess said faintly, finding enough breath to speak. "I'll just have to...think..." She straightened her jacket with shaking hands and moved past Remy to hoist up the full container of gasoline. "We should go, right? The sooner we get this back to the Rising Star, the sooner everyone will have heat and light again." Tess shouldered the door open and tromped into the blinding sunlight, squinting and aiming toward the front of the lodge. Her heart squeezed so tightly that she could hardly put together any thoughts.

Okay. Okay. This is fine, right? You wanted to know what she wanted out of a relationship, and now you know. Now you can make an informed decision.

And that kiss had been hot. Really hot. Really unbelievably hot. Tess wanted to whimper when she thought about how little time she'd had to enjoy it.

She heaved the heavy container of gasoline up onto the back of the ATV and went about securing it down with the bungee cords. *She was totally honest with you. What more do you want? She never gave you any indication that she was looking for a girlfriend. That was all you, making one assumption after another.* When she heard Remy's footsteps crunching through the snow behind her, she tried to put on a brave face.

"How long do you think it'll take us to get back?" she asked, forcibly casual. Remy didn't look at her. Her expression was completely closed.

"If we make good time, we should be there a little after noon."

"I wish there were some way to let them know we're safe. I bet Marti is worried," Tess said just to fill the silence that hung over them like a lead blanket. There was no reply from Remy. She just strapped the extra gas container to the back, got onto the ATV, and scooted forward so Tess could get on too.

"Ready?" Remy glanced over her shoulder, catching Tess's eye for the briefest of moments. The ache in Tess's chest echoed through her ribs and lungs.

"Yeah," Tess said so softly that she wouldn't have been surprised if Remy didn't hear her at all. She climbed behind Remy and hesitated before putting her arms around her, but she knew she'd topple right off the four-wheeler if she didn't hold on. So, squeezing her eyes shut and wishing she could strike the last several minutes off the history books, Tess loosely draped her arms around Remy's waist and hung on as best she could.

Chapter Ten

As the trees zipped by, Tess tried to sort her thoughts out. Everything that came to mind, though, was so damnably logical and reasonable in comparison to how she felt that it seemed like it was coming from another planet. Yes, she'd wanted to know whether Remy was only interested in fooling around. And no, Remy hadn't led her on. But that didn't mean Tess wasn't crushed by finding out that her hopes were in vain. As far as Tess was concerned, "I'd love to get it on with you but I'm not looking for anything more" pretty much erased all possibility of even friendship, let alone love.

When that word surfaced in her internal narrative, Tess thought for a moment that she might be in real danger of throwing up. Love. Is that what she'd wanted? What she'd expected? After knowing Remy for only a handful of days, she wanted Remy to *love* her?

She tried to stop before she beat herself up too much. Of course she wanted love. It's what she'd always wanted, for as long as she could remember. She wanted a perfect, romantic love, one where a beautiful woman would sweep her off her feet and treat her like someone who was worth wooing.

Remy had said she was sexy. Tess was pretty sure nobody had ever called her that before—except her friends when they were trying to cheer her up, but that didn't count. And nobody had ever made her *feel* sexy before she met Remy. But feeling sexy, feeling desirable...was that enough? She knew that if she ended up having a fling with Remy, she'd feel sexier than she'd ever imagined she could.

But would it be worth the blow her heart would take?

They spoke only as much as they needed to on the drive back through the mountain pass. Tess felt so uncomfortable this close to Remy now—as if Remy could read her mind and tell how much she'd wanted a serious relationship. Remy's confession (and it probably didn't deserve so biased a word) had driven home Tess's desire for just that. And if Remy guessed, which Tess was certain she did, it was probably a huge turn-off.

Tess cursed the long, monotonous ATV ride, where the rumble of the engine created the perfect white noise for her train of thought to spiral. The snow was melting in the sunlight and the ground was getting wet and muddy again. *Yet another thoroughly unpleasant trip on this stupid mountain*, Tess thought morosely.

When they motored up the hill and the Rising Star lodge came into view, Tess was even gladder to see it than she had been after their disastrous hike up on the first day. At the sound of their engine, the door opened and Marti dashed out, still in the process of pulling on her coat. Remy killed the ignition and put the ATV into park.

"You're okay!" Marti shouted, throwing her arms around Tess, who had swiftly dismounted as soon as they stopped. Tess hugged her back, feeling the tiniest bit better.

"We brought gas!" she said. "Did the power

come back on?"

"No," Marti answered forlornly. She let go of Tess and went to give Remy a hug as well. "But the road down is clear and we sent word with the plow guys that we're still out up here. So at least we know that the power company knows and will be working on it." She tried to take the container of gasoline off the back of the four-wheeler but Remy gently pushed her aside with a smile and a shake of her head.

"I can get this just fine," she said, anticipating Marti's objection. "Besides, you had to stay here and deal with the Tsarina while we were gone." Marti let her pick up the container and she and Tess followed Remy into the lodge.

"What happened?" Marti asked. "We thought you'd be back yesterday..." Her eyes got round when she saw the bandage on Remy's forehead. "Did you get hurt?"

"Nah, just a scratch," Remy responded, searching the lobby with her eyes for Glen. She didn't look at Marti.

"It just took us longer to get there than we thought, because of the wind and stuff," Tess answered vaguely. "And the Sweet Spring Resort had no power either. Nobody was there. It was going to be dark before we could get back, though, so we found a way inside and slept there."

Marti's mouth hung open. "There was nobody *there?* Oh, my gosh! Are you starving? Have you had anything to eat? How'd you get the gas?"

Tess smiled, patting Marti on the arm. "We found some food, don't worry. I'm just looking forward to a good shower. And we siphoned the gas out of a lawnmower," she added somewhat proudly.

"Marti, where's Glen?" Remy asked, turning back toward them. Her words were curt, and Marti frowned, glancing between her and Tess.

"Um... I think he's dealing with a little bit of flooding in the basement," she said, and Remy groaned.

"Jesus, when do things go *right* around here?"

Just then, Tess heard the familiar tapping of heels on the lobby's flagstones and Melissa appeared from the door behind the desk. Tess's hackles rose at the same time as she shrank back in defensive mode. Marti winced and Remy looked like she had already used up her last grain of patience.

"Oh, you're back, I see!" Melissa planted herself in front of Remy, folding her arms. Cold, imperious anger was on her face. "I've already missed my meeting, thanks to you, so I didn't bother to get a ride down the mountain with those...plow men." She grimaced distastefully. "I hope you got what you went for." Remy responded with a flat, silent look and held up the gasoline container. "Good." Then she fixed her eyes on Tess. "I trust you enjoyed your little sleepover."

Tess was expecting ire, especially since she'd found out from Remy how jealous and possessive Melissa could be. It was pretty obvious that Remy and Tess had gotten kind of cozy over the last few days. But when Melissa only narrowed her eyes, sweeping her gaze contemplatively over Tess's figure, Tess wasn't sure how to react.

"Sure, if you call sleeping in my clothes— again—and scrounging for food in a deserted resort 'fun,'" Tess replied. Melissa raised her eyebrows at that, turning to Remy.

"Deserted?"

"They were gone," Remy told her shortly.

"Probably heard about the storm and cleared out before it hit. Now, if you don't mind, I'm going to go get the generator running so your guests can have a little comfort."

Melissa's face stiffened and Tess could almost feel the animosity firing between them like lightning. Then Remy turned on her heel and stalked off toward the basement stairwell to find Glen.

Melissa shot one more unreadable look at Tess and then wordlessly left her and Marti standing together. Marti lifted her eyebrows at Tess; she could sense that something was amiss.

Tess merely shook her head. "I don't know what's going on, Marti," she said wearily. "I'm going to my room to take a shower."

Inside her room, Tess dropped her backpack by the door and resisted the urge to fall into bed. What was the use of having such a wonderful, soft bed if she'd only gotten to sleep in it once out of the three nights she'd been supposed to use it so far? But her clothes were dirty and she was sweaty and mud-spattered again, and she struggled out of her jacket, shirt, and pants and threw them into the growing pile of sweaty, mud-spattered clothing by the bathroom door. She hadn't even had time to send out any laundry.

Standing in her underwear on the cold tile, Tess stared bleakly into the dark shower. Of course; the generator hadn't started up yet, and that meant the water heaters would take a while to get the tanks up to temperature. She dragged her fluffy hotel robe off the peg behind the door and sat in one of the room's numerous easy chairs, pretending to read a book while she really just looped the last day's moments with Remy over and over in her mind. The lights clicked on a few minutes after she sat down, and she gave the water heaters a half-hour more for good measure.

Finally standing in the shower, as the hot water cascaded over her and she tried to untangle her hair with her fingers, Tess kept seeing Remy's face moments after their kiss. She couldn't figure out exactly what all of the emotions she saw there meant, but they combined into one clear message: Remy thought she'd made a mistake. Tess had felt so, so happy in Remy's arms, like she belonged there. But Remy obviously didn't think so—unless it was just for a night or two.

When Tess trudged, dripping, out of the bathroom, she slipped on a big t-shirt with a Super Mario mushroom on the front and wrapped her hair up in a towel. She'd just stay in her room tonight. Maybe things would look less bleak in the morning.

Tess lay back on the bed, her bare legs dangling over the rounded edge, and stared at the ceiling. It was, naturally, a very classy ceiling with flowery plaster molding around the central overhead light. Her body was exhausted but her mind raced a mile a minute, getting nowhere, like a gerbil in a wheel.

When the knock sounded at her door, Tess jolted up into a sitting position, her heart hammering. Remy? Maybe she'd come to talk, to hash out what both of them wanted out of the thing that was growing between them?

Tess was at the door before she realized that all she was wearing was the t-shirt and no pants, even though the shirt was long enough to hang below her bottom. She thought about dashing back and grabbing some yoga pants, but then she decided to check through the peephole before she wasted the energy.

Emily's freckled, anxious face peered back at

her from outside her door.

Sighing heavily, Tess pulled the door open, and before she could even say "Hi," Emily had leapt on her with a hug and was dragging her back inside the room by her arm.

"Christ on a cracker, Tess! Where were you? I heard you just got back a little while ago! We didn't think you'd be gone overnight!"

"I didn't think I'd be gone overnight either," Tess replied ruefully. "But...lots of crap happened."

Emily peered at her worriedly. "Like what? Are you okay?"

"Yeah," Tess said, waving her hand. She knew she was being needlessly dramatic. "Just tired. Nobody was there at the Sweet Spring Resort so we had to break in and stay the night."

"*Break in?*" This time, the concern on Emily's face was replaced with a shocked smile. "That's awesome! Tell me all about it!" She bounced onto the bed, kicking off her flats, and patted the space beside her. Tess couldn't help but smile. She sat down next to her friend.

"It was less awesome than it sounds, believe me," Tess told her. She explained their trip through the woods and then threw caution to the wind and described their makeshift dinner and what Remy had told her about her past with Melissa.

"Wow," Emily said when Tess paused, drawing the word out. "That's kind of sordid."

Tess grimaced. "I haven't gotten to the best part. And by 'best' I mean 'worst.'" She twisted her hands in her lap and told Emily about waking up cuddled next to Remy, then about finding the gasoline and the kiss. She couldn't bring herself to describe much about Remy's expression, but the difficulty she had in relaying Remy's words told Emily everything she needed to know.

"Aww, honey..." She put her arm around Tess's shoulders and Tess leaned into her, grateful for the contact. None of their group of friends went more than a week without seeing at least a couple of the others, and Tess realized how much she needed someone to talk to during this whole crazy trip. Especially since talking to Remy was such a minefield of confusion.

"I know, I know," Tess moaned. "My standards are too high. I expected too much of her."

"I wasn't going to say *exactly* that," Emily told her with a smile, giving Tess a little teasing shake. "I totally understand that you want something long-term. I get that. I want that with Stefan too. But you've got to be a little less rigid if you're ever going to have a chance at any sort of romance at all. So what's wrong with a fling if Remy's up for it? She's *super* hot, Tess. And sex is therapeutic," Emily added in her best this-is-my-professional-advice voice.

Tess sat back up, regarding Emily with her mouth pulled to one side. She couldn't deny that Emily had a point. Rationally, Tess knew that people had entirely satisfying flings all the time. And she wasn't *positive* that Remy would be opposed to a "friends with benefits" arrangement. But when she imagined herself and Remy grabbing a cup of coffee together once in a while and also occasionally jumping into the sack with each other, her heart ached with longing.

She could just see herself now. The two of them would be sitting together in a café, chatting and sipping lattes. Remy would be telling her a story about another dumb hiker who needed rescuing because they went hiking in high heels or something. And Remy would laugh her low, velvety laugh that made every inch of Tess's body come alive, and Remy's eyes would darken and flash, and Tess would know they'd have mind-blowing sex in an hour or two...but all she'd be able to think about would be how much she wanted to be by Remy's side, running mundane errands and cooking dinner and waking up next to each other. All she'd be able to think about would be romantic dates to the lakes and adopting a dog together and maybe, maybe one day...running around a grassy yard with a couple of kids.

Tess's heart turned a somersault in her chest. Is that what she wanted? It surprised her, felt like it came out of nowhere, but in reality she knew that dream hadn't spontaneously appeared. She'd always had it, but it wasn't until now that it felt possible enough to come to the surface.

Emily bit her lip when she saw the tears form in Tess's eyes. Tess shook her head.

"Maybe I could do that," Tess said waveringly. "Maybe I'd be okay with a fling. But I just don't know if I can disengage my heart the way I'd need to. I *wish* I could. But I don't know." She took a deep breath, rubbing at her eyes with one hand. "I've been so certain, my entire life, that what I'm looking for is a deep, passionate love that will withstand the test of time. I recognize that I might need to modify that," she added with a tired, humorless chuckle, "but the way I feel about Remy..."

Tess paused, her heartbeat quickening. Could she say it? Would that mean there was no turning back? But she had to. The words, hidden even from her for all this time, demanded to be said. "I think I'm falling in love with her."

Emily's eyes shone with sympathy and she took Tess's hand and squeezed it. "I think you should talk to her about this," she urged. "You guys always tell me that lesbians are the best communicators when it comes to romance, right? Keeping this to yourself will only make it hurt more. At least if she knows and—for some *stupid* reason—" Emily smiled, leaning close, and looked into Tess's eyes sincerely. "—she still doesn't want to date you, you both can move on."

Again, what Emily said made perfect sense. But waves of fear radiated through Tess's middle when she thought about revealing the depth of her feelings to Remy.

"She's been so badly hurt, though. I'm worried she isn't ready to trust anyone, and I just don't want to drive her away." Tess's brows furrowed. "What if I decide that I really *am* okay with a fling, that that's what I want, but she's too freaked out by the fact that I'm in love with her and she changes her mind?"

"The only way you'll know is if you talk to her," Emily said. "If she makes that decision, it's her loss, but you've got to be up front with her. You won't do either of you any favors by keeping how you feel a secret."

Tess put her head in her hands. "That feels impossible right now."

"Well, I didn't mean you have to do it right now, silly." Emily rubbed Tess's back for a moment and then sat back on her hands on the bed. "You've had a crazy couple of days. You need some rest, for God's sake. Just kick back. I hate to break it to you, though, but the TV isn't working. Except for the resort's own boring channel." Emily made a face. "The cable's still out. But Stefan and I checked out the pool last night and it's a really nice one. I bet they'll get the hot tub working again soon. And I know how much you love swimming."

After she quit roller derby when she graduated from college, the only sport Tess really enjoyed was swimming. Emily was a diehard athlete and always wanted to get her friends into whatever sport she was currently excited about. Swimming was her big victory with Tess.

"That sounds nice," Tess said, and she really meant it. Like yoga, swimming gave her just enough to do with her body while giving her mind the quiet and clarity it needed to think.

"Well, I'll let you go to it," Emily said, getting up. "You want to join me and Stefan for dinner later?"

Tess gave her a half-smile. "Nah, thanks anyway. I think I'll just order room service and stay in. I'm not really feeling very social."

"Okie doke," Emily replied with understanding. Tess stood up too and Emily wrapped her in another hug. "Come to my room if you need me okay? Any time."

Tess nodded. "Thanks, Em. I don't know what I would've done if I was here all by myself."

"Moped a lot, probably," Emily replied with a grin. "Now go get your bathing suit on. Maybe you'll meet Remy in the hallway and she'll see how cute you are and reconsider the 'I don't want anything more' thing."

Tess waved her out the door with a halfhearted laugh. Honestly, she didn't know what she'd do if she saw Remy right now. She needed to get her thoughts in order first.

She came to this resort to feel refreshed, right?

Swimming was refreshing. Tess dug through her suitcase and pulled out her bathing suit, a teal and white bikini that she'd bought just this summer to cheer herself up. As she put it on and checked her reflection in the mirror, Tess ran her eyes over her form: she was shorter than average, her hips were wide, and her breasts were smaller than she liked, but the curve of her belly was not unattractive in this suit.

Tess lifted her arms, gathered her hair into a ponytail, and turned in front of the mirror. In fact, she *did* look pretty damn cute in this bikini, just like Emily said. Wearing something like this was an infrequent treat for her, but today the confidence it inspired helped her feel just a little bit better. Maybe she didn't need Remy looking at her with those lustful eyes in order to feel sexy.

But Remy was more than a pair of eyes, and she made Tess feel more than just sexy. They'd felt *right* together. Until it went all wrong.

You'll figure this out, she told her reflection defiantly. *Remy's too important to let go just because you're scared.*

Tess grabbed her towel and hoped that water would provide the space and relaxation she needed to plan her next move.

ॐ

When Tess opened the door to the pool, she was met by a rush of warm, wet air and the scent of chlorine. *Great,* Tess thought cynically. *I'll need yet another shower after this. This resort has hundreds of things to do and services to take advantage of and I've been spending practically every minute here in the shower.*

But the moment her toe entered the perfectly temperate water—just warm enough so she wasn't cold and cool enough so she felt refreshed—Tess was glad she'd come. She lowered herself into the water and moved to an empty swim lane, then pushed herself off the wall and began to swim laps.

She went slowly, letting herself be propelled by a breast stroke and a few leisurely kicks. It was delicious to feel weightless after spending two days in several layers of clothes. Unsurprisingly, her mind turned back to Remy. No matter what she tried to think about, it was as if her thoughts were a compass needle and Remy was north.

That image she'd had before of herself and Remy in a "friends with benefits" relationship... She'd felt so miserable at the thought. But if it were that or nothing, would she rather they spend time together on Remy's own terms than never see her again?

Tess stopped at the other end of the pool, treading water. There were only a few other people here, and there were still open lanes in case anyone else came in. She turned over on her back and let herself drift, kicking every so often so that she meandered slowly toward the shallow end again.

Things would be different if she'd approached Remy as a potential fling candidate to begin with. But they'd been tossed together into this bizarre situation, and Remy drove Tess *crazy* at first. The way they'd grown close, the way Tess slowly realized that her attraction to Remy was emotional as well as physical, meant that Tess now felt too attached to her for that. In order to be okay with a fling, Tess would need to rearrange how she viewed Remy in her heart. And that wasn't something she could do.

Tess let her eyes lose focus as she drifted beneath the wooden rafters of the pool room's ceiling. All day yesterday she'd urged herself not to try to read Remy's mind. She couldn't just assume she knew what Remy had meant by "I'm not looking for anything more." But that's exactly what Tess had been doing—she'd assumed that all hope for a serious relationship was lost. In her upset over Remy's reaction to their kiss, Tess had ignored the fact that Remy was a real person with feelings and motivations that were likely as complicated as Tess's own.

Emily was right. The only way to know what Remy really meant, what she really wanted, was to talk to her. Then maybe Tess would understand what "anything more" meant and whether she could fit that into her own hopes for the future...for the romance of her dreams.

The cool swishing of the water around her body really had refreshed her. A few laps later, Tess swam back to the shallow end and pulled herself up the ladder out of the pool. Her exhaustion had shifted to sleepiness and she felt a little bit of peace. Tomorrow, she could find Remy and ask to talk. As for tonight, maybe she really would be able to sleep soundly. She wrapped her towel around her waist and padded barefoot back in the direction of her room.

Tess was lost in thought when she looked up to the sound of clicking heels and saw Melissa come around the corner ahead of her. She was wearing a similar yoga outfit to the one she'd worn for their first class—skin-tight leggings and a strappy, bright magenta sports bra top—and her incongruous white pumps somehow worked perfectly with the ensemble. When her eyes landed on Tess, there was brief surprise there, and then something else, something surer—like she'd made a pleasant decision.

"Tess!" Melissa said, quickening her pace as she came closer. "I haven't gotten a chance to thank you!"

Tess blinked, instinctively backing up a step. *Okay, breathe. From what Remy said, she's got a couple of screws loose, but you've just got to act polite. She's got no beef with you. ...Hopefully.*

"Uh, hi, Melissa," Tess offered. Melissa stopped a few feet in front of her with a bright smile.

"You know, you really saved us, bringing back that gasoline. As the owner of this resort, all of the people here are my responsibility, and I can't tell you how grateful I am." Her blue-gray eyes crinkled with happy sincerity. "We'd be up the creek without a paddle if you hadn't gone all that way for us."

"Oh... Uh, it's no biggie," Tess replied, smiling awkwardly. It hadn't been just her on her own, after all, but Melissa seemed to be purposefully leaving Remy's name out.

"Don't be silly!" Melissa widened her eyes, leaning forward with a serious air. "I don't know how to thank you, but I'll think of something before the week's over, I promise. A free spa day next season, or an upgrade, or something like that." Her smile was warm. "I pride myself on providing the very best experience for my guests, and I dropped the ball by not ensuring that we had extra gasoline. I guess I'd better start learning how to control the weather!" Melissa laughed as if she'd made a hilariously funny joke. Tess tried to join in but she was too weirded out to be at all convincing.

"It looks like you just got back from enjoying our pool," Melissa commented then, her eyes raking down Tess's body. They paused very conspicuously on Tess's breasts, and Tess felt herself go lobster-red all over. "I hope you liked it. We just had it put in last year—top of the line, very expensive." Melissa's eyes finally moved back up to Tess's face. "Oh, you've just got this...little tangle..." Before Tess knew it, Melissa had reached up with her manicured fingertips and was unhooking a curl of hair from behind Tess's ear. She gently unsnarled the strands and as she lowered her hand, the backs of her knuckles passed over Tess's cheek.

Tess was speechless, her breath hitching in her lungs with disbelief. She was so taken aback that she could do nothing but press against the wall when Melissa stepped forward, swinging one hip and then the other as she brought herself within inches of Tess.

"I can see why Remy finds you so attractive," Melissa breathed, her intense gaze cutting Tess clear to her bones. This woman had something about her— almost an aura—that made it incredibly difficult to talk back to her at all, let alone contradict her. She exuded power and control and confidence, and Tess felt like a mouse cowering in front of a cat.

Melissa reached up again to toy with Tess's ponytail. With hooded eyes, she smiled a gentle, sad smile. "Too bad you're not good enough for her."

Then her hand slid to the back of Tess's neck and tightened there, and the blast of adrenaline that shot through Tess's veins shattered into bewilderment as Melissa swooped down and locked her lips onto Tess's mouth.

The next few seconds felt like years to Tess. She was too shocked to move, paralyzed by Melissa's completely unexpected kiss. Melissa's mouth on hers was burning hot, and in this as in all other things Tess had seen from her, Melissa gave the impression of being a consummate expert. The kiss was so deep and sultry that Tess's knees buckled and she had to hold onto the wall behind her to keep from sliding down it. Her towel came untucked and pooled at her feet. That movement brought her back to herself and she planted her hands on Melissa's shoulders and pushed her away.

"Wh—?!" Tess's words were cut off by movement out of the corner of her eye, and her stomach clenched. God, had someone seen them?

She peered past Melissa's shoulder and the blood in her veins turned to gravel.

Remy stood in the middle of the hallway, her mouth slightly open, a coiled extension cord dangling from her limp fingers. The shock, the pain and betrayal were etched on her face as clearly as if she had shouted at them.

Tess's hands hung on Melissa's shoulders as the three of them stood in that frozen moment, but the only thing Tess saw was Remy's eyes. They were wide with disbelief, shifting between Tess and Melissa, hurt and disgust warring for precedence. Then she swung around and disappeared around the corner.

Tess felt like the floor was cracking under her feet. She was almost blind to Melissa's presence now, but as she pushed past, she caught a glimpse of Melissa's face—smug, satisfied, and dismissive. Tess left her towel lying on the floor and ran after Remy.

Tess called her name once, but Remy didn't turn around. Her long-legged pace was swift and she already had a key card out and in her hand. As Tess rounded a corner, Remy halted at a door, swiped her card, and slipped through it. The lock clicked shut just as Tess reached it.

"Remy!" Tess said, her heart resounding in her ears and her lungs constricted. She could hear her through the door, right? "Remy, I don't know what just happened! Melissa came up to me and kissed me! I didn't want her to!" She listened, gulping down air, desperate to hear an answer. None came.

She couldn't believe this had happened. Had Melissa known that Remy was coming down the hall? Or had she kissed Tess out of some perverse desire to mess with her head? Nothing made any sense.

Tess wanted to rattle the doorknob, to knock and pound and yell for Remy to open the door. "Remy!" Tess cried again. Then she heard a clink and the sound of metal scraping on metal.

Remy had slid the chain lock in place.

All of the blood drained from Tess's face. She rocked back, dizzy, and then took a few faltering steps away from the door, still staring at it. How could Remy think...?

Her breath shuddering, Tess turned away and went like a sleepwalker to her own room.

A few times in Tess's life when she'd been seriously, traumatically shocked, she felt like her mind was entirely disengaged from her body. At those times, it was like her consciousness shrunk to a tiny point behind her eyes and she had no awareness of her arms, legs, or anything else. When Tess's knees knocked into the edge of her bed and she stumbled and fell onto the mattress, she realized that this was one of those times.

As the numbness started to disperse into tingling horror, Tess curled on her side, her knees pulled to her chest. She dragged one of the bed's soft, fluffy pillows toward her and buried her face in it.

How could Remy think she would *want* to kiss Melissa? After everything Remy had told her? After all that Melissa had done to Remy? Remy had to know how much Tess liked her, how much Remy's feelings mattered to her. After Remy's reaction to their kiss, Tess had been afraid she'd come on too strong, and now she wondered, dazed with confusion, if she'd somehow given Remy the impression that she was fickle. How had this happened?

She shuddered as she thought about Melissa touching her, Melissa's hand grasping the back of her neck, Melissa's lips on hers. She shouldn't have let Melissa get that close, but it had happened so suddenly. And then, Remy...

The image Tess had been fighting against shattered her willpower and flooded her mind: Remy's face, so appalled and tortured. Tess had only seen her for a split second before she turned, but that split second would be seared on her memory forever. Pain crushed Tess's heart and a sob choked her throat. This misery was even worse than she'd feared. In the end, it had been pointless to try to protect her heart.

She held the pillow tight against her face as she cried into it.

Chapter Eleven

Tess's face in the mirror the next morning was puffy and red. She wrung a washcloth under cold water and pressed it onto her skin, and although it didn't do a lot for the way she looked, it made her feel a little bit better.

During the night, she'd come to a decision. She wasn't going to let Remy slip through her fingers because of something so stupid as Melissa's meddling. She would get dressed, go out into the lobby, and wait for Remy to appear. She'd wait all day if she had to. And then when Remy came out, she'd make Remy listen to her. She'd tell Remy that Melissa kissed her without her consent, and Remy could do with that information whatever she liked. And if Remy still didn't want anything to do with her, then...

Then Tess would go home. She'd had enough of everything that had gone on at this place. She hadn't wanted to admit it, because this was supposed to be her week of rejuvenation, her fresh start, but the only thing she'd gotten out of this vacation was the time she'd spent with Remy. And if there was no chance of that now, she didn't want to stay.

Tess pulled on a pair of jeans and a turquoise zip-up sweater over her favorite t-shirt (the one with a Walt Whitman quote on it). If it turned out that she was going home today, she wanted to have the comfiest clothing for the taxi ride down the mountain. She didn't feel very hungry, but she grabbed a granola bar from her backpack and took it with her anyway.

It was still early, but there were a few people in the lobby hoping to check out now that the road down was plowed. Marti was behind the desk, diligently answering their questions, and when she saw Tess, she shot her a concerned look. Tess tried to smile at her to show that despite her ragged appearance, she was okay.

There were a few cushiony chairs that faced the wing of the resort where all the guestrooms were, and Tess settled down in one of them to wait. There was no way Remy could come out of her room and into the lobby without Tess seeing her.

The butterflies in Tess's stomach kicked up a storm, and she tried to breathe slowly to overcome them. Sometime later, when all of the guests who'd been in line were gone, Marti disappeared through the door behind the desk and came out a few moments later with a muffin on a small plate. She brought it over to Tess.

Today, Marti's silky mouse-brown hair was fixed up in a banana clip at the back of her head. She had a maroon cardigan on over her usual pressed white dress shirt and black skirt. When she handed the muffin to Tess, she smiled anxiously.

"Are you okay? I thought you might be hungry."

Tess accepted the plate with a grateful nod. "I'm okay." Marti was so sweet, but Tess didn't want to confide in her—or in anyone—until she'd resolved the situation with Remy by herself. She looked down at the blueberry muffin with a wan smile. "Thanks, this looks great."

"Is there anything else I can get you?" Marti fretted. Tess shook her head. She glanced over at the hallway to the guestrooms.

"Remy didn't check out early, did she?"

Marti's frown deepened but she shook her head. "No, that that I know of." She looked like she wanted to ask more, but she didn't. Tess tried to smile at her again.

"Okay. Thanks, Marti."

Marti nodded, still looking worried, and went back to the desk. Tess tried not to watch time go by on the wall clock; she shifted in her chair so she couldn't see it and started to pick apart the muffin.

She'd eaten about half of it (very slowly) while she watched various people come and go, when the phone rang at the front desk. It had done so a few times already, but what caught Tess's attention this time was Marti's tone after she answered.

"Oh, my gosh, really?" Marti sounded alarmed, but she immediately lowered her voice when some of the other guests looked over. "Does Glen know? Oh, no, he is?" She listened for a few moments, chewing her lip and glancing around the room. "Which door was it? I can't—I have to stay at the desk," she said, her pitch rising with dismay. "But...there's got to be someone... Okay, I'll find somebody, ma'am. Thanks." She hung up the phone and came around the desk to where Tess was sitting.

"Is everything all right?" Tess asked, straightening. Marti shook her head, wringing her hands together.

"Glen's dog accidentally got out one of the back doors. But Glen's not here; one of the plow guys took him down the mountain to an urgent care center to get his ankle looked at. Cedar ran off and is nowhere in sight, and I can't leave to go look for him because I have to cover the desk." She bit her lips, turning her eyes to Tess's.

Tess opened her mouth. She had to wait here for Remy. She desperately needed to set things straight with her.

But then she remembered what Remy had said the night they had dinner together. Cedar had been rescued from an abusive situation and wasn't trained to come when called yet. Somebody *had* to go look for him or else he might not find his way back. And if he was lost, he was probably confused and scared...

Tess pushed herself out of her chair, handing the plate and the neglected half of her muffin to Marti. "I'll go."

"Are you sure?" Marti's eyebrows pinched together with concern.

"Yeah," Tess said. "I'm sure. Which door did he get out?"

"The one in the back by the pool," Marti said, following her for a few steps as she walked toward the hallway. Then Tess paused.

"If you see Remy, could you ask her to please, *please* wait for me here?"

Marti blinked, and then her expression turned sympathetic. "Absolutely. Be careful, Tess."

"I will," Tess called over her shoulder as she picked up her pace, jogging back toward her room. Once there, she grabbed her coat and hat and quickly laced on her hiking boots. It would just be a few minutes, and then she'd come back and find Remy.

Tess headed toward the pool, glancing down side corridors as she went to make sure she didn't miss any doors out. She entered the little vestibule between a main hallway and the pool, and inside, there was a door to the back parking lot. Tess pushed through it and drew her hat down over her ears.

It was sunny and in spite of the chilling wind, the snow had nearly melted completely away. This had resulted in a parking lot choppy with slush and mud and rutted with tire tracks. Tess searched the ground for signs of paw prints, but it only took her a few moments to see that finding any would be difficult.

Sloshing across the lot, Tess made a circuit of the building, calling for the dog and scanning all of the open spaces. She stopped occasionally to peer beneath a parked car or truck, but she didn't see so much as a squirrel. When she got back to the door where she first came out, she put her hands on her hips, thinking hard.

Opposite her, there was a wide trail leading into the forest. Tess glanced around to get her bearings. The trail they'd come up on the first day (well, technically the second day) was off to the right a bit; the service road was on the opposite side of the resort; and the one she and Remy had taken to the other resort was hidden around the corner to her left.

"Cedar!" Tess called again. Her voice rang in the quiet morning. There was no movement anywhere, but it was harder to see into the woods now because the snow no longer provided a white background against which something like a dog would show up sharply.

She frowned at the trail right across from the door. *If I were a dog and I just wanted to run outside and play, where would I go?* It seemed logical to her that since Cedar wasn't anywhere around the building, he would head for the first open place in the trees he saw. Tess sighed out. She had hoped she wouldn't need to delve into the forest again...but she was going to do everything she could to find Cedar, no matter what.

The mouth of the trail was less broken up than the parking lot, but it was still covered in slush and open patches of mud. Tess bent down and searched the ground. Could those little round depressions over there be paw prints?

She wasn't sure, but it was the best she had to go on, so Tess started down the trail, curling her fists with determination. If she'd lost her chance with Remy, then this whole trip would be a waste...but now, maybe she'd be able to salvage it by doing *something* worth doing. Saving Cedar would make everything she'd been through in the past few days worth it.

The wind wasn't too cutting once she got amongst the trees, and the sunlight made it cheerier than the last several times she'd been out here. The trail, as well, wasn't nearly as steep or as covered in fallen branches and trees as the one they'd come up originally. She'd find Cedar and be back to the lodge like a hero in no time.

Tess kept her eyes on the ground in front of her as she went. In the mud and the few drifts of melting snow, it wasn't easy to discern prints of any kind, let alone the prints of a smallish dog like Cedar. But every so often, she would see something she thought *could* be a print, and she knew she couldn't let herself turn around. She raised her voice, calling the dog's name over and over.

She didn't know how much time had passed before she started to wonder if this hadn't been such a good idea after all. But this trail wasn't nearly as hard to hike as the other one had been, so if she had to turn around without finding Cedar and go back, it wouldn't be to terrible, right?

Tess gritted her teeth. She didn't want to return without Cedar. She *couldn't*. Not only did she think about how scared he must be, alone in the woods, but it helped to imagine how irritated Melissa would be when Tess brought him back. There would be a lot of satisfaction in parading right into the lobby without wiping Cedar's feet and letting him get mud everywhere.

And maybe Remy would see this and would know that not only was Tess brave and capable and kind, but she also had nothing but contempt for Melissa. And then maybe Remy would be willing to talk to her, to straighten out this whole complicated mess.

The more she walked, though, the less hope she had. Maybe Cedar hadn't even gone down this trail? She hadn't seen anything resembling a footprint in a while. The colorful leaves she'd so enjoyed a few days ago had mostly all been torn off the trees by yesterday's winds. They lay scattered on the ground like a patchwork quilt, their colors deadened beneath melting snow and decomposing leaves from last year.

Finally, Tess slowed to a halt. Should she go back? Was this the point where she gave up? One last time, she shouted "Cedar!" into the trees.

And movement downhill caught her eye.

It was something brown, something that darted away so fast that she only caught the barest flash. But it was enough. Tess started forward and jogged down the hill in the direction of the movement. When she got close to the spot where she'd seen it, she stopped to listen, and she could hear a faint rustling far away that sounded like an animal moving rather than like the wind. Tess went on, pulling in breaths of cold air.

Another glimpse, and a flash of white in the brown. Cedar had white fur on his chest, right? She couldn't remember exactly, but she thought so. She picked up her pace. "Cedar!"

A crashing sound behind her made Tess jump, and she whirled around, looking up the slope to see what had made the noise. She heard the snapping of branches and crunching of brush as if something were barreling toward her. *Oh, God, it's a bear. I'm going to be eaten by a bear.*

Tess looked around wildly for a tree she could climb, but before she could move, she saw a blur of color—dark purple-red and faded blue, tumbling down the hillside through the trees.

Her heart rocketed nearly out of her chest when she realized that it was a person rolling toward her, their arms tucked in and their feet attempting to break their fall but failing to gain any purchase on the roots or rocks.

Tess shot forward. The person was close enough for her to catch if she moved quickly enough...

She stumbled to a halt just below where the figure was skidding down and she planted her feet on the ground, lowering her center of gravity so she'd be in a better position to stop them. Then she caught a glimpse of the face and all thoughts of balance left her mind.

It was Remy.

Remy crashed into her with the combined force of gravity and momentum, and Tess was so astonished that she forgot to brace herself. She toppled over Remy and then both of them were falling down the hill together.

The only thing that guided Tess then was instinct. The moment she felt Remy bump against her in their fall, she snaked her arm around Remy's middle and clamped onto her jacket with a death grip. Then Tess tried to make enough sense of the dizzying, circling blur of the world around them to grab onto something. Her arm whacked into a young tree and she hooked her elbow around it. With a scraping jerk that caused her shoulder to scream in pain, they shuddered to a halt, the soles of Tess's hiking boots bouncing over the rocks beneath them.

They'd come to rest with Remy's feet dangling over the edge of a sharp drop in the landscape.

For several seconds, neither of them moved. Tess's heart was beating so hard that her vision vibrated in time with the thumps. She lay gasping, afraid to move a muscle lest they fall any farther. Then Remy stirred, struggling to get her hands underneath her.

"Choking me," she mumbled with urgency, and Tess swiftly released her hold on Remy's jacket, which had twisted around in their descent and was all awry. Remy slowly, cautiously sat up, her arms and legs shaking.

Tess looked up at her, eyes wide, and Remy stared back speechlessly.

"Are you okay?" Tess breathed, still holding tight to the tree with one arm. All of her insides felt like jelly, quivering and threatening to come apart.

It seemed for a moment that Remy couldn't get any words out. Then she said haltingly, "I am now." She still stared at Tess, her twilight blue eyes round and astonished. "You saved me."

Tess took measured breaths in an effort to calm her hammering heart. She gingerly let go of the tree and sat up. "I guess I did," she replied finally. She ran her eyes over Remy, noting that she was dirt-covered and disheveled but free of blood or obviously broken limbs. "What are you doing here?" Tess asked.

Remy swallowed and dropped her eyes. Her face darkened with restrained anger.

"Marti told me you went out looking for Cedar. But Cedar didn't escape; he's safe and sound back at the resort."

Now it was Tess's turn to stare. "What?" That made no sense. She knew what Marti had told her.

Remy worked her jaw. "I came into the lobby after I got up and Marti told me what happened and said you'd asked me to wait for you to come back. I was going to go out and help look for him, but I ran up to Glen's office to grab Cedar's leash and his favorite treats to lure him back, and there he was, curled up in his doggy bed." Finally meeting Tess's eyes, Remy set her mouth in a firm line. "It was Melissa who called Marti to say he'd escaped in the first place."

Tess's mouth dropped open. "She... Wha...?" Remy silently continued to give her that significant look, and a distressed disbelief made Tess's stomach feel heavier than a boulder. "Melissa *tricked* me into coming out here? Why would she do that?"

"My guess is that she wanted to get rid of you," Remy said, and Tess paled. Remy rolled her eyes. "No, no, not like that. She's a bitch but she's not homicidal. I mean that she wanted to get you out of the way for a little while, and she probably figured that when you came back wet and tired and defeated, you'd just leave."

If Tess hadn't had the chance to talk to Remy when she got back—and who knew what damage Melissa was planning to inflict on their relationship in the meantime—she probably *would* have left. But that wasn't going to happen now, because Remy was here, with her. Tess felt like her heart was unfolding, a flower that blossomed with trembling petals.

"You came to find me?" Tess asked in a small voice. Remy shrugged one shoulder, looking away with reddening cheeks. Tess found this so charming she almost couldn't hold herself up.

"What Melissa did is reprehensible. I saw where your footprints led, so I took the ATV and drove down. A little way uphill from here, I couldn't get down the path on the ATV so I got off and started down on foot." She shot a chagrinned look at Tess. "When you yelled Cedar's name, it startled me and I...slipped."

Neither of them said anything for a moment, then Tess couldn't help it—she started to giggle, and then to laugh. Soon she was lying on her back again, holding her stomach and gasping for breath through her mirth.

Remy glared at her, getting even redder. "It's not—" She bit back her words, growling, and then her mouth started to quirk. Soon she was laughing too.

Their laughter rang through the woods, and down below them at the bottom of the drop, Tess saw a deer go leaping through the brush.

"Well, that explains what I was following," she said dryly. They both got quieter, and Tess looked over at Remy. The other woman was now watching her with a mixture of solemnity and wariness. Tess straightened her back and lifted her chin, meeting Remy's eyes. "Melissa kissed me without my consent last night."

The guarded expression in Remy's eyes took over everything else that had been there. She was silent for a moment, and then she said, "I figured that must've been what happened." Her voice was rough and barely audible. "I was just...shocked, and I reacted without thinking. I get all stupid when Melissa is around." Remy looked away and sighed before glancing at Tess again. "I thought Melissa was trying to mess with me. I was selfish; I just hid instead of coming to your rescue. I'm sorry."

Tess smiled, and the knot in her chest that had made it so hard to breathe since last night loosened. "I rescued myself just fine." She pulled her knees up and rested her elbows on them, not caring in the slightest that the seat of her jeans was getting soaked from the mud and wet leaves. "I think Melissa probably *was* trying to mess with you. I don't know why she would've suddenly come on to me otherwise, since I've been pretty much beneath her notice before."

Remy ran her hands back through her short hair, leaving her forehead resting in them for a moment before raising her eyes again. She gazed out into the forest, unseeing. "I guess I was kind of..." She shook her head. "This is so stupid, but I was kind of afraid that Melissa would somehow get you to believe all the shit she made up about me. And I swear I'm not trying to insult you," she added, flicking a glance at Tess. "It's not like I think you'd believe her. I just...didn't think at all. I ran away instead."

Tess regarded her with concern pinching her face. She couldn't just say that it was okay Remy'd run away. The tear-soaked night she'd spent was still fresh in her memory. But she understood why Remy reacted that way, even though it had been so painful. Remy came across as so tough, so unaffected by people, but the truth was that she hid a lot of vulnerability and insecurity. And now she was sharing a little piece of that with Tess. That, somehow, gave Tess the courage to say what she said next.

"Can I ask you something?"

Remy looked over at her with a subdued nod.

"Can you tell me what you meant after we kissed and you said you're not looking for anything more?"

Remy's face stiffened and her shoulders tensed. She lowered her eyes. Tess held her breath, but Remy didn't get up and leave like Tess half expected. For several moments, Remy fought against her unwillingness to answer.

"After what Melissa did...I'm not sure I can trust anyone that way. It's never been a big deal to me to spend a couple of casual nights with someone, but in order to have a real relationship, something long-term and meaningful...I have to trust the other person."

A dull ache began to grow in Tess's heart. She exhaled. "And you don't trust me?"

Remy's eyes widened and she opened her mouth. "No, I didn't mean that. You've saved my life twice and I only met you a few days ago. Of course I trust you. I just...it's one thing to trust that someone is reliable and competent, and it's another to trust them with...well. With feelings as strong as those."

Tess nodded, her brown eyes thoughtful. "Do you think you'd ever be able to trust me like that?"

There was silence while Remy rubbed the back of her head nervously. "I need time to think. I shouldn't have been so tactless and blunt with you, but when I saw how happy you were...it scared me. I could tell you wanted more. I was afraid of what might happen if we started to have a serious relationship, and so I thought I should set up the boundary right away."

"I get that." Tess thought back on all the dates she'd had over the years where she broke it off after seeing someone once because she didn't want to get too involved in case it didn't work out. She offered Remy a small smile. "We're a lot alike in that way," she said. "Only I've never even gotten past that boundary." *Except with you*, she thought. *You're the first one I ever decided was worth it.* "Can I make a request?"

Remy lowered her chin, cautious. "Sure."

"Would you consider a tentatively serious relationship with the caveat that it might not work out? We don't have to *expect* that it'll all go up in flames," Tess added, trying to lighten the mood with a little grin. "But if both of us know that we're not sure how much we'll be okay with, and if we communicate and both respect what the other is feeling...we could try this with a little more confidence that whatever happens, we'll be okay."

A flame was kindled in Remy's eyes, a slow burn of longing and desire, but the darkness of fear also lurked close by. The intensity in her face made a sparkling wave of warmth travel through Tess's stomach and down to thrill between her legs. Remy's breathing was quick; Tess couldn't keep her eyes off the lovely rise and fall of her breasts, her throat, the tiny motions of her full lips.

"I think I could try." Remy's voice was as deep and soft as black velvet. Her gaze was steady with a seriousness that Tess had only seen on her face a few brief times. "As long as you understand that I'm not going to be the perfect girlfriend."

Elation was slow to seep into Tess's skin, but when she felt it, she was almost light-headed with relief and joy. She smiled a goofy, incredulous grin. "You think *I* will be?" she laughed. "I'm always falling down mountains!"

Remy's face broke into a smile and she began to chuckle. "We have that in common too, apparently." Her smile softened but the light didn't leave her eyes; Tess caught her breath as she realized that she'd never seen that expression on Remy's face before. It was warm, gentle, and the caustic edge that normally characterized her was gone. She lifted her hand, raising it to Tess's cheek, and then hesitated as she noticed the dirt caking her fingers.

Tess surprised herself by trapping Remy's hand with her own and pressing the dirty fingers to her cheek as if she knew exactly what Remy had been about to do. Remy blinked and bit back a smile; then she dipped her head and pressed a lingering kiss to Tess's lips. Tess's muscles relaxed as she leaned into Remy, savoring the kiss, pleasure bubbling through her in ways she'd never even imagined.

Their last kiss had been joyful, desperate, hungry. This one was a kiss of gratitude, a release and a connection all at once. Tess felt turned on every time Remy touched her, and she did now—but there was more to it than that. There was trust and vulnerability in this kiss. There was surrender. When Remy's lips moved to her cheek, her jawbone, her ear, Tess likewise ran a trail of kisses over the bare spot between Remy's neck and shoulder. Then Remy folded Tess in her arms and they sat together on the forest floor, their breathing matched, the wind whispering through the newly bared branches above them.

After several long moments, Remy loosened her arms and Tess lifted her head.

"Tess, I don't want you to go back there." The

determination in Remy's eyes wasn't just stubbornness. "If Melissa felt threatened enough by you to send you out on this wild goose chase, I don't know what she'd stoop to next." Tess gazed at her questioningly. Sure, it would be awkward as hell to go back to the Rising Star, but she was kind of looking forward to rubbing it Melissa's face that her little scheme had only brought Tess and Remy closer together.

"What, then?" she asked. Remy's graced her with a smile that was mostly sultry but also, charmingly, a little bit shy.

"My cabin is in this direction, at the foot of the mountain. If we go back to the ATV and take another trail I know of, we could be there in a few hours. It might take a little longer to get there than it would to get back up to the resort, but..." The corner of her mouth curved more and the shyness disappeared. "I can guarantee you it'll be more comfortable."

Tess didn't bother to hide her excitement. "Lead the way!"

Chapter Twelve

The trail they took down on the ATV was even gentler than the one Tess had been hiking as she looked for Cedar. As they rode, her arms tightly wound around Remy's waist, Tess was giddy with elation. Not only had Remy believed her about Melissa's kiss, but Remy was willing to try a real relationship with her. Tess had to remind herself not to move too fast. She didn't want to overwhelm Remy, and at the same time she didn't want to push her own expectations further than was reasonable.

Their ride through the snowstorm two days ago felt like it might as well have taken place on another planet. The forest, so transformed then, had reemerged as a slightly wetter, browner cousin of the rich orange and red fireworks display it had been earlier in the week. The smell of wet leaves and earth brought a life to the mountainside that was even more exhilarating than the fall colors.

Tess couldn't wait to see Remy's cottage again, and when they rumbled down into the low foothills, she strained her eyes for a glimpse of it through the trees. It had made such an impression on her when she first saw it—a picture-perfect stone house surrounded by the trappings of self-sufficiency. And now that she knew Remy for who she was (and not just some stuck-up but admittedly hot stranger), Tess was even more excited.

Soon, the moss-bedecked roof came into view and they drove through a gap in the crumbling stone wall that marked the edge of the field. Down here, there wasn't any snow, but the ground was soaked and puddles were still everywhere. As they neared the house, a loud and impatient *baa* sounded from the goat shed.

"Oh, shit. I'm sorry, Eulalie!" Remy called. She slowed the four-wheeler and parked it in beside the shed. Tess snickered.

"You named your goat 'Eulalie'?"

"Don't you think that's a perfect name for a goat?" Remy grinned, echoing the same comment Tess had made when they were discussing Sappho's name. She jogged into the shed and unlocked the gate to Eulalie's pen, then picked up a bag of feed and filled her trough. The goat, looking terribly offended, shouldered Remy aside to have her dinner.

Tess got off the ATV and stood, gazing up at the cottage with a smile. The last of autumn's wildflowers were growing at the bottom of the stone walls, bursting in a cheery, disheveled line along the foundation. The door was fashioned of heavy wood and seemed to be very old, but it had been rubbed with something that protected it and brought out the weathered beauty of the grain. There were no welcoming wreathes or signs with cute slogans hung on its windowless front, but there was a wrought-iron knocker that looked like a traditional blacksmith had beaten and twisted it over their anvil. Tess put her hands in her pockets and waited for Remy to finish feeding and quickly tidying out Eulalie's pen.

When Remy came to unlock the door, Tess bounced excitedly behind her, eliciting a proud smirk from Remy. She pushed the door open and flourished with one arm to welcome Tess inside.

The interior of the cottage was straight out of a modern fairy tale. One side of the ground floor was dedicated to kitchen space: clusters of drying herbs were suspended from the ceiling beams, strings of onions and garlic hung on the walls, and a heavy, hand-hewn wooden table sat near the front window. The sill was populated with bottles of various colors and a large jar filled with golden liquid and lemon slices—tea that was brewing in the sun.

There were modern conveniences, of course, to distinguish this from a seventeenth-century home. The colonial fireplace was clean and empty with a rocking chair placed on the brick hearth, and instead there was a glass-topped electric stove standing against the opposite wall. Remy hung her keys up on a hook near the door and set her backpack on the table beside a closed laptop.

"What do you think?" she asked, although from her wide grin, she already knew what Tess would say.

Tess gazed around the kitchen with wide, shining eyes. The sink was soapstone and high tables had been pushed up against the wall to serve as counter space.

"This is incredible," Tess whispered, then she went back toward the door to peer into the room at the other side of the house. The hardwood floor in there was covered with an area rug and a flat-screen television had been hung above the fireplace. A cushion-strewn sofa sat opposite. "I can't believe you live here."

Remy chuckled. "Sometimes I can't believe it either." She paused as Tess smiled up at the scattering of small landscape oil paintings on the walls. "The bathroom's upstairs—I imagine you might want to get out of those muddy clothes. I can find you something of mine you can wear while we wash yours." While Remy's words were those of a casual hostess, her tone was so low and smoldering that Tess immediately looked up at her, heat blooming in her cheeks. Remy's intense gaze seemed to devour every inch of her.

A delightful starburst of flutters suffused Tess's stomach when she saw the way Remy looked at her. No matter how many times she'd seen desire for her in Remy's eyes, Tess was always caught by surprise. She'd never thought of herself as attractive like that; cute, maybe, and friendly and funny. But not sexy.

There was no way she could deny now that Remy found her sexy. Remy's eyes were dark as she slid her gaze from Tess's legs to her hips, over her curves and lingering for a moment on her breasts, then settling on Tess's face. Their eyes locked. Every part of Tess came awake, as if suddenly all of her senses had sharpened. She wanted to use all of those senses to learn the shapes and secrets of Remy's body.

Tess only had a brief moment to notice Remy's quickened breathing, her lips partially opened and full, before Remy crossed the space between them and grasped Tess's hips in her hands. Tess threw herself at Remy with the same ardor, her arms going around Remy's neck, her feet stretching up on tiptoe so she could reach her mouth. Tess breathed in Remy's woodfire-pine scent before capturing Remy's lips with her own.

The urgent passion she'd felt when they kissed in the Sweet Spring's woodshed was nothing compared to what was thrumming through her veins now. Remy clearly felt the same, judging by the way she gripped

Tess's hips and pulled them tightly against her. Remy drank her in, her warm lips already plump as she pressed Tess back against the nearest wall.

Tess would've been happy to kiss Remy's lips forever, but then when Remy bent her head and began to draw a line of kisses down Tess's neck toward her collarbone, Tess drew a shuddering breath of heightened pleasure. Soon Remy was buried in her neck, pulling on her sweater so she could caress Tess's shoulder with her cheek and lips. Tess ran her hands up the back of Remy's neck and curled them in the short strands of hair at the crown of her head. She wanted to touch other parts of Remy, to kiss her and smooth her hands over Remy's skin, but Remy's mouth was too distracting.

Then Remy moved her hands to Tess's rear and picked her up, and Tess instinctively wrapped her legs around Remy's waist. Remy tilted her head up again and Tess reclaimed her mouth. The flames that grew in Tess's body flared, overtaking her with desire, and she paused to look into Remy's eyes.

Remy licked her lips, breathing hard with a slight smile on her face. "Let's get out of these dirty clothes, shall we?" Tess almost couldn't keep herself from undressing Remy right there, but Remy set her down, seized her hand, and drew her up the stairs. Tess had started to take off her sweater when Remy looked back and held up a finger. "Ah, ah, ah. You're not doing that yourself." A giddy grin appeared on Tess's face and she pushed Remy up the stairs.

One side of the second floor was Remy's bedroom and the other looked to be a large bathroom. A few steps inside the bedroom, Remy began to draw the sweater off Tess's arms. She dropped it on the floor and then pulled Tess's t-shirt up over her stomach. By now, need was coursing so strongly through Tess's veins that she couldn't stop herself—while Remy did this, she pushed the jacket off of Remy's shoulders and set to work unbuttoning Remy's flannel shirt, which was no easy task while Remy was herself trying to pull the t-shirt up over Tess's head.

They laughed together as they helped each other get undressed, clumsily tangling their limbs and getting in desperate kisses where they could. Tess unzipped Remy's jeans just as Remy was shimmying Tess's down over her hips, and Tess smoothed her hands over Remy's muscular thighs while she kicked off her own pants. Before Tess could get her bra or panties off, Remy picked her up again and brought the both of them into the bathroom.

The tiled floor was chilly under Tess's bare feet when Remy set her down. Remy paused for a moment to lean into the large shower stall and turn on the water. While it warmed up, she captured Tess's mouth again and her hands moved to Tess's back, where she unhooked Tess's bra. Tess let the straps slip down over her arms and the bra fell to the floor.

As the water in the shower pattered on the glass door, Remy paused to take in Tess's figure. Tess had always wished for larger breasts, but the way Remy looked at them made her feel like they couldn't have been more perfect. Remy cupped one breast in her palm and ran her thumb lightly over Tess's nipple, and an urgent, tingling desire began to throb between Tess's legs. In no time, Tess pulled Remy's sports bra up over her head and began working on Remy's deliciously snug boy shorts. All the while, their mouths never left one another's.

Remy's lean, lithe frame was even more stunningly beautiful undressed than Tess had imagined. Tess ran her hands down Remy's sides, her fingertips delighting in the goosebumps that her kisses raised on Remy's skin. Remy's fingers slid between Tess's panties and her rear and Tess wriggled to help divest herself of them. Then Remy opened the shower door to a cloud of steam and they stepped inside.

The hot water, after another day of being so cold and muddy, was an aphrodisiac. It sent glorious chills down Tess's spine, and when Remy turned her around and pressed Tess's back against her front, Tess trembled with need. Remy's breasts against her were pillowy, the nipples firm, and Tess reached her hand up and slid her fingers behind Remy's head. The sensation on her fingertips of Remy's short, almost rough hair near the nape of her neck made Tess give a small moan of happiness.

Beneath the cascade of water, Remy brought her hands to Tess's breasts and began to massage them. Her fingers and palms moved a bit harder when Tess's breathing quickened, when her hips began to tighten. Swirls of pleasure and desire were flooding through her and her center pulsed insistently; as wonderful as Remy's attention to her breasts was, she turned around and pressed her front to Remy's, unable to hold herself back.

"Please," she said roughly, capturing Remy's hand with one of hers and grasping the back of Remy's head with the other. She guided Remy's hand down over her stomach and Remy happily complied. Then Remy bent down onto her knees and cupped Tess's bottom with one hand while she pressed kisses to the soft space above Tess's curly mound.

Tess gripped Remy shoulders, seeing flashes of light behind her eyelids as the pleasure mounted. Remy seemed to be teasing her, purposely running her fingers up and down the insides of Tess's thighs. Tess tilted her hips toward Remy as they began slowly rocking of their own accord, and finally, finally Remy slipped her fingers between Tess's legs.

For a few moments, she merely caressed the folds there, and Tess gasped and shuddered as waves of pleasure built inside her. Remy's lips still marked searing trails across Tess's stomach. When she thought she could take no more, she dug her nails into Remy's shoulders, and seeming to understand, Remy slipped her fingers inside. She looked up at Tess then, her eyes midnight-dark and a fiery smirk on her face. Tess focused on those eyes through the shudders that had begun to move through her. *She's so utterly gorgeous... How is this real?*

But it was real—it was one hundred percent real that a beautiful, sexy woman was making love to her in a perfect cottage, and she'd won this woman through determination and reliability and all of her own hard work. And when Remy's fingers moved inside her, when Tess's hips bucked against them and her breath caught over and over in her lungs, and when the solar flare of her orgasm sent ecstasy sheeting into every bone and muscle, Tess knew she never should've had any doubts.

Tess's knees buckled and Remy stood to catch her, winding her strong arms around Tess's ribs. Remy's face was triumphant and cocky, a gloating grin on her lips. This was exactly the Remy that had so enticed Tess and had so frustrated her—Tess realized, as she gazed up with dizzy happiness into Remy's eyes, that this mix of traits was exactly why she found Remy so attractive.

"So, you're a shower girl, eh?" Remy asked, raising an eyebrow, as if she'd just uncovered a long-sought secret.

Tess laughed, dipping her head to rest it against Remy's bare chest. "Apparently." She listened to Remy's quick heartbeat beneath the shush of the water, and as her breath began to return to normal, her hunger for Remy began to build again. She lifted her chin and kissed Remy's wet lips, sliding her hands down to caress and then dig into Remy's rear. Remy returned her kiss and then buried her face in Tess's sodden curls, chuckling.

"I, on the other hand, prefer the bed when I let somebody else take the wheel."

Tess fumbled for the faucet and turned the water off, claiming Remy's mouth again. "Oh, I'll take more than just the wheel," she murmured. Remy reached out of the shower and grabbed a towel off a shelf. She wrapped it around the two of them and they stumbled, their lips locked, through the hall and into the bedroom.

$$\mathscr{D}$$

Tess lay with her cheek against Remy's chest, her entire being suffused with a delight and pride she'd never felt before. For all of Remy's charm, all of her arrogant assurance of her own sexiness, Tess had surprised her in numerous toe-curling ways. Tess had been sure that Remy'd done it all, and that no matter how enthusiastic a lover she was, nothing she could do would blow Remy's mind. She'd been wrong.

Remy still hadn't caught her breath, and she curled her fingers lazily in Tess's hair as Tess inhaled her wood-smoke scent.

"I'll bet this isn't how you imagined today would end," Remy chuckled, her voice husky.

"In my fantasies, maybe," Tess replied with a smug grin.

"Have you been fantasizing about me much?" Remy's mouth curled cockily up at one side. Tess gave her nipple a little pinch in retaliation, pleasantly surprised by her own boldness. Any self-consciousness and awkwardness she'd felt around Remy had utterly dissolved the moment they entered the cottage.

"From the moment I met you—much to my annoyance." She slid her head off Remy's chest and onto the pillow so she could see her face. "I couldn't get you out of my head. You drove me crazy in every sense of the phrase."

Remy kissed Tess's forehead and then her mouth, allowing their lips to linger sensually. "And I thought you were plucky, but totally out of your depth. I didn't give you enough credit." She met Tess's eyes with her own, and there was a peaceful heat in their dark blue depths. "I fantasized about you, too. I could see passion in you, bubbling right below the surface. But I wouldn't let myself think about where my fantasies might lead."

"Wherever it leads," Tess said, calming the butterflies in her stomach, "we'll be ready." Remy smiled in response and kissed her again.

"I hope you know how incredible you are that you could even get me to try."

Tess's heart lit up with a glow brighter than the sun. "That's the best compliment I've ever been given."

She pushed herself up on one elbow, admiring the smoothness of Remy's breasts and stomach, and grinned. "Are you starving, or is it just me?"

Remy laughed and sat up too. "I honestly haven't eaten anything since last night. I think some supper is definitely in order. But let me grab you some clothes." Tess stayed in bed and enjoyed the view of Remy's naked backside while Remy rummaged around in her dresser and closet. The sweatshirt and pajama pants Remy handed over were big enough for Tess to swim in, but she rolled up the leg cuffs so she wouldn't trip. It was singularly delightful to snuggle in someone's too-big sweatshirt, especially when that someone had made love to you only moments before.

Down in the cozy kitchen, Tess sat at the table with a steeping mug of tea while Remy mixed together dough for biscuits.

"I know this is normally a breakfast food," Remy told her with a smile, "but there's nothing quite as comforting and filling as biscuits and gravy. What do you think?"

"I think anytime is the right time for breakfast food." Tess inhaled the cinnamon scent of the tea and looked around the kitchen. "And I feel like it'll taste extra good just by being made in a place like this."

"It does lend something to the eating experience, doesn't it?" Remy spooned the biscuit dough onto a baking sheet and put it into the oven with some sausage patties. "The spice blend I put in the gravy has rosemary and thyme from my garden out back."

Tess sighed enviously. "I have a teeny garden at my house. To have space like you do, though—to grow my own vegetables—what a dream."

When Remy set a steaming plate of creamy sausage gravy over biscuits in front of Tess, her stomach rumbled and she snatched up her fork. "This smells like heaven," she said, and tilted her head back with pleasure after taking the first bite. "You're a miracle-worker."

Remy snorted. "Nice of you to say so, but I'm not that great. Usually I only think about cooking for myself." Her wry smile softened and she glanced up at Tess fondly. "I'm about to start getting used to having a guest, I think."

Tess pinkened, lifting her shoulders with a shy happiness. She still had enough of the confidence she'd gained in bed to smile slyly. "I hope that's a good thing?"

"It is," Remy replied. "And nobody's more surprised about that than I am."

"You haven't had people over very much?" Tess asked as she scooped a forkful to her mouth. Someone as charismatic as Remy must've had tons of friends. But Remy shook her head.

"I usually just go out for beers with the other rangers or a couple of friends from my apprenticeship. It's probably silly, but..." Her mouth pulled to one side and a rueful look came over her face. Tess waited for her to continue, sympathetically silent. "After what happened with Melissa, it always felt like...if I brought someone here, that was trusting them just a little too much. I couldn't do it."

Tess's brows drew together and her brown eyes shone with concern. For the moment, she promised to rein in her anger and resentment toward Melissa for Remy's sake.

"She really hurt you, didn't she?" Tess's

Marian Snowe

heartbeat sped as she recognized the signs that Remy was pulling back into herself, but then Remy's shoulders relaxed and she raised her head. When she met Tess's eyes, hers were subdued but frank.

"I thought she loved me. All those times she threw tantrums because she was jealous of what innocent attention I'd give other women... I thought her possessiveness just meant that she was totally smitten with me. I liked the idea that I'd make someone feel that much passion." Remy's gaze dropped to her plate and she pushed around a piece of sausage, then scooped it up and ate it.

"I can understand that," Tess said softly. That was one of the things that had drawn her to Remy in the first place, after all—Remy made her feel desirable. "I'm sorry she broke your trust like that."

Remy shrugged as if it were no big deal, but Tess knew it was. "She wasn't always that crazy. She just bought into that whole 'Can a woman have it all?' myth, where 'having it all' is some just arbitrary goal determined by the patriarchy. She wanted to prove that she could balance a successful career and a successful relationship, and anything that threatened either of those brought out her insecurities. She was always hypersensitive to anything I'd say about her needing to ease off on the amount of hours she put in at work, and then at the same time she'd flip out if she thought something was threatening our relationship."

"So...that's why she thought you were cheating on her?" Tess frowned. She supposed that made Melissa a little more understandable, but it didn't endear the woman to her any, or forgive the way she'd treated both of them.

"Yeah. I should've seen it coming. I didn't think

our relationship was perfect, but I was pretty blind all the same."

"I think you're amazingly brave," Tess said, leaning forward. "After all that, you still kept going back to the Rising Star and helping them out. I've never been that brave."

Remy quirked an eyebrow at her. "Says the woman who survived falling down a mountain multiple times *and* broke into a building to get help for me?"

Tess couldn't help smiling, but she waved her hand dismissively. "I mean about relationships." She paused, watching Remy, noting the charming messiness of her hair and how her lips were still rosy with their kisses. Even in a faded long-sleeved t-shirt and pajama pants with ducks on them, Remy was still unbelievably attractive. Remy's expression was attentive, and Tess resolved that the candid communication they'd promised each other would start today.

"I've always had an unrealistic idea of how a romance should go," Tess said. "When I was a teenager, I couldn't tell anyone I was gay, so I poured all my romantic frustration into daydreams. And in them, the woman I met would be perfect in every way, and we'd meet in a wonderfully romantic scenario and it would be all roses and sunshine forever. I ended up scared that any relationship that *didn't* immediately feel like that was doomed to failure."

Remy listened carefully, her cheek resting on her fist, but Tess could see the worry growing in her eyes. Tess smiled and shook her head reassuringly.

"That kept me from giving anyone a fair chance for years. But when I met you..." Tess's heart fluttered and she was washed with a sudden wave of gratitude that this was all really happening. "When I met you, I realized that you were worth it."

Slowly, Remy's eyes widened and she lifted her head, her fist loosening and dropping from her cheek. Her lips parted but she didn't say anything. Tess had witnessed a lot of emotions on Remy's face over the past few days, but she'd never seen her this deeply moved.

"Tess..." Remy's voice caught. "After all the times I pushed you away, you still gave me a chance. I wanted you the moment I met you, but I wrote it off as something that I just couldn't let happen. But if you're willing to trust me this much...the least I can do is try to trust you, too." She swallowed and moved her hand on the table toward Tess, and Tess readily took it in her own. "I can't promise that I'll be able to get past all of those fears...but hearing you say that goes a long way to making them smaller."

Tess breathed a sigh of relief and squeezed Remy's hand. "Will you promise to tell me if I do anything that hurts you? I don't want you to ever think I'd manipulate you the way Melissa did."

Remy ducked her head to hide the emotion on her face. "I promise. You have to do the same, okay?"

"I will." The fluttering in Tess's chest burst into sparks of joy. This could work. Maybe it wouldn't be perfect, but this could really, truly work.

It was past midnight by the time they finished dinner. Tess snuggled next to Remy in bed, relishing the feeling of Remy's arm beneath her and the soft, delicate circles Remy was drawing on Tess's back with her fingernails. For the first time in her life, Tess was contented with the idea that the future was uncertain. Right now, she and Remy were enjoying the hell out of each other—and that was all that mattered. She didn't need to give up on her dream romance; all she had to do was realize that dreams can be malleable.

Chapter Thirteen

In the morning, after a quick breakfast and another lovely shower together, Remy and Tess drove the ATV to the park ranger station across the road from the Rising Star Yoga Resort's trailhead. There were a few rangers sitting around desks inside, and one of the younger ones hopped up when Remy opened the door.

"Labelle! Geez, you've been having some adventures, huh? We were afraid a bear had got you."

Remy chuckled. "No bears so far." She shared a look with Tess; bears or not, the past few days had been enough excitement for a year. "And you guys didn't even send out a search party!"

The other ranger looked uncomfortable. "We knew you'd gone to find the hikers, so we figured you went up to the resort with them and got stuck in the snowstorm…" He put up his hands conciliatorily. "But the girl from the front desk called down when they got the phones back and said you'd been there, but you left on a four-wheeler yesterday morning. We were going to send someone to check at your house today to make sure you got there safely."

"Sure, sure," Remy replied, snatching his hat and ruffling his hair. He scowled at her.

"Marti thinks of everything, huh?" Tess smiled, sure that the "girl from the front desk" had to be her.

"We should let them know we're okay."

"Yeah, absolutely." Remy gave the ranger his hat back. "Can we borrow a truck? I want to get the four-wheeler back to the resort in case somebody needs it."

And I need to pick up my luggage and get the hell out of that crazy place, Tess added to herself.

"Give them a call for me, will you, Bryce?" Remy caught the keys when he threw them at her and he waved a hand in agreement.

"Need any help getting the four-wheeler into the truck bed?"

"Nah, just remind me where we store the ramp and we'll be all good."

Tess climbed up into the truck bed after she and Remy moved the metal ramp into place and stood there to direct Remy as she positioned the ATV's wheels on the ramp. Soon they had the vehicle safely strapped into the truck bed and were on their way around the mountain to the service road on the opposite slope.

The road up the mountain got them there in less than an hour from the base. Tess watched out the window as the road wound in switchbacks up the tree-covered slope. She shook her head; it was so much faster than hiking up that it seemed ludicrous that they'd spent all that time dragging themselves up difficult trails. *I guess it was all part of the experience,* she thought with a sarcastic twitch of her lips.

They pulled up to the Rising Star Resort to find the parking lots cleared of slush and guests hurrying to and fro as they got ready to depart. Power had been restored, as Tess saw by the multitude of lights that sparkled, even in the morning sun, through all of the windows. Only a portion of them had been rigged to the generator and now the Rising Star looked the way Tess expected it to.

Marti was on the phone when they came in the door, but her eyes flew wide when she saw them. She hung up as quickly as possible and rushed over to them, throwing her arms around Tess first.

"I've never been so relieved as when the ranger station called this morning! I thought for sure you two had fallen to your deaths this time!"

"It was a near thing," Remy replied dryly and returned Marti's enthusiastic hug. "Looks like things are back to normal here, huh?"

"Mmh." Marti's eyes darted back behind the desk uncertainly. "You-know-who is on the warpath. Not that that isn't normal," she murmured. At that moment, as if to prove her statement, Melissa slammed the door open and entered the lobby on a cordless phone, talking a mile a minute in an irate, superior tone.

"Fine! If he refuses to reschedule, he can kiss his commission goodbye—"

Melissa's mouth dropped open when she saw Remy and Tess standing there, and she hung up the call. Tess blinked as the angry voice on the other end of the line was cut off mid-sentence.

"You have some nerve to come back here," Melissa growled, stalking toward them. Tess wasn't sure which one of them she was talking to, but she bristled nonetheless. "You," Melissa said, pointing at Tess, "need to leave. Now."

"I was going to leave anyway!" Tess shot back. "I don't need to be put through this kind of crap!" Then Remy placed a hand on her shoulder and stepped forward.

"Melissa." Her voice was hard as stone, and Melissa's eyes snapped to her. She looked surprised and wary to hear that Remy's typical anger toward her had turned into something more assured. "We know that you sent Tess out looking for Cedar when he was, in fact, safe in Glen's office. That was a dangerous, childish stunt you pulled. Tess could've been seriously hurt." Remy didn't even look like she wanted to shout at Melissa; her fury had hardened into calm rationality, which unsettled Melissa much more.

"What are you talking about?" Melissa scoffed, putting a manicured hand to her chest. "Cedar hadn't gotten out? I was quite sure!" Tess had always found Melissa to be a convincing actress, but this time she was clearly bluffing. She'd lost some of that absolutely certainty in her ability to control others.

Tess snorted, and Melissa turned a glare full of barbs on her. "And how was *I* supposed to know," Melissa continued, "that Tess would be the one to go looking for him? After all, I didn't even know who was in the lobby when I called down."

"But you'd been through just a couple of minutes before," a soft voice said. Marti stood to the side, her hands clasped nervously in front of her chest. She stared at Melissa with hurt, disbelieving eyes as she put the pieces together. "You stopped to ask me when the phones would be working, remember? And yesterday afternoon you said Cedar came up to the back door and you let him in. Ma'am, you lied to me?"

Melissa gritted her teeth, somehow unable to fabricate another story in the face of Marti's genuine distress.

"Marti," Remy said gently. "I'm sorry I didn't come right down and tell you that Cedar was okay."

"I understand," Marti said shakily. "You needed to find Tess." She turned to Melissa again, her eyes flashing. "But ma'am, you let me think he was lost! And you let me worry about Tess and Remy when you knew they'd gone out for no reason!"

"Now, Martha, look," Melissa said, patting the air in a classic "calm down" gesture. Nevertheless, she seemed nervous. "It was only a—a prank. I didn't think—"

"You don't pull pranks, ma'am," Marti interrupted. "I've been working here since high school. I know you're not the kind of person who plays pranks on people." Marti's hands balled into fists and she dropped them to her side. "I'm sorry, Ms. Hart, but this is too much. You put Tess and Remy in danger on purpose, and you lied to me. I've looked the other way all those times you haven't filled out the expense reports correctly..."

At this, Melissa stiffened. She shot a piercing look of warning at Marti, but Marti stared her down.

"I know you keep buying things you think will improve the resort," Marti continued, "but you have to document it the right way. And you can't spend money meant for repairs and upkeep on new things when you never let us fix the old things!" She shook her head. "I have to tell someone."

Tess felt such a surge of pride that she had to hold herself back from punching the air and cheering. Remy looked tense, though, keeping her eyes on Melissa. Melissa slowly folded her arms over her chest, reining in the dangerous rage that had stolen over her face.

"As a *secretary*," she spat, "you have no authority to do any such thing. And you're about to have no authority here whatsoever. This resort has no place for someone as disrespectful as you—"

"Melissa!" Glen's shocked voice sounded from the hallway and his crutches creaked as he made his way hurriedly over. "What do you think you're doing? You can't *fire* Marti! Nothing would get done around here!" He looked at all of their faces in turn. "What on earth is going on?"

Remy stepped forward, tossing a disdainful, quelling glare at Melissa. "Glen, I'm glad you're back. Melissa sent Tess down the mountain on foot to look for Cedar, who she *said* escaped." Glen's forehead wrinkled in confusion.

"But Cedar's..." He pointed with his thumb over his shoulder in the direction of his office. Remy nodded.

"I know. He was safe here the whole time, and Melissa knew it. I don't know what she was trying to accomplish—" With this, Remy's glare turned colder than a razor-sharp sliver of ice. "—But she purposefully put Tess in danger." Tess watched Remy's face with a shiver of excitement mixed with awe. Remy could be a little scary when she wanted to—and it delighted Tess that Remy felt so strongly about keeping her safe.

"I didn't!" Melissa protested. She was starting to sound desperate. "I really thought your dog got out..."

"You just said it was a prank!" Marti looked utterly scandalized. Glen turned to her and then to Remy and Tess, who nodded grimly.

"It's the truth," Remy stated. Tess decided to stay silent—it would be better if she let Remy, who Glen clearly trusted, handle this. "Melissa has it out for Tess because she and I are dating."

A silence fell among the five of them, and

Marti's hands flew to her mouth to hide a squeal of excitement. Tess's heart thudded against her ribs and sparks of heat flowed through her veins. Remy had said it. She'd said it to all of them. It was almost as if that made it official. Tess felt like she might burst with joy.

Melissa's eyes fell on her, and they were full of venom. "You'd better watch out for that one, *Tess*," she said, as if Tess's name were a mocking slur. "Pretty soon you'll realize that I sent you off for your own protection, to get you away from *her*."

Tess shook her head slowly. "I won't believe, not for one second, *anything* you say about Remy." She looked over at Remy and held out her hand; Remy took it, her eyes narrow with gratitude. To Melissa, Tess said, "Nothing you do is for anybody else's benefit."

A feverish red flush appeared in splotches on Melissa's face. "How dare you," she hissed. "I've dedicated my *life* to bettering this resort—"

"That's the problem," Glen broke in. He stepped closer to Melissa, leaning on his crutches. "You're fixated on adding new things in an attempt to stay ahead of what's in vogue, while at the same time you're unforgivably rude to guests and you refuse to let us spend money on improving what we already have! How many times has Marti or someone else had to smooth over a visitor's ruffled feathers after you chewed them out for no good reason? Not to mention the family who'll never be coming back because you threw them out after you accused the wife of having an affair with Remy!"

Glen was growing red in the face too, now. This was clearly the last straw, and everything Tess had heard about the resort's problems since she got there was only the tip of the iceberg.

"I've been giving you the benefit of the doubt," Glen went on. "But this has to stop. You've been mismanaging the resort for as long as I've been here, and longer if I can trust the accounts of the other employees—which I believe I can. I'm going to tell your mother and father, Melissa. And they won't be happy to hear that you're running this branch of your family's business into the ground."

The flush on Melissa's cheeks had bled away and now her face was pale. She looked from Glen to Marti, then to Tess, and finally her eyes fell on Remy.

"You were out to ruin me this whole time, weren't you?" Her eyes were filled with hatred, but there was something else there too—she sincerely believed that Remy betrayed her, and the pain was evident.

Remy breathed out a long sigh. "Look around, Missy," she said softly. Tess glanced at her in surprise to hear such an intimately childlike nickname. "This isn't what you wanted. You drove me out. Your resort is held together by a few rusty nails and Glen's willpower. I know the only reason you offered all of those tickets to local companies to raffle off was to drum up more business. You can't keep holding onto this and pretending a fresh coat of paint or a shiny new mud bath is going to make it perfect. 'Perfect' doesn't exist. You'll only make yourself miserable trying to find it."

Melissa stared at her like a breathing statue, her posture rigid, her chest rising and falling with each rasping inhale. She was silent, as if someone had told her utterly shattering news and she was paralyzed with absorbing it. For the first time, Tess felt a twinge of sympathy for her.

Then Tess heard the tapping of high heeled shoes—a sound she'd only associated with Melissa before—and she turned to see one of the white-shorts ladies walking toward them with a curiously serious expression on her face. She stopped right in front of Melissa, earning various confused glances from the others.

"Thousand-Dollar Handbag Hannah?" Tess asked with surprise, then clapped her hands over her mouth. Remy couldn't contain a snort of laughter. "Hannah" spared a dismissive glance for Tess, then locked her eyes on Melissa.

"Ms. Hart, I've heard enough."

"*Excuse* me?" Melissa had apparently recovered herself enough to sound both condescending and indignant, but "Hannah" didn't appear at all cowed. In fact, her expression and posture were nothing like the inept socialite Tess remembered from the hike up. She pulled a business card from her pocket and held it out to Melissa with two fingers.

"My name is Rhiannon Colt, and I've been employed by your mother and father—the owners of Celestial Resorts Incorporated—to investigate your business practices. They have concerns about the allocation of your budget, and I've gathered what I need to present them with a true account of how you're running this resort."

Melissa gaped at her, at a loss for words. She snatched the card from Rhiannon's fingers and angrily read the printed name and title.

"This is..." Melissa sputtered. "If this is some kind of idiotic joke, I'll make sure you regret it." Her glare was fiery, but there were definite cracks in it where uncertainty shone through.

"This is no joke, Ms. Hart." Rhiannon folded her arms, matching Melissa's confident, steely posture. "Now that the roads are open again, I'll be taking my evidence to your corporate headquarters."

"Evidence?" Melissa cried scornfully. "What on earth kind of evidence could you possibly have?"

Tess's mouth dropped open. "Your stupid vlog!" she said, and then once again winced at her poor choice of words. All of those times "Hannah" had taken insipid videos with her smartphone, she'd actually been documenting the way the Rising Star was being run?

Rhiannon smirked at her. "It's gratifying when my cover fools people so completely."

"You're lying," Melissa spat. "My parents would never..." She gritted her teeth, realization and anger blending on her face.

"Call them and ask, if you like," Rhiannon replied, waving a hand. "But I suggest you take a few days off, until this matter can be addressed. It's in your own best interests."

Tess, Remy, Glenn, and Marti all looked on in stunned but somewhat eager silence as Melissa's mouth twisted. She said nothing, though, only turned on her heel and stormed to the door behind the desk.

"Marti!" she shouted. "Call me a goddamn cab!" Marti hurried to the reception desk and picked up the telephone, sharing a look with Tess that said she couldn't have been more pleasantly surprised if she'd just won ten thousand dollars. Tess turned to Rhiannon.

"Holy cow, you're a private investigator?"

"Corporate investigator," Rhiannon corrected. Then she smiled slyly. "How else do you think I could afford a thousand-dollar handbag?" With that, she inclined her head and took her leave. Tess turned her eyes to Remy and Glen, her mouth hanging open.

"Did that really just happen?"

Glen let out an incredulous chuckle. "I guess I won't have to be calling her parents after all. Corporate's more on top of this than I expected."

Remy gazed at the door Melissa had disappeared through. "If anyone is in desperate need of a reality check, it's her. Sometimes the only remedy is a hard kick in the ass."

"Or a hard fall down a mountain?" Tess suggested mischievously. She twined her fingers through Remy's, delighting in the warmth of their palms pressed together. Remy chuckled and smiled fondly down at Tess.

"Yeah, that works too."

Glen shook his head at them, smiling. "I'll see you two later. I've got to talk to Marti about our new plan for running this resort."

Left by themselves, Tess pulled on Remy's hands, dragging her down for a long kiss. In a burst of affection, Remy wrapped her arms around Tess's middle and lifted her off the ground. Tess laughed, and when Remy set her back down, she cocked her head up at her gorgeous girlfriend.

"So, how much is it going to take to convince you to come with me to a yoga class?"

Remy laughed too, burying her face in Tess's hair. "I think the odds are better than they were a few days ago, I'll say that much."

With a grin, Tess drew Remy toward her room. "Let's find you some yoga clothes. And then after class..." She ran her eyes up and down Remy's form with a sultry lift of her shoulder. "My room has a *really* nice shower."

One Year Later

The lobby of the Rising Star Yoga Resort was fairly quiet until a cascade of four- and five-year-olds tumbled through the doors. Tess walked at their back like a farmer herding geese.

"All right, guys, let's huddle over here and go over the rules. The Rising Star invited us to their lodge and we want to show them how well we can behave." The children crowded in and gathered at one side of the door, gazing around at the high ceilings and glass-paned walls with amazement.

"How many of you have stayed in a hotel before?" Tess asked. A few hands shot up. "This is like a hotel where you can take fun classes, so we want to behave just like we would back in our classroom, okay? That means inside voices and no running." She looked over at the reception desk, where Marti was beaming at them. Marti bent down to open one of the desk drawers and then came over with a big smile on her face.

"Welcome to the Rising Star Yoga Resort!" she said, then held out two fists bristling with lollypops. "We're so glad to have you here! I'm Marti, the assistant manager, and I've got lime, orange, and cherry lollypops. Who wants one?"

Over the clamor of kids requesting their favorite flavor, Tess searched the lobby with her eyes.

Her whole face lit up when she saw Remy come sauntering over to them from the far fireplace.

"How's my favorite director of maintenance?" Tess asked, her eyes sparkling. Remy tossed her head with a proud grin.

"I'm happy to report a milestone—today it's officially been a whole month since something broke down."

"Congratulations," Tess laughed. Then she heard a voice pipe up behind her.

"That's her!" one little girl cried, pointing. "That's Miss Monroe's girlfriend!"

All of the children crowded closer to get a look at Remy.

"She's tall!" one said.

"She has hair like a boy!" said another.

"Are you gonna kiss?" asked a girl in a tone that was both eager and appalled. Tess, laughing, went up on her tiptoes to place a quick kiss on Remy's lips. Squeals and cries of "Aww!" and "Eww!" went up from the assembled preschoolers.

"All right, guys, quiet down," Tess chuckled, patting the air. "The resort has set up a special kids' yoga class for us, and that's why I asked you all to wear sweatpants or leggings today. The instructor will be meeting us here any minute."

At that moment, Emily appeared out of the hallway that led to the classrooms, a wide, bright pink headband holding back her shock of red hair. Tess waved to her, unable to contain a little bounce.

"Hi, kiddos!" Emily came over, planting her hands on her hips. She was outfitted in sparkly green yoga pants and a black tank top with Tinkerbell on the front. "I'm Emily, and we're going to be doing yoga together today. In yoga there are a lot of poses where we pretend to be animals, so who here can hop like a bunny?" Everyone's hands flew into the air. "Great! We're going to hop down to the studio!" Emily winked at Tess and led a conga line of hopping children away toward the classrooms.

When they were gone, Remy grabbed Tess by the waist and drew her close, kissing her again. This time it was deep and lingering. Tess leaned her forehead against Remy's and sighed contentedly.

"Ready for the big day?" Remy whispered.

Happiness swelled in Tess's chest. She looked up into Remy's eyes and bit her lip with a smile. "I think so." She pecked Remy's lips again. "Although I should really be the one asking you that."

Remy chuckled. "I'm definitely ready. I have the day off tomorrow, and if our emergency-free track record holds, I'll have all day to help you move in." She locked her fingers at the small of Tess's back and smiled down at her. "And even if something does come up, Glen can handle it."

"You're sure he'll have time, now that he's managing the whole place?"

"Sure he will. He's got Marti. And nothing's going to happen anyway." She nuzzled Tess's cheek but then pulled back, searching her face. Tess's eyebrows drew together with worry. "What's wrong?" Remy asked.

Tess tilted her head. "Do you think Sappho and Eulalie will get along?"

Remy blinked at her and then burst out laughing. "Considering that Sappho is a *house* rabbit and Eulalie is a *garden* goat, even if they don't become best friends immediately, they'll have their own separate spaces to get used to this new arrangement."

A soft smile appeared on Tess's lips. "Thanks for being willing to try out not having separate spaces ourselves."

Remy tucked a curl of Tess's hair behind her ear, her fingers moving over Tess's cheek reverently. "I've found I don't like being alone the way I used to. I always wish you were there." Tess leaned her cheek into Remy's hand, closing her eyes with contentment. "But still," Remy said seriously, "I'll probably do things like nag you for leaving your socks on the floor."

Tess opened her eyes and gazed up into Remy's, delighting in the deep ocean blue that she'd become so fond of losing herself in. "And I'll keep forgetting to pick my socks up. I don't want a perfect romance anymore. I want you. Being with you is a hundred times better than what I imagined perfection to be."

Remy, her eyes shining with trust, tightened her arms around Tess and lifted her off the ground. Tess squealed and held on tight, then took Remy's exquisite face in her hands and kissed her with a joyous fervor. It was amazing how taking a risk was so much easier when you knew how sweet the reward would be.

The End

CPSIA information can be obtained
at www.ICGtesting.com
Printed in the USA
LVOW08s1713270417
532419LV00003B/596/P